I0831346

The Timekeeper's Daughter

The Timekeeper's Daughter

C.J.M. NAYLOR

C.J.M. Naylor
cjmnaylor@yahoo.com

Cover Design by Alexander von Ness

Printed in the United States of America

Second Edition

For Paula.

This book was unfinished the last time I saw you. It is finished now because of you.

CHAPTER ONE

December 1943

My mother always told me that God gave people their own personal trial in life. She said everyone had their own personal struggle—something that they had to work through on their own. But she also said he rewarded them for this in heaven.

I have lived my entire life with a personal struggle. Every single day, as I walk to and from my classes, and the library, I have my own trial. It sometimes feels like an endless war that is raging inside me, a war that never wants to come to an end. I wonder if the people I pass by every day can truly see me. I know that they see the face of a girl, almost eighteen, with minimal makeup. A girl with her hair tied back and on a mission to complete something—a girl that doesn't care what other people think of her. At least, that's what I'd like for them to see. But the truth is, I do care.

I don't want them to think I am insane.

For as long as I can remember, I have heard disembodied voices. I am the only one that can hear them, and they are there. They aren't inside my head. They live in the empty space around me. And they aren't cruel. At least not yet. They are kind. Sometimes, I hear a mother speaking to her child. Sometimes, I hear people reminiscing about life after the war. I'm not sure what war they are talking about. I'm constantly reminded there is a war going on. Signs are pasted all across the city that warn citizens to wear their gas masks. Just the other night, we spent some time in the bomb shelter again. It isn't as bad as it used to be, the attacks. At the beginning, they were terrible. London suffered lots of property damage, but more important, we lost the lives of innocent people.

The sounds of traffic through my window disrupted my thoughts. The everyday sounds of London were attempting to wake me up. The voices returned and once again they were soothing.

"She's beautiful, because she looks just like you," a man spoke.

"I love you," the woman replied. "I love our daughter."

Silence. My eyes popped open. I could not control when the silence came and the voices stopped. The voices were in control, not me. When I had first heard them, they were only whispers. I couldn't hear what they were saying or what gender they were. The only sound was constant whispering. At first, it had scared me when I heard them. Hearing voices, not thinking them, hearing them, was enough to scare anyone though. At ten years old, if you start to hear things that aren't there, it might be cause for concern. The secret was my own though—I kept it locked away in my heart.

At a younger age, I liked to live in my own little world. Imagining was my favorite past time. Because of my imagination, the whispers were welcomed into my head. I had only confided in two people about the voices: the first was Bridget. She was my closest friend. The first time I told her, she thought it was great. She thought perhaps it was some kind of magical ability. But as the two of us got older, she thought I should seek some professional help. Seeking help was the last thing I wanted to do. My mind came up with the wildest fantasies. If I sought help, then that must mean an insane asylum waited for me. If it was hundreds of years ago, then there was a stake ready for me. I could see the villagers already.

"Burn the witch! Burn her!"

I realized it was the effect of an overly active imagination, but still, if someone came up on the street and told me they were hearing things, well, I would probably think they were insane. However, in my case, I probably would consider we had something in common.

One of the reasons I did not want help for this was because of my past. I was adopted when I was a child. My mother and father could not have a child of their own and decided to adopt. However, the way I was given up was quite sad. My biological mother dropped me on the doorstep of an orphanage and walked away. She didn't leave a note. She didn't leave a reason why. She just got rid of me like I was trash. My friend Bridget did not even know this about me. I chose not to tell her. My parents told me when I was nine. I felt ashamed of it. I felt unworthy of a mother's love. I knew that I shouldn't feel unworthy, but I did.

A knock at my bedroom door distracted my attention. I waited. My mother would knock, to simply announce she was coming in, and then she came in.

"Abigail!"

I pulled my covers up to my nose and tried to feign sleep.

"Wake up."

My mother pulled the covers off my bed and I was exposed. She stood before me, the short woman she was, hands on hips. She was already dressed to head out to the hospital for a day's work, but she had haphazardly thrown on an apron to cook breakfast no doubt.

"Sleeping in is a gift." I pulled the covers back toward me and turned on my side.

The covers were pulled off again. I would never get one day to sleep in. My mother was one to wake up and enjoy the day. I prepared myself for her usual statement about every day and smiled when it came.

"It isn't necessary to sleep in and waste another day on God's good Earth," she said. "You never know..."

"When it could be your last," I finished. I did know. She told me all the time. My mother and father had raised me in the Catholic faith. My faith was something that was important to me, especially in this time. In a time of war and death, people needed faith in God to do the right thing. I needed it.

"Of course!" my mother smiled at me. She was older now, but her beauty was still there in her soft, black hair. She often wore it in a bun, like today. "Besides, you need to get out of bed and seize the day, because tomorrow is your eighteenth birthday and we will be having endless celebrations, like always."

My birthday was tomorrow. The last time I had thought about it was a week ago, and now it was tomorrow. It amazed me how quickly time could fly by.

"Phillip is downstairs."

Before I knew it, I shot out of bed like the sheets were on fire.

"Why didn't you say something?"

She smiled at me and simply shook her head.

"Young love," she said as she left my room. "I was there once."

My heart pounded as I thought about Phillip waiting for me. He was the other person who knew my secret. He had proposed to me a couple of weeks ago. It hadn't exactly been formal, and there wasn't a ring, but I said yes, and every day since I was thinking about our life together. We had met two years ago when I started university at Birkbeck College. He had been a junior at the time. He was now working at the London Library.

"Abigail, you will learn the truth."

I stopped frozen, my hand on the doorknob to my bathroom. When the voices came, I usually had the ability to keep going with my day. But this was different. The voices had never said my name. They had never said anything to me. When I was younger, I used to respond to them. I used to ask them questions. But when I never got a response back, I grew out of the habit of doing that. I decided to try again now.

"Hello?"

The wind rustling outside. A sound of a double-decker bus's horn. Those were the sounds I could hear, seeping in through my window. I did not hear a response, however.

I decided to try one more time.

"Hello? Are you there?"

"You will learn the truth. Be ready."

I wasn't sure why it was, but I could always tell when the voices were leaving. This voice was leaving.

"Wait! What truth will I learn? What will I be ready for?"

But then the voice was gone. I wasn't sure how much more I could take of this. If conversations between *the voices* and I were going to happen, then that was something different altogether.

The water from the tub was warm against my bare body. I had my eyes closed, and I let the water take me to a different time. Imagination was powerful, especially during a war. I would rely on a warm bath to erase my thoughts and my fears. I would allow it to take me away, but it could only be briefly. I used the soap and shampoo briefly, keeping in mind that it was all being rationed.

After the bath, I brushed my hair, admiring my reflection in the mirror. My wet, brown hair was what I liked most about myself. My hair fell down to the middle of my back. I knew that a person should not be too vain, but I liked to admire myself in the mirror. I was always a simple girl. I did not like to wear lipstick, but occasionally I would put some powder on my face and redden my cheeks, as my mother would call it. Like I said, minimal makeup.

I curled my hair and let it fall down one shoulder, matching one of the styles that were in. My mum had washed my button down striped blouse. I put it on and then pulled out a pair of black slacks. Finally, I wore my favorite black flats that had what looked like a flower at the tips.

The voices of Mrs. Baxter and Phillip could be heard from the upstairs landing. I did not go downstairs just yet. I liked to visit my father in the morning. He would not always be down for breakfast when I was; I liked to make sure he knew I was nearby.

My mother and father's door was slightly ajar and I was able to peek in. My father was sitting on his bed, staring at the wall. I could feel my heart pounding, as it did everyday, when I was about to see him. I would always go in, not knowing what he would say or what he would remember. His memory loss had grown substantially worse this last year. Some days, he would seem entirely there, but recently, he seemed dazed and confused. He remembered me though—it was my mother he had forgotten first. My father no longer knew who she was anymore. He assumed she was his second nurse and frequently asked where his wife had gone. It broke my heart.

I pushed the door inward and walked quietly into the room. His back was facing me. He was sitting on the edge of the bed, his hands in his lap. He had put on his pants and his undershirt, but his shirt was only partially buttoned up.

I sat down on the edge of the bed next to him and he took my hand, placing it in both of his.

"I knew you would come to see me, Abigail Lu."

He had called me his Abigail Lu for as long as I could remember.

"I come see you every morning, Dad," I said. "You know that."

He nodded his head and then let go of my hand. His hands shook, but he brought them up to work on the buttons on his shirt. He managed to get one button buttoned, but his hands began shaking more and he struggled on the next one.

I knelt down in front of him. "I'll help you."

"No."

He put his hands out in front of me.

"I'm fine. Why don't you go down and help the nurses with

breakfast?"

The *nurses.*

"Mum and Mrs. Baxter," I said. "Mrs. Baxter is your nurse, and mum is your wife."

A confused expression enlightened his face.

"I think I meant that. Yes. Go on."

He shooed me out of the room. I walked down the landing, down the stairs, and into the main hallway. I had lived in this house since I was adopted. My mother and father, older than most mothers and fathers, had raised me in this house. Pictures of the three of us adorned the walls. Phillip always said there wasn't one room he could walk into in this house and not find a picture of me.

"These pancakes are delicious, Mrs. Jordan."

I heard Phillip commending my mother on her cooking as always. It made me smile.

Upon walking into the kitchen, I found Mrs. Baxter, my father's nurse and my old nanny, sitting at the table reading her newspaper. She had worked in this house for eighteen years. She began as my nanny, raising me in the day while my parents worked. When I went off to school, she was our maid, and was here to watch me when I returned home. Finally, when my father began to lose his memory, she was his nurse. She cared for him during the day while my mother continued to work at the hospital. She was a short, stout lady, even shorter than my mother. Phillip often had to crane his neck all the way down just to look at her. She had the cutest glasses a little old lady could have and she always wore her hair back in a tight bun.

"Good morning, Abigail," Mrs. Baxter addressed me over her

paper. She couldn't see me, but she always knew my footsteps coming into the kitchen when everyone was already there.

Phillip had his back facing me, but he got up from his chair immediately.

"There she is," he said. He pulled me into a hug and kissed my forehead. Phillip quickly pulled away and smiled. The look on his face told me he wanted to kiss me, but he never had the courage to do it in front of my mother. What was with men and mothers?

"You act as if we've been a part for days," I said. "I saw you yesterday, in case you've forgotten."

"Darling," Phillip remarked, "every minute apart from you, is like a century in my heart." He said it very theatrically and I giggled.

I sat down at the table and helped myself to the limited pancakes. My mum did the best with the supplies she had. Items like sugar, flour, and the essentials came rationed in the time of the war. One thing I loved about my mother though, was that she would do her best to get these items and make us simple treats. She would use just enough ingredients that would make just enough for us to enjoy. I looked forward to the days after the war—the days when things would not have to be rationed, and the days when we wouldn't have to worry about waking up during the night to an air raid.

"What are you two dolls doing today?" Mrs. Baxter asked.

I looked at Phillip for that answer. I wasn't entirely sure. I didn't have class on Tuesdays, so I assumed we would probably spend the day at the library. Even though he was off, we still spent our time there. He was given his own office for his studies and work, and we both loved books and falling into worlds we couldn't have.

"The library," my mum said. She was standing at the sink and had a dishtowel thrown over her shoulder.

"We didn't say that," I protested, a grin appearing on my face.

My mum pointed her index finger at me.

"Abigail Lu Jordan," she said smiling, "I see it on your face. I admire your tastes in books, the both of you, but you don't have to spend all of your time there. Remember, we don't want to waste another day on God's Earth—"

"Because you never know when it could be your last."

I looked over at Phillip after he said it. He knew my mother to a "T". He appreciated her positive outlooks and views on life.

"Right, you are, Phillip Hughes," my mum said. "Now, both of you, off. I have a kitchen to clean and work to be attending."

Phillip came around and pulled my chair out for me.

"Such a gentleman," I joked.

"No need to be joking about those things Abigail, dear," Mrs. Baxter commented, "I was at the market the other day and spoke to a most interesting woman. She thinks the days are a coming when men won't be as polite as they are now."

"Mrs. Baxter, that day has come and gone," my mum said, "you simply need to take a day off and experience it."

"Nonsense!" Mrs. Baxter said. "Now, Annette, you get to work and I'm going to finish these dishes."

Phillip and I left Mrs. Baxter and my mum in the kitchen. All the way out the front door I could hear their bantering about who would finish the dishes.

Phillip pulled the door closed behind him. "Those two will never agree.

As soon as the door clicked, I felt him tug at my arm and I twirled into his arms. We stood there on the steps for a moment, looking into each other's eyes. I wondered if this is how my parents felt when they were in love, or if it was different for everyone. Phillip tilted my chin up just a bit and then our lips met. They moved in perfect unison with each other, his lips with mine. The kiss ended and we looked into each other's eyes a bit longer.

"We can kiss in there," I said. "It doesn't have to be on my front stoop for the city of London to see."

"I know," he said, "but I want to show the world how much we love each other."

"Okay, let's show them."

I took his hand in mine and we strolled down the walkway, arm in arm, toward his car. I let my mind wander for a while—how could a war be going on when our love and the love of many others was in the world?

Phillip drove his black, 1940 Riley Twelve in the direction of the London Library. My body vibrated in the left passenger seat as Phillip drove through the streets; occasionally he would hit a bump in the road and I'd bounce up and down. He was excited about spending time with what we loved: books. Books made up an important part of my life. My schooling had always included reading novels of many genres. Having developed an interest in school, I enjoyed books of almost all kinds.

My eyes averted to the window, and gazed at the passing scenery.

The car was journeying through Trafalgar Square. The fountain attracted my attention as I admired the water within, frozen in place.

"Abby, you are sitting next to *me*." I turned my gaze on Phillip. His attention was focused on the road, but his eyes darted over to look at me and then back to the road again. My attention focused on his eyes. He looked back at me again, an odd expression on his face. I realized he was waiting for me to speak.

"What do you mean?"

"Well, you are here, but your mind is somewhere else today. Talk to me."

Why was my expression always so readable? My mum could read me, Bridget could read me, and even Phillip could read me. I considered what to say. I told him about how strong the voices were today.

"Well, my love, tomorrow is your eighteenth birthday. Naturally, the voices are preparing you for adulthood." He smiled at me. His answer to everything was humor, and most of the time it comforted me. But today the voices left me with questions; I didn't want to be comforted. I wanted answers.

"Why do you think this is funny?" Life could not be fixed with a joke or a laugh. Sometimes, it was necessary to take things seriously. If anything bothered me about Phillip, it was his lack of seriousness.

"Abby," Phillip said, "I was just trying to make you feel better. I'm sorry."

I ignored him, but then I felt his warm calloused hand.

"I'm sorry." He squeezed my hand.

"But what do you think about it?" I wanted to know. I needed to know.

"Well, it is probably just something new. At first, they were whispers, and then conversation, and now they are talking to you."

"You think I am insane." I folded my arms and lowered my head.

"Did I say that? I don't think you're insane. If you were insane then you wouldn't be normal and quite frankly, you are. When you first told me about this, let's call it an ability, you were perfectly calm and straightforward. You didn't ramble on like an insane person, you didn't say the voices wanted you to kill people or do horrible things. I don't think you are insane. I've always listened with an open mind, you know that."

He did have an open mind.

"Let's get to the library," Phillip said, squeezing my hand again, "and I will look up some books, or at least try to find some books, on supernatural phenomenon. Okay?"

"Okay, but knowing you, you'll probably end up in the history section."

The library always had a draft and today was no exception. Cold, bitter air seeped in through the cracks of doors and windows. The iciness clung to my skin like icicles cling to the edge of rooftops in winter. I rubbed my hands against my arms as I poured over a copy of *A Tale of Two Cities*. My imagination left the war we were living in and fell into the world of 1775 London and France.

"Melanie?"

I looked up. For a split second, I feared a voice was talking to me, but it was actually a young man. He was around my age, and had a muscular build like Phillip. He towered over me at around six feet—just like Phillip.

"I'm sorry?" I responded.

The man looked at me for a moment and then said, "What are you doing out?"

I'm sure my puzzled expression was enough to tell him I was confused. "I'm sorry, my name isn't Melanie..." What was he talking about?

A strange look appeared on the man's face, but then it was gone.

"I'm sorry," he said, "you just looked a little bit like someone I knew, from far away though, close up you're different. I didn't mean to interrupt you, but oh, that book is my favorite!"

"I've reread it quite a bit," I admitted, a smile appearing on my face.

The man pulled out an empty chair and straddled it. He smiled at me and brushed some of his sandy blond hair out of his hazel eyes.

"Ian Cross," the man said, extending his hand. I shook it. "Sorry about the confusion."

"Abigail Jordan, and it's okay," I replied. Was this man being flirtatious with me? Or was he being friendly? I tried to steer the conversation toward friendly.

"Hello, hello."

My glance left Ian and gazed up to see Bridget standing in front of the table. She was wearing reading glasses but took them off and placed them in their case. Her dark black hair was braided up, falling down her back. She too pulled out a chair and took a seat. Finally, she looked over and met Ian's gaze.

"Hello stranger," Bridget said, smiling. "Who might you be?"

Ian introduced himself again; Bridget did the same. The two of them began a discussion about *A Christmas Carol.* I fell out of the conversation, but I noticed Ian looked a bit annoyed.

I excused myself for a moment and wandered off to find Phillip.

I found him in the historical section. What a surprise. He was reading a book on the civil war. He liked historical non-fiction just as much as fiction; I could not blame him for getting sidetracked.

"How can you read a book on war, during an actual war?" I felt the question was worthy of an answer. The idea baffled me. I knew Phillip had a different take on the war, but I woke up every day fearing the worst.

Conscription was something I feared. In my heart, I knew it was a noble ordeal to serve in the war. But the selfish part of me feared it just the same. Because I was not yet eighteen, and also a student, I was not yet required to serve. But that did not mean it would never happen.

Phillip, being twenty and fresh out of school, could be called at any given time. That was more so my fear—losing him.

"History fascinates me, love." Phillip grinned at me and then placed the book back in its spot. "I'm sorry," he continued, "like you predicted, I got distracted..."

His voice fell away and was replaced by a dark, distinct whisper.

"Do you trust him? Do you trust her? Do you trust anyone? Death is near."

My eyes shot to the area I felt the voice was coming from. I followed them.

CHAPTER TWO

The voice began to merge together with other voices and they became whispers; a moment passed and I could no longer tell anything apart. It was simply a constant barrage of whispering.

"Abby."

I could hear Phillip's voice—I processed it. But I continued to follow the whispers. It felt like the whispers were summoning me. It scared me, but at the same time, it fascinated me as well.

My course of direction was skewed as I weaved my way through different sections of bookshelves. I passed books upon books, smelling the paper of all of them. The smell of old library books at times wafted into my nose, but I continued my search for the whispers.

I turned a corner and then I walked right into a body. I caught the scent of wood and lavender as I gazed up into Ian's eyes. He had a crooked smile on his face; his hands encircled my arms, stopping my body from moving any further.

"Careful, there." His tone was light, joking, and sensitive.

"Sorry," I mumbled. My eyes glanced to the side, straining to see any destination point for the whispers. But as quickly as they had come, they were now gone. Silence was all there was now.

"No need to be sorry," Ian replied. "It seems to me like you were on one hell of a mission."

I smiled. It was true; I probably had been a bit frantic. Footsteps, then Phillip appeared from around the corner. My face blushed; I realized Ian still had his hands on my arms.

"Abby, why in the—" Phillip stopped and gave Ian the *look*. The jealousy look. I rarely saw it on Phillip of all people; the only time was when a man flirted with me on the street, but one of Phillip's looks quickly changed that. Ian let his hands fall and he placed them in the pockets of his trousers.

"Ian Cross." Ian extended his hand. Phillip looked at it for a moment with distaste, but shook it in the end.

"Phillip Hughes," he replied.

"Pleasure." Ian sounded bored with the introductions. I would be too, after three different people in the span of an hour. "Abigail, I need to be going. But I just wanted to let you know that Bridget was looking for you, and she invited me to your birthday tomorrow, if that's okay."

Bridget was being her outgoing self, as always. I remembered last year, we were in a boutique shopping, and she invited a stranger out to lunch as a joke. The man followed us around for a good hour until we lost him. She found humor in the strangest things. But the idea that Ian could potentially be a friend or more for Bridget came to mind. I really wanted her to have some more people in her life. She had not had a man in her life since before her father died last year in the war. "I think that's a great idea." I could see Phillip tensing out of the corner of my eye. "Did she give you the address?"

Ian reached into his pocket and pulled out a piece of paper. "Nineteen Barton Street," he read aloud.

"That would be the one," I said. "My mum should have dinner ready around five. See you then?"

"Alright." Ian said his goodbyes and walked away. Once he was out of earshot, I turned to Phillip, bracing myself.

"Who in the hell was that?" he asked.

It was quite difficult to ignore Phillip's anger. I could tell he was restraining himself from getting too angry with me, or from going after Ian and doing who knows what.

"Ian Cross," I responded. "I think he said that."

"I know he said his name, but he obviously knows you."

As we walked back in the direction of where I had left Bridget, I casually explained that I had met Ian a while ago before I had come looking for Phillip.

"And now, he's coming to your birthday?"

"In my defense, I didn't have anything to do with that."

We found Bridget reading the copy of *A Tale of Two Cities* that I had left behind. When I sat down across from her, she looked up at me through her glasses.

"I wondered where you went off to," she said. "Did you see Ian?"

"The birthday guest?" Phillip blurted out. "We met him indeed. Bridget, it is not your place to invite strangers to Abigail's events."

The Phillip and Bridget argument of the day commenced. In whole, the argument was probably around five minutes long. The average was ten minutes, but at one time they had argued for at least an hour. The arguments usually revolved around me, politics, me, my voices, and me. Phillip and Bridget were friends at heart, but they definitely did not see eye to eye on certain issues, such as politics and me. Bridget suggested I needed professional help for my *problem* whereas Phillip thought I was perfectly fine. He was indignant when he had found out that Bridget had been all for the voices when I was younger, but in her defense, she had been ten.

"I don't like him," Phillip said, "there is something different about him."

"He's a man," Bridget responded, "and the reason you don't like him is because he talked to Abigail. She is perfectly capable of making her own decisions about who she talks to and what she does."

"Which explains why you took it upon yourself to invite him to her birthday?" Phillip counteracted.

"I invited him more so for myself," Bridget responded. "He was actually quite pleasant and I'd like to get to know him. We talked for quite a while about Charles Dickens."

"Oh, Charles Dickens!" Phillip exclaimed. "Well let's just invite him to the wedding then! I mean the man knows his Charles Dickens, therefore, why the hell not?"

"Would you two stop your arguing? Bridget, I would appreciate next time that you ask me first before you invite him to an event of mine. However, Phillip, I am perfectly fine with Ian coming. He seems nice and is definitely a person I would not mind knowing. Now, I don't know about you two, but I'm ready to leave."

I had actually interrupted because the voices were back, and they were speaking to me again. But the last thing I wanted was to make that the topic of their next argument.

Who do you trust? Who do you trust? Who do you trust? Who do you trust? The voices said it over and over and over again. What scared me was that it was definitely the voices talking to me, but I knew it was a legitimate question too.

Barton Street came into view as Phillip turned the corner. The car moved slowly down the street, past the familiar row of terraced houses until we came to mine, number nineteen.

"Would you like me to come in?"

Phillip turned the key and the car ceased to run. I looked in his direction, and for a moment I wanted to say yes. But I felt worn down by the arguments and the voices that had arisen during the day. Rest was all I wanted.

"I think I'm going to have dinner and turn in early. I'll see you tomorrow."

"Goodbye, love."

The smell of pot roast engulfed my senses. I almost ran to the kitchen, but stopped myself from doing so. Especially since I was eighteen tomorrow, running in the house would get me nothing but a talking to from my mother.

I calmly entered the kitchen and before I could even say one word, my mother said it for me.

"Pot roast for dinner!" she exclaimed.

"However did you get it?" I couldn't control my excitement. Meat was not cheap in the war, and I knew this couldn't have come without a high price.

"For your birthday," my mum said, "tonight and tomorrow, there will be no war. We will eat like royalty!"

My laugh came out of joy. My mum did her best to make us happy in a time when happiness was difficult to come by. She would surprise me anytime she could.

"It must have cost a fortune."

My mother beamed at me. "Oh, it did. But don't you worry about that dear. This is your eighteenth birthday and we are going to celebrate!"

Twenty minutes later, my family and I were feasting on pot roast and fried potatoes. It wasn't a complete meal, but it was more than we had had in a while. I was used to tinned meats and broths, not pot roast!

"This turkey is delicious, Diane!"

My heart ticked faster when my father said that. I peered at him out of the corner of my eye. My mum had told me only moments after exclaiming about the pot roast, that my father had been calling her Diane all day. Apparently, Diane was an old lady friend of my father's from when he was back in school.

"Dean, my name is Annette, I am your wife, and you are eating pot roast."

My father simply smiled at my mother and took another bite. I tried to dismiss it, but I felt another crack in my already damaged heart.

* * *

After kissing my father goodnight, I informed my mother about Ian coming to my birthday the next day. She seemed thrilled by the prospect of meeting someone new. After that, I couldn't wait a moment longer; my bedroom was calling me after the long day and my warm bed was waiting.

I pulled my covers to my chin and curled up in my bed. Though the room was dark, I could still hear the sounds of nighttime London. Fairly soon, the city would be going to sleep. After a few years of the blackouts from the air raid, I figured many people in the city turned in as early as I did.

Sleep made its way through my veins, calling me, and then it took me...

The dark of night was upon the city, but there was moonlight shining down in my mother's garden. It was springtime, and the flowers were blooming. Butterflies flew through the garden. And then the alarm sounded. The alarm started out soft, but got louder, and louder, and louder.

"ABBY!"

I looked ahead, my mum was standing just outside of the bomb shelter, and she was looking at me with pure panic in her expression. She was waiting for me to come to the shelter. I looked up into the sky and I saw the small black dots, getting bigger and bigger and bigger.

"ABBY! HURRY!"

I ran forward, but every step I took, my mum and the shelter got farther and farther and farther away.

"Abigail."

I stopped. The voice was different from my mother's. It still had a motherly quality to it, but it was softer, and younger. I turned around.

She was standing just in front of the back door to our kitchen. Her long, wavy, blonde hair fell elegantly down her back. It blew in the wind along with her pure, white dress. The woman held out her hand, palm up, like she was waiting for me to come and take it.

"Stay away," the woman said.

It was too late.

The bombs dropped.

My whole body went upright as I took a gasp of air. My heart was racing so fast I thought it might burst forth from my chest. The silver nightgown I wore was now drenched in sweat. My eyes looked around in the darkness, but that was all I saw—darkness. I lay back, placing a hand over my heart, hoping to calm it down. I stared up at the ceiling, wondering what I had just dreamed.

Cold air wafted into my room. I shivered underneath the covers of my bed. Weren't covers supposed to be warm? I stopped my thoughts and listened. But there were no voices right now—all was quiet. Quiet, until there was a creak outside of my door and it opened.

"Abby..."

My mother's soft voice drifted over to me and my eyes cracked open a little, and then I was awake.

"Happy birthday, my sweet girl."

The door opened all the way until it was ajar and my mum stepped into my bedroom. She walked over to the edge of my bed and took a seat, placing a hand on top of mine.

Today was December 8th—my birthday.

"Why don't you get dressed?" my mother whispered. "We'll be off to church in a few."

I was pressed in between my mother and father at St. Patrick's Church in Soho Square. The church was packed today; everyone chose the same mass time it seemed. I let my eyes wander up to the vaulted ceiling with its intricate designs. But when I felt the soft touch of my mother's hand on mine, a gentle "pay attention" statement, I refocused my attention back toward the altar.

After the mass, we resumed the day at number nineteen with a special breakfast prepared by Mrs. Baxter. My mother had taken the day off, to be with me she had said, but the nagging worry about our need for money remained constant. I brushed it off. Birthdays were once a year.

"Tinned sausage, cooked, some wheat toast with a dash of cinnamon, and we have some browned potatoes," Mrs. Baxter announced. She placed each dish on the kitchen table and put her hands on her hips. "It isn't much, but it's my birthday treats for Miss Abigail, here."

"Mrs. Baxter, I'm sure it will be delicious," I assured her, "thank you very much."

Mrs. Baxter planted a kiss on my cheek and then began cleaning the pots and pans she had used.

"Did you tell the guest five o'clock?" my mum asked after she had swallowed some of her potatoes.

I nodded as I chewed on some sausage. The taste was salty and delicious, but there was still a hint that it had been tinned and not fresh.

"Will my wife be there?"

My heart skipped a beat and I turned my attention toward my father. His expression was sordid, and he looked like he was about to cry.

"Dean." My mum placed her hand on his. "I'm right here, sweetheart. I'm right here."

It wasn't fair for my mum. It just wasn't fair.

I was combing my hair when it happened. One moment, I was in front of my bedroom mirror, my hand combing through my hair, and then I had fallen out of my chair. My breath had left me.

The waves rattled against the seashore. I was looking out on the ocean. Seagulls flew through the air. The whiteness of their feathers caught my eye. Suddenly, a light mist of sea waves sprayed me and I smiled as it touched my cheeks. I wondered what was happening, how was I here? I could hear the waves. I could feel the mist. How did I get here?

"Abby."

A man came up from behind and placed his hand on the small of my back. It wasn't Phillip. I knew that. But this man, I felt like I knew him. I felt like I loved him. What was going on? What was going on? I began to panic and—

My lungs cried for breath and finally it came. The ceiling was above me. I was looking up at it. I was probably convulsing on the floor, judging from the amount of gasping I was doing, trying to catch my breath. What had just happened? Something different had happened, that was for sure. I had felt the ocean. I had felt the man's hand on me.

The door to my bedroom opened and closed and then there were footsteps.

"Abby." I heard Phillip's voice and then his arms were around me, pulling me into his chest.

"Honey," he said, "are you okay? Talk to me."

I opened my eyes just a bit and looked into his blue eyes. We held each other's gaze and then I curled into him. He stood up, lifting me in his arms and carried me to my bed. He carefully placed me in the bed and then knelt down by the side of the it.

"Something happened," I whispered, "I think I went away."

"What do you mean?"

Phillip meant everything to me. I trusted him with my life and I knew I could trust him with this; therefore, I told him.

I told him how I was standing by the ocean and felt the sea spray against my face. I told him how another man, someone I loved, placed his hand on my back and had called my Abby. I told him how it wasn't like a dream; I had been there. I had felt it. I had seen it.

"I feel like I've betrayed you," I said, and I did. Why was there a different man in whatever this had been? Was it a vision? But I had felt it. It had felt real.

"Abby," he said, "you haven't done anything. Please do not think you've betrayed me. Never think that."

The door to my bedroom opened again and my mum was in the doorway.

"Are you okay?" She looked concerned. I assumed she had come in to tell me to come downstairs, but I could see the concern in her face.

I nodded.

"Well, let's go," she said. "Ian, is that right? Well, he's here."

"Lovely," Phillip said, "let's go talk about some Dickens. Shall we?"

He stood up and held out his hand. I took it, feeling comfort and warmth. Today was my birthday; it was a time of celebration. I wasn't going to let these things in my head get to me tonight. Tonight, I would celebrate. Tomorrow, I could worry.

CHAPTER THREE

Phillip insisted that I hold his hand as we walked downstairs. I refused, knowing that he only wanted to make it obvious that we were together, but he grabbed it anyway. I could hear my father talking to Ian from the landing and felt peace knowing he could still talk to others.

"Abby," Ian announced as I walked into the sitting room. I felt Phillip tense up at my side, but he quickly relaxed again. Ian held out his hand and I dropped Phillips and shook it.

"It's a pleasure to see you again, Ian!"

"Abby." I heard Phillip's voice and then his arms were around me, pulling me into his chest.

"Honey," he said, "are you okay? Talk to me." My eyes popped open and Phillip was leaning over me. The whole thing had been another dream? Maybe I would worry today after all.

"Honey," Phillip said, "please talk to me."

And then I was telling Phillip about the sea spray on my face and how I could feel it. After that, I was telling him about the man. I did not normally curse, but what the hell was going on? Had I not already said these things to Phillip?

I realized that Phillip had lifted me up and carried me to my bed. My mum should be coming through the door by now and sure enough...

The door to my bedroom opened again and my mum was in the doorway.

"Are you okay?"

I nodded.

"Well, let's go," she said. "Ian, is that right? Well, he's here."

"Lovely," Phillip said, "let's go talk about some Dickens. Shall we?"

He stood up and held out his hand. I didn't feel stable enough to go and join the party. The safer bet was to stay in bed, but I knew I couldn't. The next several moments passed by like they had before and then I was shaking Ian's hand. My mum announced that we would begin when Bridget arrived. I took the opportunity to pull Phillip to the side and talk to him. I needed to figure this out now.

We walked into the hallway and then I began to whisper to him.

"Something is wrong," I said. "It isn't just the whispers anymore, I had some sort of vision. I saw everything that just happened, before it even happened. I saw you come into my room and help me off the floor, after I had had the first vision and then we went downstairs and Ian had said hello to me. And then I woke up and everything happened as I had seen it."

Before Phillip could respond, there was a knock at the door.

"We'll talk about this later," he said, "okay?"

I nodded. I turned and was about to walk over to the door when a picture on the wall caught my eye. It was a picture of me out in my mother's garden. I was not looking at the camera, but playing in a flowerbed. I remembered the day because it was the day that I had fallen out of the big willow tree in our backyard. My thoughts drifted for a moment to who I was becoming—because who I was becoming was starting to scare me.

I realized my hand was shaking from fear as I undid the chain on the door and turned the lock. Bridget stood before me in the cold London air. Snow had begun to fall and the ground was already blanketed with some of it.

"Come in."

Bridget did not wait in the cold a second longer; she stepped through the doorway and I shut the door to the cold.

"Happy birthday!" she said. A smile appeared on her face as she took off her jacket and gloves. She pulled me in for a birthday hug and I returned it graciously.

"Thank you," I whispered.

"Who do you trust, Abigail?"

My bones rattled; my body froze. Why were the voices talking to me? I felt like I was unraveling at the core.

"Are you alright?"

Snapping back to reality, I realized Bridget was speaking to me. I nodded and made my way back to the sitting room before she asked another question.

"Happy eighteenth birthday, my love!"

My mum placed a round cake, frosted with white icing in front of me. The words 'Happy Birthday' were written on top in red. It was simple, but at the same time I felt gratitude. My mum went to great lengths to find enough ingredients to make a cake. With the war, they were more expensive every day.

"Thank you, mum," I said.

She planted a kiss on my forehead and then she cut the cake. The party was small and quiet, made of my parents, Mrs. Baxter, Phillip, Ian, and Bridget. It was simple, but it meant the world to me.

Music erupted from the sitting room and I realized Mrs. Baxter must have turned on a radio station.

"Let's dance, Ian!"

I couldn't help but let out a laugh at Mrs. Baxter's youthfulness. She was always trying to be young again. Phillip held out his hand and I took it. He led me to the living room to see the horrors of Mrs. Baxter's dancing. She had Ian glued to her body and they were dancing. Ian looked a tad bit uncomfortable.

"Diane," I heard my father say, "would you like to dance?"

Diane. He just wouldn't stop calling her that. I heard my mum say yes and then Phillip pulled me behind him and we were dancing, too. I realized Bridget was standing by the wall, smiling, but she still looked alone.

"Bridget," I said, "come dance with Ian."

Mrs. Baxter gave me the look of death, but I ignored her. Ian stepped aside and held out his hand for Bridget; such a gentleman he was.

"Well, if that's how it is going to be," Mrs. Baxter said, hands on hips. She walked forward and held out her hand for Phillip and he took it. "I'll be stealing your man, youngin'. Watch and learn how us old ladies get jiggly with it."

"Mrs. Baxter!" My mum attempted to sound stern, but it ended up coming out as a laugh. I laughed too; it was all in good fun. I stepped to the side and watched Phillip and Mrs. Baxter get "jiggly with it". My heart melted a bit when I saw Bridget; she truly looked like she enjoyed Ian's company. I wondered.

"Are you ready?"

Phillip and I were standing in the kitchen, alone. We had been talking about the night. The rest of the party was still in the sitting room, chatting and dancing. Bridget had left a little early to do some studying.

"Ready for what?" I asked. I was still eating some cake; I played with it with my fork.

"My proposal to you."

The fork fell to the plate. I had forgotten that Phillip was going to "propose again" on my birthday when he had a ring, as he had said. He had asked me a few weeks ago simply because he couldn't wait any longer, but now this was it! My mind couldn't come up with words to say, and therefore I only nodded my head.

Phillip stood up and then bent down on one knee. He reached into his pocket and pulled out a small black ring box.

"Abigail Jordan," he said, "I love you. I will always love you. Will you be my wife?"

He clicked the box open, and I stopped breathing. Literally.

The snow was falling around me. I didn't feel it, though. I didn't feel cold; I wasn't freezing. The blackout rules were still being enforced and thus all the windows of homes were dark, shuttered up or covered by dark curtains. One house still had a light emanating from it and I saw an Air Raid Protection (ARP) Warden bang on the door of a house.

"Please, put the light out!"

Immediately, the light went out. The moonlight shown on the street though and I could still see figures walking down the street. The street. I realized then I was on Barton Street—my street.

A double-decker bus was making its way down one end of the street and because of the blackout rules, the bus was emanating the smallest amount of light possible.

"I don't understand why you have to go!"

A woman's shrill, upset voice from behind me caught my attention. I turned around and saw a man and woman arguing at the steps of a terraced house down the road. I walked toward them, slowly, casually.

"Margaret," a man replied, "it is an honor to go and serve my country. Please understand."

The woman's face—I could tell now—was streaked with tears. It looked like they were a couple and had been out for the night, for a date, perhaps. But the night was being ruined now as the man broke the news.

"You are my husband," Margaret replied, "I will not understand. Please, don't leave me. Don't."

She was in hysterics now. She wasn't thinking clearly. Margaret stepped out into the street and turned. The bus! I had forgotten about it. It came out of nowhere in the darkness. She was facing the other way; she wouldn't have known. The man screamed for his wife, but she was hit.

"Bloody hell." I heard the ARP warden yelling and then curtains were being pulled open and what was supposed to be a blacked-out neighborhood was now lit

up by the lights. The bus had stopped, but too late; it had hit her. Margaret lay in the ditch, where she had rolled after being hit. She was dead.

My eyes fluttered open and directly in front of them were Phillip's eyes. He was leaning over me when I came to. I gasped for air and coughed violently. My body was shaking.

"The street." It was all I could say. And then finally, I came back completely to reality. I pushed myself up, much to Phillip's surprise, and walked out of the kitchen, and down the hallway.

"Abigail?" I heard my mum say, but I was too focused to respond. I threw open the door. I couldn't see anyone.

My mum and Phillip walked up behind me, followed by Ian.

"What's wrong?" my mum said.

"A woman is going to be hit by a double-decker bus."

But just as I said it, the bus rolled by and there was a scream. My mum, being a nurse, pushed past me and ran out into the dark street. Lights began to pour forth from within the other terraced houses.

"Bloody hell."

My eyes followed the voice. The ARP warden was running to the scene. My mum was already there. She was on the ground, leaning over the woman. Margaret's husband was kneeling next to his wife, crying. They were trying to do something, anything. But I knew. I knew she was already dead. Because I had seen it before it had happened.

In the midst of the chaos, I ran back up to my room and closed the door behind me. I was still shaking. I knew my reaction to the whole event was probably strange, but the only thing that kept running through my head was the fact that I had seen an event before it actually happened.

I slipped into my bed and pulled the covers up to my chin.

I wasn't sure if hours or minutes had passed when my bedroom door opened and light seeped in. The door shut again and I could smell the scent of his mint lotion.

Phillip crawled into the bed next to me, pulling the covers up and over him. I felt his arm around my waist, pulling me into him. I felt him turning me to face his eyes in the dark.

"What are you doing?"

If my mum came in and saw us like this, she would have a heart attack.

"I came to protect you."

Protect me.

"Your mum," Phillip said, "is at the hospital with the husband. He was in hysterics; I can't blame him."

Phillip's hand came up and brushed my cheek. He caressed my cheek for a moment, gazing into my eyes.

"If anything like that ever happened to you," Phillip whispered, "I don't know what I would do with myself. You are my everything."

My eyes watered. I realized I was crying. He pulled me into his chest and his scent engulfed me. It smelled so soothing, calming.

"Don't cry, love."

"Phillip," I said, "I saw it. I saw it happen, before it happened. You heard me predict it. Please don't tell people; don't tell Bridget."

"I know, and I won't. But you should tell her at some point. There is something special about you. There always has been."

I wasn't sure if I wanted there to be anything special about me. It scared me. I told Phillip that and he shushed me. We laid like that. I in his arms. Him in mine. Together, we fell asleep.

CHAPTER FOUR

The next morning, after Phillip had left, the snow had stopped falling. It had left a soft, white blanket over the city. I heard the crunching of the snow beneath my feet as I walked down Barton Street. My mind was toiling over the events of the previous evening—the fact that my mother, and even Ian, now knew I wasn't exactly a normal person. I had not seen my mother since the previous evening—she was already gone when I woke up that morning. I was walking in the direction of the tube, to head to class, when a hand touched my shoulder.

"Abigail."

A little shriek came from me and I turned around. I put my hand to my chest to calm myself when I saw it was only Ian. He had his long, brown walking coat buttoned up around him.

"I didn't mean to scare you," he told me. "I was about to stop at your house when I saw you leaving. I wanted to see if you were okay."

I nodded. "I'm fine. But I need to go. I have class, sorry."

I turned, but he spoke up again.

"I know what you are. I know you hear voices. And I think I know where you come from, if you will let me explain."

My whole body froze. He knew about the incident the night before and he knew where I came from. But how?

I turned around again. Ian was closer to me. If I reached out, I could touch him. His eyes—there was recognition there, as if he'd finally achieved something he'd been working toward for a long while.

"You think you know where I come from?"

Ian nodded. "If I'm correct, I work with your father—your biological father. When I found you at the library, I felt like it was you. I've seen pictures of your biological mother and you look exactly like her, except for your hair color. But I still didn't know for sure until last night. That confirmed it for me."

The cold of the weather and the surprise of his words were causing me to shiver.

"Are you okay?" he asked.

"No," I said. "I don't understand any of this. How do you know about all of this?"

I realized that my eyes were tearing up and I quickly turned my face and wiped them away. Ian put a comforting hand on my shoulder and I looked back at him.

"I really need to go to class," I said.

"I know, but I thought I could—I thought I could take you to your father. What happened to you yesterday, what's been happening, I can't imagine how it all must feel. But I feel that seeing him would be better for you."

I never skipped class, but this felt like a good reason to. After a minute, I nodded. The world I lived in was getting bigger.

Ian and I took the tube to the building of Parliament. We didn't talk to each other; or at least, I didn't talk to him. He attempted to make conversation, but after so many nods and grunts from me, I think he gave up. My mind was in disarray. Who was this person? How did he know my father? I had never thought before that I would receive answers to many of my questions, and in turn be rewarded with even more questions.

"Do you hear them too?" The question probably surprised him after minutes of silence. I figured I should elaborate. "The whispers, or the voices. Do you see things?"

"Yes," Ian replied. "Believe me, there are hundreds of people who have this, let's call it, an ability. But I want you to hear it from him, not me."

A part of me wished Ian, or my father, had found me sooner. I felt if I had not known Ian a part of me would feel like succumbing to insanity. The thought scared me. I decided to think about Phillip, but that only made it worse. What would he think if he knew Ian had some sort of connection to me?

The train began to brake and finally came to a stop. As we began to make the trek out of the tube, my attention diverted to a poster for the war. *Hitler will send no warning—so always carry your gas mask.* The picture of the mask, being held by two hands, brought my thoughts to my mask at home. I had stopped carrying it a long time ago. The purported gassing from Hitler had never come, but they kept the signs up to remind us. We weren't safe. What if someone had had a vision about this war and all the death? I wondered if it could have been prevented.

"Abigail."

My eyes averted back to Ian. I realized I had paused, one foot on the step and the other on the ground, my attention being taken up by the sign.

"I'm sorry."

I ran forward to keep up and followed Ian out of the tube. The cold air was not friendly to my cheeks. I pulled my coat tighter around me and followed him out of Westminster station. The streets were busy today as we crossed over and entered the building of Parliament through the public entrance. Ian led me through the Lords Visitor Route and then we stopped at a door that was clearly for authorized individuals only. He took out a set of keys from his pocket and unlocked the door. I followed him through the open door and he shut it behind us.

"Isn't someone going to be suspicious that we are coming in here?" I asked.

It was then that I realized he had put on a badge for U.K. Parliament maintenance.

"My profession during the daytime, miss," Ian replied, a grin on his face. "How else would I have keys? Besides that, we have ways of gaining access. We were here first, in all technicality."

We. Who were we?

Ian led me down several flights of stairs until I was sure we were at the very bottom of the building. He led me through several chambers used for ventilation and heating, until finally we faced an older brick wall. Ian then took out a key inserted it into a very small crack, and then turned it. The wall began to slide over, revealing an entrance. Beyond that, there was only darkness.

"Do you trust me?"

My eyes widened as I considered his question. He held out his hand.

"No," I said. But I took it anyway.

I followed him into the darkness and could tell he was inserting the key into another crack on the other side of the wall. The wall began to slide into place until we were entirely consumed in darkness. A sudden jerking motion made me scream and lose my balance. I felt Ian's arms around my waist, steadying me. We were descending.

"A lift," Ian said. "This is where the secrets come to light."

The lift continued to take us farther and farther below Parliament, until finally it stopped. We were in front of an old, iron, fence door. Ian inserted the key into an actual keyhole this time, and unlocked the door. He slid it to the side and I stepped out into a long corridor.

"Well, I took a tour of Parliament when I was younger," I said, "with my parents of course. I definitely don't remember this being part of it."

Ian laughed. "No. Abigail, I know this may be difficult for you to understand, but the world that you live in, that we live in, is not privy to everything that is a part of humanity. Come with me."

I looked up as I followed Ian down the corridor. The vaulted ceilings captivated me. I felt like I was inside an underground castle. Pictures adorned both sides of the walls. They were portraits of people. The older ones were painted, but as we moved further down the corridor, a few were actual photographs.

Finally, we entered a round, oval shaped room. It looked like a small library and sitting room. An enormous fireplace was at the opposite wall, a fire roaring in its grate. In front of the fireplace, there was one mahogany desk.

"Ian."

The shock of a nearby voice almost made me scream. I turned slowly, realizing that this voice must belong to the man that was my biological father. Turning around, I saw him exiting a door to the side of the hall, closing it behind him. He was taller than me, probably around six feet. His hair was a dark brown, like mine, but it was quite long, almost down to his shoulders. He sported a light shadow of a beard on his face and appeared to be in his early forties.

"The rules, Ian," he finally spoke. "You are not supposed to bring anyone into the—"

He stopped. Realization came over his face as he continued to gaze at me.

"You look like my wife," he said. "Elisabeth."

"Mathias," I heard Ian speak up. *Mathias.* My biological father was *Mathias.* "This is Abigail. Your daughter."

A look appeared on his face, portraying some kind of internal struggle. But then it was gone, replaced with an everyday look, void of any struggle. Mathias walked over to me and held out his hand. I looked at it for a moment, questioned myself, and then shook it.

"Abigail Jordan," I finally spoke.

"Mathias Benedict," he replied. "I suppose you must have many questions."

I only nodded.

Mathias turned his head back toward Ian.

"How did you find her?"

"I met her at the London Library," said Ian, "a couple days ago. She looked so much like the picture that you showed me of Elisabeth and then, last night at her birthday, she had a premonition and I knew it was her. Abby, come sit."

Ian led me over to a dark, leather couch that sat just in front of the desk. I took a seat, and he sat down next to me. It was a little too close for me, but I let it go.

Mathias walked in front of the couch and turned to face us, hands behind his back. He looked almost like one of my professor's while I was in class.

"This place," Mathias began, "was built long ago. Abigail, you are part of a society of individuals that has been in charge of something very powerful for thousands of years. This society of people is very involved with the governments throughout various countries. We remain hidden, for our powers would be too much for the human race to handle and understand.

"Our place in government allows us, certain privileges. For example, our society has quite a few influential people also working in the government. We were able to persuade, shall we say, where U.K. Parliament would be built so that we could preserve our secret location. We are called the Timekeepers."

I had taken in everything Mathias had been saying, but the words that continued to be on repeat in my head were *powers* and *Timekeepers*.

"The Timekeepers have the gift of the sight," Mathias continued.

"We are able to travel to the past as well as foresee events that might happen in the future. Our role in society is to record time, measure it, and keep it protected. Humanity and its history could very much be lost if it was not for our role in this world. We use a powerful force called the Time Line to help us measure and record history. It is our job to keep time constant and moving, otherwise, time could easily stop and that would very much affect the future of this planet."

My mind was producing one question after another.

"I can hear voices," I finally said. "They talk to me."

"Those voices," Mathias answered, "would be part of the sight. They are usually one of the first signs of the ability to appear in a child Timekeeper. Once the Timekeeper turns eighteen however, those voices will usually manifest into full-fledged premonitions."

I passively nodded.

"I saw someone die," I said, "yesterday. Before it happened."

"That was when I knew it had to be your child," Ian spoke up.

"I should have prevented it," I admitted.

"No!"

Mathias had raised his voice. A slight flush graced his cheeks. I suddenly felt ashamed of something I had said. What was so terrible about wanting to prevent someone's death?

"Mathias," Ian said, "she doesn't know."

Mathias' expression cooled off a bit.

"I'm sorry," Mathias said, "I forget sometimes that not everyone knows everything about our world. Abigail, if you would be interested, I'd like for you to come here as much as possible to learn about this world. To learn about us. I understand you've never been a part of it, but I'd like for you to join us. I understand that all of this might be a bit much for one day, but if you come back, I promise you answers. But I want to let you know of an important rule. That rule is that we do not inform outsiders of our abilities, except in the case of a spouse. There are people that know about our world, but these people are approved by the council to know. You must seek approval, and have a very specific reason, if you want outsiders to be knowledgeable of our world."

I nodded; however, I was more focused on him giving me answers —the one thing that I had been searching for for so long. I had an answer for the voices. I had an answer for the visions. But did I have an answer for who I was? Why my mother left me? I still wasn't sure of my place in this world—what I was meant to do. Joining this world—being a Timekeeper—it scared me. But it also fascinated me. I wanted to learn. However, I was not sure if this was something I wanted to confide in everyone else, just yet.

There was no going back now.

"I will."

The fire crackled in the grate in Phillip's apartment. Warm air touched my skin; it made me feel comfort. Phillip was studying at his desk, several books out in front of him. I was reading the copy of *A Tale of Two Cities* that I had checked out.

I continued to read the same quotation over and over again. It brought back memories of the things that I had learned today.

I read to myself, *"If, when I hint to you of a Home that is before us, where I will be true to you with all my duty and with all my faithful service, I bring back the remembrance of a Home long desolate, while your poor heart pined away, weep for it, weep for it!"*

Finally, I tore my eyes away from the book. I looked at Phillip. His focus was entirely on his studies. He looked peaceful and vulnerable. How could I not tell him? I had to tell him.

"No, you don't. Don't trust them."

I did not understand these voices; they could not be from the future.

"Don't trust her."

Her? It sounded like two different voices going back and forth, but they both sounded the same in some aspects. But Phillip I could trust; I didn't have to listen to the voices.

"Phillip."

Phillip looked up from the book he was reading and gazed in my direction. He grinned at me, his dimples going up in both directions.

"Yes?"

"Will you come here for a second? I need to tell you something."

He pushed the chair back and was over to the couch before I could say another word. He sat down next to me, pulling me close to his chest.

"I didn't say cradle me," I joked.

"What is going on?"

Would he be mad at me for not telling him sooner? Maybe. Would he still love me? Yes. He always would. I told him about Ian knowing that I could hear voices. I told him about Ian taking me to Parliament, and finally about meeting my father. And finally, I told him about being a Timekeeper and having powers. I knew that I was technically breaking a rule, but were were engaged, so I felt like it was okay.

"Holy shit."

Really? That was his response. It was entirely Phillip. I shouldn't be surprised.

"I'm going back tomorrow with Ian."

"I don't like him."

I couldn't help but raise my eyebrows.

"I'm assuming you don't like him because I consider him a friend and like to spend time with him—as friends."

"You are perfectly capable of spending time with people," Phillip countered, "I'm not the jealous type. There is just something about him that rubs me the wrong way, that's all."

After informing Phillip that Ian was a nice person, that he was just a friend, and how I didn't see anything wrong with him, we talked about the Timekeeping.

"I just don't know if it is something I want to do."

"It's your choice," Phillip said, "but if you don't mind my saying, I think you should."

"I think I will," I said, "I'm just afraid. I've wanted to find myself and here I am. Finding myself. But it feels like more and more questions are coming up."

Phillip kissed my forehead, and then whispered to me softly.

"Don't be afraid. It will be okay. I promise."

CHAPTER FIVE

The next morning, snow stuck to the ground. The city of London was blanketed in white powder. It wasn't terrible. The snow had already finished by the time day broke and the roads were not treacherous. Ian and I had come up with a designated time to meet outside the Parliament. He stood in front of the visitor's entrance, hands in pockets. He had his usual grin on his face and his sandy blond hair was disheveled.

"Afternoon, Miss."

"Afternoon," I replied. He had on black trousers and a tweed jacket. On his jacket was the usual badge that said he was an employee in maintenance. I couldn't help but giggle when I saw it.

"Might I ask what is so funny?"

"Why, your maintenance badge, sir," I responded.

Ian led me down the same hallways and into the basement of Parliament.

"Are you able to get into the clock tower?" I asked.

"Of course. I am maintenance after all. I'll take you up there someday."

"I'd like that."

For the first time in a while, things felt like they were going in the right direction. Ian was someone I liked being around and I hoped he'd consider us being friends. I needed more friends in my life.

Mathias stood in front of his mahogany desk, leaning on it just slightly. Ian sat in the chair behind it.

"Today," Mathias began, "I think we should start with the history of the Timekeepers. What you might find fascinating about us is that at some point in time, we lost our history. This is why we consider it even more important to record history, not only for us, but for the human world as well. Thousands of years ago, it is rumored that there was one family who had the power to control time, manipulate it, and use it. The family supposedly took great care in this gift and passed it on to their children. However, at some point, they decided to start a society, because it was shown that they could not care for the whole world's history on their own."

"Why did we need Timekeepers in the first place?" I asked.

"We need them to keep the Time Line going," Mathias said. "If for some reason, the human history is lost, we have it. We can keep the Time Line going. We keep time. It is what we were called to do."

I decided to ask about my mother. I needed to know about her, just as much as everything else.

"Tell me about my mother."

Ian got a little tense behind Mathias, but he stayed quiet.

"Abigail," Mathias began, "I'm going to be honest with you in all of this."

I nodded. The truth was what I was here for.

"First," Mathias began, "your mother, my wife, Elisabeth, is dead. She was an amazing woman—always happy. If she ever had difficulties, she did not show them. Which is why I believe she did not tell me some of the things that went on in her life before she died. What I know is that in the last few months of her pregnancy with you, she began to act strange. She began to herself in her room and I have no idea why. She did not wish to speak with me. I assumed she was mad at me, but now I believe she was trying to protect me from something. Obviously if I had found out what it was I would have done everything I could to protect her and help her. Which is why she probably didn't tell me anything."

Mathias reached forward and poured himself some tea from a pot on the coffee table. He sipped at it casually like we were at a tea party. He offered me a cup but I declined.

"Toward the end of her pregnancy, she disappeared," Mathias said. "She left no note; no clue as to where she had gone. The next day, her body was found hanging from the Tower Bridge. Obviously, it was deemed as a suicide, but I felt in my heart that this wasn't the truth. She was a strong, courageous woman, your mother. She wouldn't leave her family like that, not without good reason. I feel she was in danger, and the reason she did not tell me was because she wanted us both to be safe. But I had no way of knowing you were alive either, until Ian brought you here. Otherwise… well, otherwise I would have been searching for you."

"Are we still in danger?"

Mathias simply shrugged his shoulders. "That I cannot answer. I have not received any threats from outsiders in all these years, nor I have ever considered myself to be under any danger. I trusted that if you were alive, you were safe. I had to."

I sat motionless for a moment. I felt like the only thing I was getting were more questions instead of answers. I had a strong desire to understand what happened to the woman who protected me. She was the reason I was left with Mr. and Mrs. Jordan. My father had nothing to do it with it. I knew she was trying to protect me, but from what, I didn't know. I had to know.

"So...this time thing," I said, "does that mean I can time travel?"

"That is not possible," Mathias stated. "We can visit events in the past, but that is all. With the future, we only know what we think will happen based on the premonitions, but there is no way for us to actually travel into the future, as far as we have discovered anyway."

"But what about the visions I've seen of things," I asked, "they can only be from the future."

"While we cannot travel into the future," Mathias continued, "we can predict. Timekeepers receive what are called premonitions. These visions or voices we hear are a premonition of what could happen. However, whether or not they do happen, is up to the person in the vision. They can always change. These premonitions can be quite annoying, as some are so trivial and minor we wonder why we even bother to get them."

"But if we need to, we can change them?"

"No."

Mathias suddenly became very stern. His whole body tensed up, like it had yesterday, but then, just as fast, as he became less tense and settled down.

"I'm sorry," he told me, "I've forgotten again there are many things you do not know yet. But one of our greatest laws as Timekeepers is that we do not change or interfere with what we see. We are not protectors. We are not God. We simply oversee the course of time, record events, and correct mistakes as they happen. We have to allow people to make their own decisions. If they choose to walk in front of a train we cannot interfere with them just because we saw it in a vision. It can be difficult, but is naturally right. Free will is an important element of a being a human with a soul."

"But what do you mean about correcting mistakes?"

Mathias hesitated, but then continued. "You have to understand that there have been Timekeepers that have broken the law and interfered. We correct their mistake in the best way we can. Usually it is stripping them, unfortunately, of their Timekeeping ability. However, these have been small mistakes. If a Timekeeper foresees someone's death, they are not to interfere with the course of death. If they do, death will take them instead."

"So, what you are saying is, is if I had told that woman about her dying, I would have died instead."

"Yes," Mathias responded.

I felt relieved that I had not told that woman about her death, but a part me of also felt frightened. What if Ian had never found me? What if I had done something like this in the future? Why would my mother put me in this situation?

"Why didn't you tell me this yesterday?" I asked. I felt like it was something I should have been told right away.

"I apologize. I just didn't want to overwhelm you. I realize that is something I should have told you now." I nodded and took a deep breath and decided to continue asking questions.

"Can we travel to the past and change it?"

"No. When we time travel, all we can do is observe. No one can see us. There is no way we can interfere. We simply observe, and then when we travel back, it is to the exact spot we left."

"Can time be reversed?" I could only think of question after question to ask. I was very curious.

"No."

"Who enforces the laws of time?"

"There is a group made up of Timekeepers from different countries," Mathias replied. "They make up a small council that makes sure the law is enforced. They serve on the council for ten years, before electing new members."

I was going to ask more, but Mathias held up his hand, signaling me to stop.

"Abigail. I understand you are curious. But there is a lot that I have to teach you and—forgive my pun—but a lot of time to teach you it. I would like for you to come here each day for lessons. I will allow you to choose whenever you want to come. I will always be here."

I thought about it for a moment. Was I really going to do this? But I had to. I wanted to learn about my mother and I was interested in it all.

"Okay," I said.

Mathias smiled.

"Will I see you tomorrow then?" he asked.

I nodded.

"Ian, will escort you out. You can meet here at the same time, tomorrow."

Later that night, after dinner, I helped my mother take my father upstairs. He kissed us both goodnight and I went back down with my mother to help wash dishes.

"You seem off today," she said while scrubbing a greasy pan.

"I'm fine." I methodically dried the dishes, not really paying attention to what I was doing.

"Are you sure?"

I didn't look at my mother. I kept drying the glass in my hand, but I knew I had to respond.

"I am." I could tell she didn't buy it.

"You don't have to tell me anything." I felt my mother's hand on my shoulder. A gesture of comfort that was both simple and powerful. "Just tell me everything will be okay."

I smiled then. She always understood and that is what I loved about her.

"Everything will be okay," I responded.

She leaned in and hugged me. As she did, there was a knock at the front door.

"I'll get it," I said.

As I walked to the door I began to hear the wind outside rustling the house. I opened the front door and then Bridget was standing in front of me.

"Come in," I said.

"Bridget, hello dear," my mum said, coming into the hallway.

"Hello, Mrs. Jordan," Bridget said.

"Why don't you two head upstairs and I'll bring up some tea and cookies," my mum said.

"That sounds like a plan," Bridget said, a smile appearing on her face, "if Abigail doesn't mind."

My mother's face shifted into a confused expression and then she smiled.

"Of course, she doesn't mind," she responded. "My dear Bridget, what a silly thing to say."

My mum smiled again and then went back to the kitchen. I began to make my way up the stairs and Bridget followed.

I shut my door as soon as we were safely in my room.

"Listen Bridget," I said, "there is something I want to tell you."

"Are you hearing the voices again?" she asked.

I caught myself before I said anything. What should I say? Honestly, I felt like Bridget wouldn't believe me. She would probably suggest professional help again.

Bridget and I had been friends since childhood. We had grown up together. Even when her father and stepmother had moved to another neighborhood, my mum made sure we stayed friends. We occasionally hung out in a group with some friends from university, but Bridget was truly my best friend. I could talk to her about anything, but ever since I grew closer to Phillip, it felt like we had grown apart. I decided to tell her a few things.

"I might have another parent."

Her eyes widened. "What do you mean?"

I launched into the story of the past two days, but I left out the

Timekeeping. I decided to leave out the premonition at the party as well. I simply told her I had met my father at Big Ben and that we talked briefly, but that he wasn't a very personable type of person.

"How did you know where to find him?"

Another lie. "I've been doing some research."

Bridget was smart, and I could tell she didn't quite buy that response, but she let it slide for the time being.

"Are you going to go back?"

"I think I might go tomorrow," I responded. I looked over my shoulder and out the window. The snow had begun to fall. It was beautiful and for a moment I thought, why was I lying to my best friend? I didn't want to, but at the same time I felt like this thing that I was needed to be kept private. I would tell Phillip of course. I was going to marry him after all. But if Bridget and I were growing apart, then I didn't know if I could tell her.

"I didn't think it was going to snow again," Bridget said, "I'd better get going."

She said this just as my mother came in.

"Are you sure?" my mother protested. "You could spend the night here dear."

"I need to get back Mrs. Jordan," Bridget responded, "thank you though. I've just got a lot of work today and it's all at home."

My mother saw her to the door. So much for the cookies. I ate one as I continued to look out into the night. The cold snow fell from the sky. Was I a cold person? The thought scared me because I felt like I might be.

CHAPTER SIX

I went to Big Ben via a bus, due to the snowy weather. Ian was at the same spot as yesterday.

"How are you today?"

"I'm okay."

"I want to show you the tower."

The questions that ran through my head were never ending. Ian led me on a different course today. He led me to a door that simply said, *Clock Tower*, on it. As he did with the other doors, he pulled out a set of keys and unlocked the door. And then began the long trek of stairs.

It felt like the stairs were never ending. Every time we turned a corner, I hoped we were there, but there were only more stairs. Further up he led us, until finally we entered a square shape room with the bell, Big Ben, in the middle. He led me over to the round window with the clock hands and I looked out upon the city of London.

"It's beautiful," I said.

"It is," Ian responded.

We stood like that, for a while, admiring the city—tranquility surrounding us.

Mathias met us just outside the lift.

"Ian," Mathias said, "would you mind leaving us alone for a while? I would like to spend some time with Abigail, privately."

Ian nodded, even though I longed for him to stay. I still felt more comfortable around him than Mathias. I once again admired the long corridor leading down to the study. I stopped to look at the pictures on the walls.

"Am I related to these people?" I asked.

The pictures were mostly of men, but there was an occasional woman here and there.

"Yes," Mathias responded, "these are your ancestors. This one here is my father, your biological grandfather."

I looked at the picture Mathias motioned me to. It was of a man, slightly older than Mathias, but it was clearly Mathias's father. His eyes were the same cerulean blue and he had the same prominent cheekbones Mathias had. He didn't feel like family to me though. None of these people did.

"But my mother wasn't like the rest of you?" I questioned him.

"No," he said. He was silent for a moment as he closed his eyes. A smile crept onto his face as he spoke. "She was a simple human being."

I wanted to question him more and began to speak, but he held up his hand.

"There will be more time for personal questions later," he insisted, however I had the feeling he didn't have any intention of answering questions about my mother unless he had to. "The first thing that you need to be taught today is the Time Line. The Time Line is the most important part of being a Timekeeper. Come and see for yourself."

Mathias led me into the circular study, but instead of stopping by his desk we walked further. The fire was not going in the grate today and I was astonished when Mathias walked into the grate. He beckoned for me to follow him and I did, into a small opening in the left side. The room beyond had a faint, blue glow and as soon as we entered it, I realized why.

In the center of the room, floating above an intricate design of a clock, engraved in the floor, was a horizontal line that stretched from wall to wall. The line appeared as if it was made of some gas or chemical.

"What is it?"

"This is the Time Line. The Time Line is made up of a magical energy, from the force of time itself."

"It's amazing."

"The Time Line consists of important events in the history of the United Kingdom as well as other countries," Mathias said. "It is our job to ensure that time moves like it should—in this country that is. Every country has its own Timekeeper to ensure the events of that country are properly kept as well as that time continues.

"The Time Line is almost like a person with a mind of its own. The Time Line we have here is the same all Timekeepers have. They run together and are filled with information of the future together. However, as I have said before, there are events of the past that we do not know; events that were not recorded. That we cannot know.

Further, it will only let you view events that are most important, or significant, to the history of the planet. This means that you cannot go back into a single person's past and view their everyday lives. Believe me, I've tried." I assumed he was referring to my mother. I'm sure he tried many ways to try and use the Time Line to figure out what happened to her.

Mathias continued, "The Time Line automatically updates itself at the midnight hour of every day. The most important events can be viewed. The Time Line will also record all premonitions that a Timekeeper had. The Timekeeper knows that time is in check if the Time Line continues to be a straight, constant line."

"Is it magic?" I asked.

Mathias looked at me for a moment, a curious glint in his eyes.

"You could call it that," he replied, "however it is more commonly thought of as a force with powers."

"Show me."

Mathias shook his head.

"First you must understand the laws of this world. You must know what we do and why we do it, as well as the limitations we have."

A small table stood next to the Time Line. There were several items on it, such as books and papers. Mathias picked up a very worn piece of parchment. Elegant handwriting was scribbled across it.

"The laws of the world," Mathias said. "First off, a Timekeeper cannot interfere with the free will of another. Free will is something that every human being has the right to and no force has the right to take that away. As human beings, we are given the right to choose, so why should a force like time give a person the opportunity to take that away? Now, if you choose poorly, what happens after this life in the next is a person's own fault."

Mathias explained how time would react in the worst ways if someone interfered with the course of another human's free will.

"I don't understand that part," I broke in. "How come horrific occurrences do not occur in everyday life if a person murders someone? Is that not against another person's will?"

"That is correct," Mathias answered. "However, you must remember that those people are not Timekeepers. They do not know what may or may not happen, whereas we do. Timekeepers are given these premonitions to prepare us for what might come, therefore it would not be fair or right for us to interfere with a person's course because we know what may or may not happen. Even if that person were to die, it would not be fair to anyone if we were to save them. Time could almost be considered a temptation. It isn't something that is naturally good, but it is something we are plagued with nonetheless."

He continued to explain how the Timekeepers had the power to observe the past, watch over the present, and see what might happen in the future. He explained how Timekeepers lived outside the Time Line, meaning that no events of a Timekeeper were recorded in the Time Line and also that Timekeepers were able to maintain memory. If for some reason time were changed, Timekeepers would be able to remember. I questioned how time could be changed if we weren't allowed to interfere with it.

"Supposedly," Mathias answered, "the original Timekeepers had the power to change an event in the Time Line. But once again this is a supposed myth in our world."

Finally, Mathias beckoned me over to the Time Line. I followed him. The straight, blue line had intricate dates engraved in it. Mathias extended his arm and touched the Time Line with the tip of his finger. He slid his finger across the Time Line and it began to move and I realized it began to show dates from the past. He slid the Time Line century by century. The Time Line stopped however on 1400 A.D.

"Why did it stop?" I asked.

"This is when the first Timekeeper took up their place in each country," Mathias answered. "Before then, it is said that the one family was in charge of all Timekeeping duties, however information and facts have been lost throughout the years due to a lack of recording. Some say this Timekeeping family is a myth and that one day a human discovered the Earth's Time Line, a Time Line of all events in history—all events—even events that humans of today have no recollections of in their history books, such as battles and wars that were never recorded. Or events that changed everything. Once again though, this is a myth. No person has ever found this Time Line of Earth; believe me we have tried. And no one has ever discovered this Timekeeping family."

It amazed me that even this magical world had myths and legends that they considered just that—myths. Mathias reached into his pocket and pulled out a pocket watch.

"You will receive something like this at your ball, which is your initiation into our world," he said. "This pocket watch allows me to access the Time Line and go back in time to review particular events in history. Take my hand—the one with the pocket watch."

I took hold of his closed hand. As I did, he reached out with his other hand and touched the Time Line.

The room dissolved.

Screaming filled my ears. Mathias stood next to me and before us was the worst sight I had ever seen. Fire was everywhere. The city of London was on fire, but it was not the city I was familiar with. I knew immediately where we were. I was literally standing in the middle of the Great Fire of London that occurred in 1666. However, as Mathias had said, I could not interact. Screaming men, women, and children were running about but paid no attention to me. If they happened to run through me, I was like solid matter whereas they faded into particles like the whole thing was a projection. I understood then the power of the Timekeepers. They were powerful. This was magic in some way, shape, or form. I remembered Mathias calling it a force. I literally could not believe my eyes, but then it was gone.

I was standing back in the study and Mathias was staring at me.

"That was phenomenal," I said.

He smiled at me.

"The first time," he spoke, "is always something *special.* Now, all you have to do is hold the pocket watch and touch the Time Line year of your choice. Once you do, you will see several events at once that happened during that year and you will then think of which event you want to see. Since you traveled with me the first time, the event was of my choice. So now it is your choice. Go on."

He handed me the pocket watch and I took it. I reached out my hand and touched the year 1700. There were a few events to choose from, I chose the first. It was the treaty of 1700 in London. It was a big event in history, but viewing it was nothing special. I was simply watching the treaty being prepared. The room returned to normal and I nodded at Mathias, signaling I had grasped the concept of it. I handed the pocket watch back to him and he tucked it safely inside his jacket pocket.

"I guess I don't really see the point of it," I said.

"It isn't meant to be fun or exciting. This is a job, a duty. We have the power to view these famous events of history over again as a tool. A tool to use to help us prepare for the future."

"But if we can't change it, what are we preparing for? What is the use of this and our premonitions?"

Mathias shook his head. Clearly, I was missing something.

"Abigail, what did I say about Timekeepers? We record and measure time. We keep track of it. That is it. Our premonitions come to us so that we can see the big events that will occur. While we cannot change it, or interrupt it, we know we need to be there to see it, to record it. All of the events in that Time Line were put there by previous Timekeepers. It is like a movie. They recorded it. We place those events on that Time Line. To make it simple, we keep track of time, we record it, using the objects given to us as well as our Time Line."

"Well then, who keeps track of that Time Line of earth you spoke about?" I asked.

"Like I said, that story is a myth."

"Mathias."

I turned and saw Ian standing in the entryway of the chamber. He had a small piece of paper in his hand.

"What is it, Ian?" Mathias asked.

"The council has sent us a letter regarding Abigail starting her training," he responded. "They will be arriving in an hour to discuss preparations."

"Very well," Mathias answered, "Abigail, we will resume training tomorrow."

He walked away rather abruptly, taking the letter and sweeping past Ian.

Ian walked into the room and stood next to me, standing over the Time Line.

"How was it?" Ian asked. "I know Mathias can be a little too focused on learning, sometimes."

"It isn't your fault. I guess I'm just a little hurt that he doesn't seem to talk about my mother that much. I really wanted to know more about her."

"I understand. But as you learn more from Mathias, I feel like he will open up to you more. What I can help you with is this. Do you have any questions about the Time Line?"

"I'm the kind of person that wants to know why we do the things we do," I said, "so why is this Timekeeping important? Why are we given these powers?"

"Mathias has already somewhat explained how many Timekeepers are influential in government as well as in society. By having such influence, our people have the ability to deliver history correctly, as it happened. Humans have had the ability to record history by writing it down, but as Timekeepers, we have the ability to have recorded history as it happened and we have the ability go back in time and revisit that history. I'll have to admit that society is getting more creative with how they can record history. We now have the ability to take a picture and even record video of things, but Timekeepers will always have the Time Line. We will always have history at our fingertips in case anything gets lost."

"Literally then," I responded, "you record time, measure it, and make sure it stays kept. That is utterly fascinating. But is this power a good power? Can it be evil in a way? I've always been taught that things like powers could be wrong."

Ian inclined his head as he listened to me, clearly pondering my question.

"That is a good question. I think that what we do is good. We help society move forward. We make sure we don't lose the history of our people. But there is evil just as there is good. I'll save it for Mathias to explain to you, but there is a way that the power we have can be abused and used for wrong."

Mathias was back, standing in the entryway.

"Abigail, I understand you are interested," Mathias said, "but that is all for the day."

Ian smiled and said he would show me out. As I walked past Mathias, I felt a coldness trickle down through my body. I couldn't explain why I felt it. And as I walked away, I could feel his eyes watching me as we went. Ian led me up in the lift and out of the basement, and as always told me he would wait for me the very next day.

CHAPTER SEVEN

The London Library was freezing. It was always freezing. I was wearing a coat, but I hugged myself anyway, rubbing my hands against my arms to keep warm. I would be facing the wrath of Phillip tonight. I had not met up with him since the day I met my father and he wouldn't be happy. I knocked on the door of his office. There was silence for a moment, but then I heard footsteps behind the door and it opened.

Phillip stood in the doorway. His hair was messy as usual and he was wearing his glasses today. He had a more disheveled than usual look—as if he had woken up on the wrong side of the bed. I was sure he had.

"Well look who it is," he said. His tone was condescending and he smirked at me. He stepped aside, signaling I should come in.

I walked inside and turned to look at him as he walked back around to his desk, leaving the door open. I smiled shyly.

"I'm sorry," I said. I kissed him and he kissed me back. I could tell he was still frustrated though. I took his hand and our fingers intertwined with each other. We walked over to the couch and sat down. Phillip was silent. He extended his arm and touched my hair. I watched as a lock of my hair slid through his fingers. He would always play with it whenever he could. He touched the side of my face and we stared at each other. His baby blue eyes—and my dark brown eyes—locked on one another. He leaned in and kissed my lips. I felt a feeling of warmth that was genuine and true. In that moment, I felt protected by Phillip. I felt like nothing bad could happen to me while in the protection of him. But, then he pulled away.

"Bridget is here."

I turned my head and sure enough Bridget was striding toward us.

"Don't say anything about the Timekeeping," I whispered to Phillip, "she only knows I met my father."

"What's going on, you two?" she asked, entering through Phillip's office door.

I didn't have time to respond. I stopped breathing.

A bridge.

Tower bridge.

I saw the bridge, I saw the figures. Two people, a rope.

A flash of a body could be seen going over the bridge. Were they being hung? I couldn't tell. I thought I saw a woman, but who was the other person? Everything was too dark and blurry for me to figure it out or make sense of it.

"Abigail!"

My eyes popped open. Once again, Phillip's baby blue eyes were staring back at me. Bridget was kneeling over me. I realized that behind them was the ceiling. I was on the floor. My head was pounding.

Phillip gently placed his hand behind my head and lifted me up into his shoulders. I felt out of breath. I felt tired.

"You just slipped off the couch and hit the floor," he told me. "Did you see something?"

Phillip lifted me back onto the couch and then sat down next to me—cradling my hand in his own. I rubbed the back of my head with my free hand and thought about it for a moment. Bridget sat down next to us and I looked from her to Phillip in confusion. I was trying to make sense of what I had seen.

"I saw the Tower Bridge and I'm pretty sure a woman was there," I told him. "It looked like someone was being hung. Phillip, I think I saw my mother's death. Mathias said her body was found hanging from the Tower Bridge. It was deemed as a suicide."

"Wait," Bridget interrupted, "your mother committed suicide? You didn't tell me this yesterday."

A feeling of panic shot me through me. I forgot I had left this part out, along with my secret Timekeeping abilities.

"I'm sorry," I replied, "I forgot to tell you."

"You forgot to tell me? How peculiar, considering that when *my* father died I remembered to tell you."

"Bridget I'm sorry. A lot of things happened yesterday and were going through my mind."

"I feel like you're not telling me something else," Bridget pestered onward. She stared at me with a look of confusion and hurt and finally she stood up.

"I'll leave you two to your secrets. I'm sure there are many you need to discuss." She turned on her heel and pulled the door shut behind her. It slammed loudly and the noise echoed around the office.

Phillip looked back at me questioningly. "Why did you tell me everything and not her?"

"Because I'm marrying you. I don't think Bridget should know about these strange...powers...at least not now." Another thought occurred to me. "Do you think you would have the paper of the day they found her body?"

"Maybe," Phillip said, "we could check several. It just depends on whether they published the information or not. Do you know the day? It would have been in December 1925 right? Since you were turned in at the orphanage the day you were born."

I nodded and Phillip stood up. He took me to where they kept their older newspapers and we were in there for a while looking through them. It wasn't too difficult to find however. We looked up the date of my birthday, December 8, 1925 and sure enough, it was there. I realized then, something I had not thought about before. My mother had died on my birthday.

December 8, 1925—Mysterious Suicide on London's Tower Bridge

Investigators are puzzled today after a body was found hanging from the London Tower Bridge in what appears to be a suicide. The body was a young woman who appears to be in her mid-twenties with long blonde hair. The body is being identified as Jane Doe at this time until further information becomes available. Anyone with information is asked to come forward.

The article was not too helpful, but Phillip managed to find another paper for a few weeks later, which furthered the story.

December 20, 1925—Mysterious Tip to Investigators Identifies Jane Doe

Investigators have been unable to identify the body of the woman in what is deemed a suicide from a few weeks ago. Investigators received a tip from an anonymous public source identifying the body as that of Elisabeth Callaghan, but have been unable to confirm this. Unless further information is discovered about the case, investigators will not be pursuing further. The body will be buried at the City of London Cemetery at the end of this week under the name given.

I folded up the paper and gave it back to Phillip. He took it. My mother was buried at the City of London Cemetery. I knew her full name as well—Elisabeth Callaghan.

"Are you going to go and see the grave?" Phillip asked a look of puzzlement on his face.

I nodded. I had to. I owed her that much, but I still wouldn't be done. This wasn't a suicide. Mathias knew that and I knew that. I wanted to know who did this to my mother, who destroyed the family she loved so much to protect.

That night I returned home with a strange feeling in my stomach. I was afraid to visit my mother's grave. Phillip was going to take me tomorrow and we would do this together. I felt like he should meet the woman he would never know—the mother of his fiancée he would never know.

When I walked through the front door of my house, I saw Mrs. Baxter and my mother playing cards in the kitchen. I heard Mrs. Baxter shout "you cheat" real loud. She was a very competitive woman. I decided to go up and see my father.

I entered my parents' room quietly in case he was asleep, but he was wide-awake. He was propped up against some pillows and reading a book. He loved to read, but I wondered if it had the same feeling it did before his illness. I wondered if he understood what he was reading. I also wondered if it was terrible of me to think that way.

"Father."

He looked up from his book and smiled. He placed it down on the bedside table.

"Come over here," he said, still smiling.

I walked around to his side of the bed and sat down next to him. I remembered the nights when I used to run in this room afraid as a little girl. My parents would wake up immediately and comfort me.

My father put his arm around me and I fell into his shoulder. He had the same familiar smell I associated him with—a clean spring scent. His head was balding around the top with his gray hair around the middle. He still wore his spectacles, but his blue eyes had a glassy look to them that they didn't use to have.

"How are you, Lu?"

"I'm fine," I responded. "How are you? What are you reading?"

"I feel good today. I'm reading, uh, oh what is it?"

A feeling of despair arose inside of me. Maybe he had not been reading at all, but trying to read, or trying to remember.

A look of pain came onto his face. He usually looked like he was in pain when he couldn't remember something. I took his hand in mine and held it.

"It's okay. You don't have to tell me."

His face became sad and I hugged him. I missed our moments together. We used to go out all the time—to see a play at the theater or to see a film. He would take me out on the town. I had always been close to my father.

"I'll let you get some rest now," I told him. I kissed his cheek and then helped him to lie down. I turned off his bedside table lamp and walked across the room to leave, but he spoke up.

"Good night, my little Susie Lu."

There were no tears this time. Only silence.

"I win!"

"Yes, Mrs. Baxter," I heard my mother say, "you've won, again. Congratulations."

"Well this gambling has run me down low," Mrs. Baxter said, "I'd better be getting home now."

"We didn't even play with real money!"

"Church going people don't gamble, Annette!"

Mrs. Baxter was standing up from her chair as I entered the kitchen. She smiled at me and gave me a quick hug.

"I'll see you fine ladies in the morning," she announced.

"Good night, Mrs. Baxter," I said as she shut the front door.

I sat down at the kitchen table across from my mother, who was sipping a cup of tea. She smiled at me.

"Would you like some?"

I shook my head. "I'm fine."

I thought about it for a moment and then decided I wanted to tell my mother everything because she deserved to know.

"I've found my biological father."

My mother was in the middle of taking another sip of her tea as I blurted it out. A brief look of heartache flitted over her face. She slowly set down her cup and pushed back her chair. She looked at me for another brief second—it felt like forever—and then she stood up from her chair and walked out of the kitchen. I realized I had been holding my breath and quickly let myself breathe. I heard my mother's footsteps go up the stairs, down the landing, and into her room. I heard the door open and close, followed by the click of a lock. It was not the reaction I had been anticipating. It was not the reaction I had imagined would ever possibly occur. I had broken her heart. And that isn't something you can reverse.

The next day was colder than the day before. My mother was already gone the next morning and with the fresh memory of what I had done to her, I decided I didn't want to go see Mathias today, so instead I phoned Phillip and was waiting for him to pick me up. I wore a dark sweater and long dark skirt with a heavy overcoat protecting me from the cold. Phillip picked me up around noon. He stood in my doorway, shaking. He looked sweet waiting out in the cold for me. His hands were protected in the warm pockets of his brown overcoat. His long brown hair was once again shaggy and messy. He really needed a haircut.

The drive to the cemetery took about a half hour with the traffic. When we arrived, Phillip got out of the car and walked around to the passenger side to let me out. We held hands as we walked up to the gates of the cemetery. We quickly found directions to the gravesite after stopping to ask someone that worked there. My heart was pounding as we approached the location that the directions had led us to. I looked around at all the gravestones as well as the mausoleums around the cemetery. Finally, Phillip spoke up.

"This is it."

He gestured toward a grave a few feet in front of me and I walked ahead of him to observe it. I knelt down next to the grave and read the engraving.

Elisabeth Callaghan

Birth: Unknown / Death: December 8, 1925

I reached forward and touched the stone and let my fingers touch the letters of the engraving. A branch snapped nearby and my head turned.

Birds flew up from the trees. In that single moment, I felt like someone was watching us.

I stood up and walked back over to Phillip and took his hand.

"Did you hear that?" I asked.

"Yeah."

We stood there for a moment, watching the trees and looking around the cemetery. I didn't see anyone, but I knew someone had been there. Something made a branch snap. Something made the birds take off. I looked back at the gravestone again.

"For some reason. I thought this would make me feel better. About everything. But nothing's changed."

I felt Phillip's hand touch the small of my back as he spoke.

"This is all still new to you," he said softly. "You need to give it time."

"I'm ready to go."

I pulled away from Phillip and began walking through the cemetery back toward the car. He followed closely behind, as if he meant to say something more, but I was too busy in thought to talk to him. I wasn't thinking about the branch snapping. I'm sure it was someone just walking through. I was thinking about my mother. I was now more determined than ever after seeing the gravestone of the woman who was my mother. There was no date of birth because they didn't know it. They didn't know she was a loving wife and mother. They wouldn't have even known her name if it hadn't been for the tip.

I saw the car up ahead, and something else as well. There was a piece of paper taped to the windshield. I assumed it was a ticket or something, but Phillip hadn't parked against regulations. I picked up the paper as soon as I got to the car and unfolded it. It was a note, quickly scribbled. My heart dropped as I read it.

I saw you. I've been waiting for so long. Please, come to me.

Phillip had finally caught up to me.

"What is it?" he asked, leaning over my shoulder. I looked up and out over the cemetery parking lot.

"Hello!" I called out. "Who is there?"

"Abigail, what are you doing?" he took the note out of my hand and read it.

"What the hell?" he muttered under his breath. "Let's go. This place is giving me the heebie jeebies."

I stood there for a moment—looking out—hoping to see someone. Who left the note? Why had they been waiting? How could I come to them if they didn't tell me who they were? I got into the car feeling further away from the truth than I had when we had arrived.

CHAPTER EIGHT

"Please come into the shelter, Abby!"

I was in the back yard again. It was night and the only light came from the stars above and the moon. My mother stood a few feet ahead of me, a look of panic etched on her face.

"Abigail."

It was her voice again. I turned around and there she was. It was windy tonight and the wind whipped her hair around her face.

"You need to stay away," she said.

"Stay away from what?" I asked her.

"Time," she responded. "Within time, there is only darkness. Within darkness, there is only death."

I heard the sound of the planes and I looked up. They were flying over us, like birds in the sky. But they weren't birds.

The bombs dropped.

I sat bolt upright in my bed. I was breathing heavily and drenched in sweat. It was still dark as I looked around my room. I looked over at the clock by my bed and could make it by the moonlight. It was 3:00 in the morning. Why was I having these dreams?

I fell backward on my mattress and stared up at the ceiling. Eventually, I drifted back to sleep.

"Abby."

I opened my eyes to my mother's face. She was leaning over me, smiling softly. I immediately sat up and pulled her to me tightly.

"I'm sorry," I whispered.

She laughed quietly and rubbed my back before pulling away.

"I'm not angry with you honey," she said. "I just needed some time to think. I was angry with myself."

"Why would you be angry with yourself? You didn't do anything."

"Because we should have had this talk when you first found out you were adopted," she continued, "and because the man you think is your father is not your father."

She reached into her pocket and pulled out an old piece of folded paper and handed it to me. I gave her a questioning look before taking it and unfolding it. I quietly read it to myself. The handwriting was very sloppy, as if the person who wrote it was in a hurry or under some kind of pressure.

Whoever reads this has taken my daughter in. For that I thank you. I only have two requests that I hope you will honor. First, name her Abigail. It was my mother's name. Second, please tell her when she asks about her biological family (if she ever asks) that she has none. After I am finished writing this, she won't. I will be dead within the next few hours. Her father died not long after I was with child. We had no living relatives. Please care for her as if she were your own biological child. Her birthday is December 8, 1925.

-Her mother.

"The sisters at the orphanage said that she refused to give any information and insisted this be given to the adopting parents," my mother said.

“I thought you said I was left on the steps?”

"I felt it was only right to honor her request, so I never told you there was any communication between the orphanage and your mother. I realize now that this may have put her in a bad light for you, and I apologize for that, but Abigail, I'm not sure how you came to find this man who claims to be your father, but I am concerned for your safety."

I didn't look at my mother, because I knew she was wrong. My biological mother was lying. She had to be. There was too much evidence on Mathias' side to counteract what this letter said. And if Mathias was not my father, he at least knew my mother. He had pictures of her after all. But then I realized he hadn't shown me any. I had just bought into what he had told me. But I couldn't discount everything entirely. I knew now that I had to lie to my mother and that was the worst feeling in the world. But I had to.

"I won't see him anymore."

My mother smiled at me and pulled me in.

"I'm sorry this has happened," she said quietly. "But you're a young woman now and I trust you to make the right decisions."

I suddenly realized how easy it was to spin a web of dishonesty. After my mother left, I continued to wonder why my mother wouldn’t want me to know about this world. What if I interfered with a premonition of death? I would die. Why wouldn’t she want me to know that? Something just didn’t feel right about all of this.

* * *

As I made my way back to Parliament, I decided the only person I would confide this in would be Phillip. I didn't believe I was in danger. The only thing that was clear was my biological mother was trying to protect me from something, and whether she was telling the truth or telling a lie, I felt in my heart it was done for my protection. So, for now at least, I wouldn't tell Mathias or Ian about what I had discovered. Even though I still didn't understand why my biological mother wouldn't want me to know about my dying if I interfered with a premonition of death, I still knew that I was at least safe now. I was safe because I was learning about this world. I just had to be smart about things. As I approached the building, I could see Ian just ahead. He was waiting for me like he had previously.

"Why didn't you come yesterday?"

I suddenly felt guilty. It hadn't occurred to me that he had probably been waiting a while yesterday before deciding I wasn't coming.

"There were some things I needed to get done," I said. "Do you wait here for me every day?"

"I've actually been having premonitions of when you come," Ian whispered. "They've been coming in handy. But a lot of the time, when Mathias isn't teaching me that is, I like to stand up in the clock tower and watch the city. I can see you come that way as well."

Ian seemed like a simple person—someone who didn't need the world to make them happy—pleased by the simplest desires. I liked that about him.

"Can I ask you, well, does Mathias expect me to come every day?" I asked. "I mean, I guess I could, but I do have classes that I have to attend and such."

"I don't think he does, but you need to tell him what you want. He was expecting you to come yesterday, and you didn't. Let's go though. He's waiting for you now."

Ian led me into Parliament and then in the basement and down the lift.

Before long, I was standing in the middle of the study. Ian had gone off to do something and Mathias sat at his office desk, scribbling on a piece of paper, not bothering to look up at me.

I awkwardly cleared my throat. No response.

"Good morning," I said. No response.

I wanted to throw something at him. I was suddenly angry. Not only was he ignoring me this very minute, but he also he wouldn't tell me about my mother and wouldn't act like a "father." Was I just a student?

"I didn't realize I was obligated to come waste my time every day." I threw my bag down on the couch and sat down. I was startled and looked up when Mathias banged his hand on the table. His face was red and this time he was staring directly at me.

"What is your problem Abigail?" he yelled at me from across his desk. "Do you think this is a waste of time? Please tell that to whoever gave us this Timekeeping ability and let me know the response you get."

I didn't respond. My breathing was heavy and all I wanted to do was scream my head off. Due to my civil upbringing however, I refrained.

Mathias stood up and walked down the hallway off of the study. I sat there for a while, wondering what I should do. Was he going to come back? I looked around the room. It definitely held the exterior of an office or study. There was nothing that felt like a home. I think a little homeliness could've added some warmth to the place. I wished there was a picture of my mother somewhere, but there wasn't. It was only where he kept them locked away. Surely someone that was my father would keep pictures of his wife? I guess I could see why he wouldn't, but what my mother had told me was still nagging me.

Approaching footsteps made my head turn back toward the hallway. Mathias was coming back. He was carrying what looked like a very old book. He sat it down on his desk and took his seat again.

"Today we are going to discuss more of the laws of Timekeeping," he said, "specifically a power that is forbidden to all Timekeepers."

I honestly couldn't believe he was just going to shrug off the outburst that we had just had. Weren't we even going to talk about it? I decided to say it.

"Show me a picture of my mother."

He looked up, flabbergasted. It took him a moment before he finally spoke.

"Why?"

We stared at each other for a moment. His eyes were questioning me, but mine, I knew, were doing the exact same thing to him. I figured we were both wondering about each other.

"I feel like I deserve that at least," I said. "Mathias, I have no idea if you are honestly telling the truth. You haven't given me any information to prove you are who you say you are. Give me this."

He didn't hesitate any longer. He opened a drawer on the side of his desk and reached in. Immediately he withdrew a tattered and worn looking photograph and handed it to me.

"I look at it every day."

I felt as if that was the first emotional thing I had heard him say. I took the photograph and immediately turned my eyes to it. My mother and Mathias were staring back at me. They both looked happy. My mother was exactly as I had dreamed her. She had beautiful blonde hair that fell down her back in curls. Her face was bright and happy. Mathias looked quite different. He was handsome like he was now, but younger. His face was vibrant and happy. It held no sadness or despair like I saw in it today. I handed the picture back to Mathias.

"Thank you." It was all I said.

Mathias took the picture from me and placed it safely back in his desk drawer. He cleared his throat and then turned his attention back to the book he had brought with him.

"Specifically," he began, again it was as if the moments we had just shared had never occurred, "we are going to talk about a force known as An Am Phorse feiniméin. However, it is more commonly referred to today as the forbidden powers because it is illegal and detected use of it will receive a Timekeeper immediate stripping of their duties."

"What language was that?" I asked.

"Gaelic," Mathias responded. "Most of the information we have is written in Gaelic. It is thought that if there were an original family, they were based in Ireland. But again, there is no confirmation of that."

I gave Mathias my undivided attention. He had given me something special today and I would give him my attention in return. The subject seemed interesting too. It also seemed to be pretty important to Timekeeping.

"The forbidden powers," Mathias continued, "are the deliberate abuse of the force of time."

"So is it when someone tries to take away someone's free will?" I asked him.

"No, this is something different. Taking away someone's free will is usually not done in spite or in wrongdoing, but more to prevent suffering. It is usually done as an act of good intention, resulting in horrific consequences."

Mathias turned the pages of the book to a specific page and began to look it over before speaking again.

"As in your world there is evil from regular humans, there is evil from Timekeepers in ours. This force is kind of like a spell for evil Timekeepers. After successful completion of the criteria, it allows a Timekeeper to use time in any way they please. While they cannot change time or mess with the balance of time, they can use the energy force of time itself to cause damage or harm to innocent people. They can also use this to gain immortality by using time as a means to keep them young."

Mathias reached out and handed the book to me. I gently took it, seeing how fragile it was, and turned my attention to the page before me.

An Am Phorse feiniméin

Use of this force has been deemed forbidden by the council. This force is used to abuse the energy force of time and used to cause damage or harm to innocents. This force can also be used to extend life. The criteria are as follows: The Timekeeper wishing to gain this force must take the life of another Timekeeper. The Timekeeper must then give up their soul to the forces of evil. The Timekeeper finally, must convince another Timekeeper to trust them completely. These three criteria are three of the most horrific acts in Timekeeping and are illegal to perform. As such, a Timekeeper who willfully performs these is no longer considered a Timekeeper, but a person of evil.

"So, there isn't a consequence?" I asked. "How come time won't react or anything?"

"If the force of time reacts, it faces the force of evil. Only the force of good is strong enough to face the force of evil. Have you ever thought of it like that before? I believe that is why."

I had no words to describe my feelings. Just like individuals in our world created weapons to harm others, so had these people. The acts that the book listed were horrible— irreparable. Why would anyone want to commit any of these acts? I could only imagine the horrors that would ensue if someone had access to this kind of power.

"Has it ever been done?" I asked.

"So far in Timekeeping history, to the knowledge of the council, no. However, it could definitely have occurred before the Timekeepers. Perhaps, in the Timekeeping family itself. If the myth is true, that is. There is a rumor that a small group of Timekeepers—evil Timekeepers—exists and may or may not have access to this power."

"Why is this even listed for Timekeepers to know about?" I asked, "this is dangerous information in the hands of the wrong person, isn't it?"

"But it is useful information in the hands of people who do not want to see this happen," Mathias countered.

I guess that was true. We had to know the horrible sins that could be committed if we wanted to prevent them. Then again, I hoped no one would ever want to commit these horrible acts.

"Well," Mathias said, "I know this information can be quite hefty so I think that will be all for today. Come back tomorrow if you can."

I didn't want to leave, however. I wanted to know more. I wanted to see more.

"Can you show me around this place?" I asked. "I mean, I'm sure there's more than just this study and that hallway." I gestured to the long narrow hallway. Mathias smiled at me; it was a genuine smile.

"Follow me," he said. He withdrew a ring of keys from his pocket and I followed him across the room to the hallway. Instead of going straight, like we normally would if we were leaving, we took a sharp right into a little crevice in the wall. Inside the crevice was a large wooden door. Mathias put one of the keys into the lock and turned. The door opened into a small room with a hole in the floor. A spiral staircase led downward.

Mathias shut the door as I entered the room and I began to follow him as he descended down the stairs of the spiral staircase. The further down we went, the darker it got. At one point I reached ahead and rested my hand on Mathias' shoulder so that I wouldn't lose him. His shoulder felt strong and rugged. It felt like the shoulder of a man who was a protector. I don't know why I thought it, but I just did.

Finally we reached the bottom of the staircase. A tall double wooden door stood in front of us. The shape of a clock was engraved into the doorway. There were no clock hands however. I found this strange. The times were written in numerical numbers.

"Why are there no clock hands?" I asked Mathias.

"This clock represents all of time," Mathias said, "all of time is unending and is not necessarily designated a specific time. Therefore, the clock means all time."

"Cryptic," I responded.

Mathias laughed and placed another key in this door. He then pushed against the doors and they swung open to reveal a large ballroom. I walked ahead of Mathias. My mouth was literally hanging open in awe. I gazed up at the vaulted ceilings. The room was circular. The walls were beautifully engraved with signs and symbols so ancient I wouldn't be able to even decipher them. The floor was marble, a beautiful dark, sleek marble.

"This room is used for gatherings," Mathias stated, "or Timekeeper weddings. When you take my place as Timekeeper, there will be a ceremony that will be celebrated in here. Your mother never saw this place. I wished she could have. The London ballroom is considered one of the fancier Timekeeper ballrooms if I say so myself."

I looked at Mathias. His attention was elsewhere; he was gazing around the room like I had been. I could tell he missed her. I could tell he would do anything to have her back. A part of me felt he had to have been telling the truth, but then a part of me continued to rest on the knowledge of my mother had told me.

"Where do you live?" I asked. I then decided to rephrase it somewhat. "I mean I know you live upstairs in the study, but where is your room? Where would people stay in this place?"

Mathias gestured to a door at the other end of the ballroom. "Let us move onward then. The London Headquarters is also known for its elegant rooms of rest."

I followed Mathias as he walked across the marble surface to the door at the opposite end of the ballroom. Once again, he turned another key. I really didn't understand why he locked this place up so tight. Was he expecting someone to break in?

The door he opened led to yet another set of stairs. We descended downward again into more unknown darkness. At the bottom of the stairs there was one last long hallway. There were two doors on each side and at the very end there was one tall door.

"This is my room," Mathias told me, beckoning toward the first door on the right. He opened the door and I looked into his room. It was very unkempt. Clothes were littered across the floor, books in various places, and his bed was not made.

"You could use some housekeeping," I told him.

He laughed and showed me the remaining three doors. Each one led into yet another spare room.

"If you ever want, you can stay here, he said.

I smiled. The gesture was nice, but I had no intention of living here. It was far too large in size for me and I felt like I would get lonely quite fast. But then I had a feeling. If I eventually took over for Mathias, wouldn't I *have* to live here? I shrugged the feeling off. It was not worth worrying over now.

Mathias turned to go back up the stairs and I followed.

Mathias and I made our way back up to the study. I thanked him for showing me around and then left rather abruptly. Once again, I was thinking about why I was doing this. Was it worth it? I knew it was, but this life, this ability—it all seemed too much to me. Once again though, I fell back on my main reason. It was the main reason for all of this—the woman who had protected me—my biological mother.

"What's wrong?"

Phillip and I were having dinner at his apartment. He had prepared spaghetti. It was good, so that wasn't why I wasn't eating it, which he could tell.

I put down my fork and looked at him.

"Do you think I'm strange?

"Phillip put down his fork as well and looked at me, his eyebrows raised.

"Is that a joke?"

I shook my head and gave him a dirty look.

"Why would I ask something like that jokingly?" I asked, my tone upset.

"No. I don't think you're strange. Is this about the fact that you are a Timekeeper?"

"Well, isn't this whole experience a bit out of the ordinary for you?" I asked him.

"Of course, it is Abigail," Phillip said, "it isn't every day you find out your fiancée is a Timekeeper. But then again, I already knew about the voices and visions, so I wasn't too surprised."

I sighed.

"I just don't know if this something I want to do with my life or not," I responded. "I don't know if this job is cut out for me."

"Only you can make that decision Abby. It isn't something I can decide for you, you have to make it for yourself."

Phillip continued to eat, but I sat there in silence.

After dinner, we decided to go out for a walk. We would just do a quick walk around Phillip's apartment building. It was too cold for anything else.

As we walked, I admired the sky and how bright the stars were. I wondered if time existed among these balls of gas that lit up our solar system. I wondered if they were immune to the effects of aging and growing old. Did they stay up there forever? Did they always guard over us? Did they watch us humans in everything that we did?

Phillip's hand was warm in mine. I swung his arm as we walked. It had been quite a long day and I was fairly tired. I leaned in against Phillip and he put his arm around me, keeping it firm on my shoulders.

"Are you tired?" he asked me.

"Very. Mathias and I did a lot today at the Headquarters."

He suddenly leaned down and kissed me. We stood there for a moment, in the middle of the sidewalk, sharing a small but passionate kiss. He held my face in his hands as he moved his lips with mine. Finally, he pulled away from me so I could breathe.

"I don't think I can walk now," I joked, "that was very

unexpected."

Phillip laughed. "Alright then."

I was suddenly pulled off my feet and into Phillip's arms. He had never done this before, but it felt nice, trusting him to hold me. I smiled and put my arms around his neck. He smiled back and began to walk back into the apartment.

"Are you sure I'm not too heavy for you?" I asked him.

He laughed again. "You are as light as a feather my dear."

All sense of humor and laughter faded however when we got back to the door of Phillip's apartment. Attached to the door was another note, just like the one from yesterday, written in the same handwriting.

You look so happy with him. But I can tell you don't share the same feelings with your father. You yearn to know about your mother, don't you? Come to me.

"What the hell is this?" Phillip muttered. He ripped the note off the door and tore it into pieces. I simply stood there, motionless. Whoever was leaving these notes was following me. They had watched us at the cemetery and had watched us tonight. What was going on? And then the conversation I had had with my mother that morning came back to me. I realized I still needed to confide in Phillip what I had found out.

Phillip unlocked the door of his apartment and pulled me in after him. He immediately locked the door behind him, bolting it as well as putting up the chain. He went through his apartment and searched in every closet, looked in the bathroom, his bedroom, and made sure all the windows were locked.

"The place is clear," he said, coming back into the living room.

I sat down on the couch and beckoned him over.

"I need to tell you something," I said as he sat next to me.

I confided in him the events of that day and how Mathias may or may not be my father. I told him my feelings and how either my mother was lying to protect me—or telling the truth to protect me—but she was doing something. I also expressed my yearning to learn more about my past and why I wanted to go back, despite telling my mother I wouldn't.

Phillip surprised me when he said he understood why I was continuing to see Mathias, but to be cautious and careful.

"I can tell you're very passionate about this," he said. "I know I tell you what you should or should not do sometimes, but that's just me trying to protect you. But I realize you need to make your own decisions, so I respect the one you are making."

I smiled at him. "I'd better get home. I shouldn't be out this late."

"Okay, here goes the protection thing. I'd rather you stayed here. Obviously, someone is out there watching you, and I would just feel more comfortable if you stayed."

I supposed that I needed to respect that from him, so I stayed, but worry was still in the back of my mind.

I ended up sleeping on the couch with Phillip. I didn't feel it was as inappropriate as sleeping in a bed together. I was curled into Phillip, his arms held tightly around me. I was comfortable. By all means I should have fallen asleep, but I couldn't sleep. I was thinking about the notes and who had been leaving them. Why were they following me? What did they want? Was Mathias really my father? Was my mother lying? The endless questions raced through my mind.

My thoughts were broken up when the window above the couch shattered into a million pieces. Glass hit my face and I quickly shut my eyes to protect them. I felt pieces of glass digging into my skin and I screamed. Phillip awoke immediately and was cursing. He stood up and ran across the room, flipping on the light. I looked down onto the floor. In the middle of the room was a large brick that had been sent flying through the window. Attached to the brick was a piece of paper, this one different from the one the notes had been written on. I bent down and pulled off the paper and looked it over. It had clearly been written by someone other than the person who had left the previous notes.

My heart was racing. Phillip looked down at the note and then yelled out in fury. He ran to the window and bent out it, trying to see if whoever had thrown the brick was still there.

"I will find you, you fucking maniac!" he shouted into the streets of London, "you stay away from her!"

My attention was still on the note. Phillip's screams and curses were only in the background. I was disturbed by the note, disturbed by what it meant, and disturbed by what I was getting myself into. I kept rereading the note and letting the words sink in—letting them fill me with more terror.

I killed her. I'll kill you too.

CHAPTER NINE

"Shit! That fucking hurts!"

I gave Phillip a look. Men could be such babies sometimes. They would give up their life for women—I knew Phillip would—but when it came to cuts and bruises they were babies.

Phillip sat on the stool of the toilet in his bathroom. I had alcohol out and I was cleaning the cuts where the glass shards had hit him. We had already cleaned and bandaged mine. He insisted I go first.

"Don't be such a baby," I muttered.

I dabbed a bit more alcohol onto the cut and he winced. I rolled my eyes and began to bandage the larger cuts. Luckily, neither of us had been hit too bad by the flying glass.

"Also," I continued, "your use of foul language has exceeded its limit for the night. So please, bite your tongue."

Phillip scowled at me. I ignored it and placed all of the supplies back into the medicine cabinet. It was fairly late when we got back to sleep. We didn't report the incident, because well, because of my "condition" as a Timekeeper. Luckily, none of Phillip's neighbors had called down or showed up at his door about the noise. Because we didn't want to sleep below a shattered window, we ended up in

Phillip's bed.

We lay in his bed for a while. He had me pulled in close to him, his arm around me.

"So, you think the notes are from two different people?" he asked.

"They have to be. It's different handwriting. I feel like maybe I have a person watching over me and a person trying to kill me at the same time."

"Do you think it could be *him*?" Phillip asked.

By him, I assumed he meant Mathias.

"I mean, if the letter that my biological mother left for mother is anything to go by, then possibly. But I've been with him multiple times now. If he wanted to kill me, he's had the chance."

"Maybe he's waiting for something," Phillip responded. He turned to me then. I could barely see him in the darkness, but I knew he was looking right at me. "Please promise me you will be careful.

"I put my hand on his cheek. "I will."

We didn't talk anymore, but he continued to pull me close to him. I was practically glued to him—he wouldn't let me go. I managed to fall asleep this time though.

The Thames was calm today. Phillip and I sat on a bench near the river. I stared out at the water. We were waiting to return to Phillip's flat. The window was getting fixed, so we had left for lunch and a walk.

"Maybe we should talk to Mathias about the notes," Phillip suggested.

"I don't know if we should trust him. Remember what you said last night."

He didn't respond. I continued to stare out at the river. It was beautiful. Works of nature were beautiful.

"Abigail."

I looked at Phillip. He looked concerned. I couldn't blame him. He was probably very worried about me right now, but this was my life, I couldn't change it. Could I?

"I just don't trust him," I finally responded, "I feel like he hides things from me. I know he does. He should have told me everything about my mother when we first met. Why should I have to pester him for questions? And obviously, my mother didn't want me to meet him for whatever reason, or else she wouldn't have said he was dead. Or my true father really is dead."

I got up and walked toward the river. The river flowed calmly, slightly hitting the bank. I stopped breathing. I heard Phillip shouting as I did.

The bombers were coming. My biological mother stood before me, her hand outstretched. Her blonde hair was still whipping around her face in the night's wind.

"Abby," she said, "Stay away."

"Abby!" My mum was screaming behind me from the bomb shelter. "What are you doing? Why aren't you coming to me? Why aren't you listening to me? They are coming."

The bombs dropped.

My eyes flashed open and water was all around me. I was slowly sinking into the abyss of the Thames. Cold, freezing water was numbing my entire body as I sank further down. I felt a tight grip on my arm and turned my head to see Phillip. He pulled me upward and we broke the surface.

The next hour or so was a blur. I remembered Phillip pulling me out of the river. I remember getting back into Phillip's car and driving back to his flat. The window had been replaced when we got back inside. I stood in the middle of Phillip's living room and suddenly realized I was freezing cold. My body was soaking wet. Water dripped off my clothes.

"Abigail," Phillip said. "Are you listening to me? What happened?"

"I don't know. I was having a vision or something and then I woke up in the water."

"Why did you fall in though?"

"I don't know!" I was shouting now. "I just did. I'm sorry, I must've fell in during my vision."

"Alright. Alright fine." I could tell he was frustrated.

Phillip pulled his shirt off. I was suddenly exposed to his muscles and half naked body He then unbuckled his belt and pulled off his pants. He was standing in front of me wearing only his knickers, which he began to take off.

"What are you doing?" I asked.

"Undressing," he responded, "I'll warm up faster if I'm completely naked."

"Phillip, please stop. We aren't married and this isn't appropriate."

"Oh, forgive me," Phillip said, "I just thought that I could do something out of the norm for you since you decided to jump in the

Thames!"

"I didn't jump!" I shouted back. "I fell in. There's a difference."

Phillip had almost completely pulled off his knickers. I did the only thing I could think of. I undressed too.

I took off my shoes and reached behind me and unzipped my dress. I stripped it off and stood before him wearing just a slip and he finally stopped undressing. I breathed a sigh of relief.

"I'm sorry," I said to him, "I didn't mean to fall in. The vision was just consuming me."

"You have no idea how crazy you sound right now," Phillip said.

"People do crazy things. We're standing in front of each other almost completely naked. I mean that's not really crazy, but you know we're not married and well..."

Phillip walked up to me and pulled me into his arms and kissed me. We began to kiss passionately. He lifted me up and we moved into his bedroom. He dropped me on the bed and we continued to kiss, but finally I placed a hand on his chest.

"Phillip, I'm sorry. I didn't mean to get you, well, excited."

Even though I was apologizing for getting Phillip excited, the truth was that I was a little excited too. I had never been that close to him intimately and it made me want to get married even sooner.

"Sure," he said, rolling off of me onto his back. "You just took off your clothes because I was doing it."

"Exactly," I responded. I thought about it for a moment. Why did I take off my clothes? I wanted him to stop so I did it anyway. This whole day was turning into a ball of insanity.

"I just want to wait until we are married," I told him, "before we get this close again."

Phillip rolled onto his side and touched my chin with his fingers. "Let's get married now then. We don't have to wait."

"Phillip," I said, trying to make him understand, "we are going to have a wedding. Our families will be there. It will be beautiful. Why let that go?"

"Why do we need such a big extravagant wedding?" he asked. "Why can't it just be me and you. And maybe a few people."

"That's fine, and I want to get married to you as soon as possible, but I also want to be engaged for a while. For some reason, I want to enjoy being engaged to you as much as I want to enjoy being married to you."

"I suppose you're right," he said.

"Of course, I am. I always am."

He rolled his eyes at me and I got up out of the bed. I went to his dresser and pulled out some clothes and threw them at him.

"Now get dressed," I said, "I'm going to take a shower."

Phillip got up and walked toward me.

"A shower sounds like a great idea!"

I slammed the door in his face.

"Alone," I yelled, laughing.

The water felt warm against my skin. It made me feel good, especially after the jump into the icy river. I ran my fingers through my wet hair and let it fall against my back. I thought about the day and wondered why I had done the things I did. I turned off the shower, dried off, put on the pair of clothes that I left at Phillip's in case of emergency, and walked back out into the bedroom.

Phillip was already in bed and I began to walk out of the room.

"Abby..."

I sighed and turned to look at him. He patted the empty bed next to him and I rolled my eyes. I shut his bedroom door and crawled into bed with him.

He pulled me into his side and held me close. I could tell he had just put on deodorant. He smelt fresh and clean.

"Abby, Abby, Abby," he said softly in the darkness. We stayed like that for a while, the two of us in each other's arms. Slowly, I nodded off to sleep.

After the events of the previous day, I decided to go to confession. I had not been in quite a while and I felt it would be good to go. But there was also something else I wanted to ask. As I walked into St. Patrick's, I admired the vaulted ceilings and the intricate designs of everything. Incense engulfed my senses. I had always liked the smell. It made me feel calm and safe. The small confessional at the side of the church was empty. I slipped inside and slid the door shut.

The small window in front of me slid open, and the priest began with the sign of the cross. He had a thick Scottish accent that was kind of soothing. I told the priest my sins and he said the blessings and forgave my sins, telling me to go in peace. I didn't leave however.

"Father?"

"Yes, child?"

"Do you believe God gives us trials and sufferings?"

There was silence for a moment. I could hear the breathing of the priest on the other side of me.

"What do you mean, child?"

I hesitated for a minute. What should I say?

"Recently. I've met my biological father and I've discovered some things about myself that have begun to change my life. These things have caused a struggle. Sometimes I don't know if I can make it through."

"I believe," the priest said, "that God gives us trials in life. Every person has to deal with things that they do not want to deal with in life. However, I believe that these are gifts that get us closer to heaven. The more we work through these trials in life and the more suffering we endure but make it through, the more we are rewarded in the next life."

It was what my mother had always told me, but I felt a feeling of clarity I hadn't felt before. I knew my mission was not over. It was only just beginning. But I felt like the path ahead of me was going to be okay.

"Does that answer your question child?"

"It does. Thank you Father."

I stood up to leave and reached to slide the door open when the priest spoke up again.

"Child."

"Yes, Father?"

"I'm not sure what trials you are enduring right now, but I will pray for you. But be careful of temptation to do wrong. It will come when we are at our strongest, and our weakest as well."

The idea of temptation frightened me. I did not want to be

tempted. I wanted to do good.

"Thank you, Father," I said.

"Go in peace."

The clock tower bells at Big Ben were chiming as I came up to the building. Ian was standing nearby, waiting for me. I was just about to enter the large building when I heard my name being called.

"Abigail!"

I turned around and saw Bridget running up toward me. I began to feel a lump in my throat. I didn't feel like now was the best time to talk to her.

"Did you follow me?" I asked Bridget as she came up to me. My tone was very suspicious, more than I wanted it to be. However, I did not like being followed either.

Bridget looked like I had slapped her across the face.

"Of course, I didn't follow you Abby," she snapped back, "are you saying that you think that is the kind of friendship we have?"

I turned my face away from her and looked back up at the building. Ian was still waiting for me, but he didn't try and come out to see us. I could tell he was trying to be discreet so that Bridget wouldn't see him. I really did not want to deal with this right now. Bridget and I were growing further apart, and the more I wanted to know about myself, the more I had to keep her out of it. But did I have to keep her out of it? Could I trust her?

"Well?"

My thoughts had made me forget where I was for a moment and I turned my head back to look at her.

"No," I said.

"It still sounds like you are accusing me of something," Bridget said.

"No, Bridget, I'm not accusing you! Please stop putting words into my mouth."

"Honestly Abby," Bridget said, "I saw you coming this way so I stopped you. But I feel like you are hiding something from me."

Bridget moved closer and looked me directly into the eyes.

"Please," she whispered, "are you telling me the truth?"

I looked directly into her eyes. I could feel the truth trying to erupt from me, but I forced it down within. I lied to her face.

"Yes. I am telling you the truth. But I have to go now."

I left Bridget standing there and made my way toward the building. Ian was standing there, still slightly hidden so that Bridget could not see him. My thoughts consumed me. What kind of person was I becoming?

Once we were inside, Ian left me in the study with Mathias and then wandered off. Mathias sat at his desk. He was reading over a book. I walked around the study and admired it. The room was very intricate. Designs were etched into the walls of different periods in time. Whoever had built this place, I presumed it was our ancestors and past Timekeepers, had put a lot of thought into it. Mathias finally finished what he was reading and closed the book. I turned to give him my attention.

"So, what are we learning today?" I asked.

"Actually, I thought we'd try something a little different today.

Instead of picking a topic and teaching it to you, how about I answer some of your questions."

Finally. There were many questions I wanted to ask him. But then I remembered they were mostly about my mother. I figured those weren't the questions he was talking about. I thought about it for a moment.

"How long does it take to become a Timekeeper?" I asked him, "I mean how long do you usually train someone."

"Timekeeping training itself takes about two years," Mathias answered, "however that is usually for a Timekeeper who was raised learning things as a child. What I have been teaching you so far would be knowledge that most Timekeeping children would be taught all their life before they actually begin the official training. I suspect it will take about three years to train you."

Three years to train. It amazed me there could be that much knowledge to learn.

"Much of the training involves learning the laws, how things work, how things can be abused," Mathias said. "There will also be a lot of history to learn. Time traveling with the Time Line will also take a while to learn. It is not possible to simply learn it once and know it. In order to time travel, you have to do it over and over again. Returning from wherever you travel also takes time. There is also potential learning from other Timekeeper's that will take time as well."

My next question was a little broader.

"What happens when time stops?"

Mathias gave me a puzzled expression. He clearly was not

expecting a question of that magnitude. He answered it anyway however.

"That is quite an interesting question. Obviously I cannot give you a correct answer because it hasn't happened, but I presume it would simply be the end of the world. We cannot continue unless time is moving us forward. Right?"

"Right," I said. At least I thought. Time was a force and we needed it, but what was time. Could we live without it? I assumed the answer was no, but who knew?

I didn't have any more questions. I really wanted to talk to Mathias about myself. I wanted to try and trust him.

"Would you like to go out for a night? With my fiancé and I?" I asked.

Mathias looked taken aback by this question.

"I—I, well, like I said I don't go out much. I appreciate the offer though."

"Well we could have it here," I suggested.

"He cannot come here until you are married, remember?" Mathias said.

"What would happen? Would he drop dead? Surely my mother was allowed in, right?"

"Your mother was allowed in because I was working from a different Headquarters at the time," Mathias said. “My father was here, dying, and I didn't want to be here. She never met him."

I felt a feeling of sadness for Mathias. He didn't want to be here while his father was dying. I wondered what kind of relationship they had.

"We cannot risk your fiancée knowing our secrets about this place," Mathias continued, "until he is bound to you in marriage."

"Well then come out with us. It's the least you could do."

Mathias stood there silent for a moment. He seemed to be contemplating whether or not he should actually go through with this, and finally he sighed.

"Very well," he said.

I smiled. I figured this should be interesting.

I stood before my bedroom mirror and assessed the situation. I was wearing a short black dress that came down to my knees as well as my black heels. I grabbed a black cardigan to place around my shoulders and made my way down to the hallway.

"You look beautiful!" my mother told me.

My mother and Mrs. Baxter were standing by the front door.

"Woo wee," Mrs. Baxter said in a high tone. "I remember the days when I had a figure like that, I would just let myself go and dance the night away." She began to snap her fingers and shake her hips. My mother's eyes looked like they were going to roll back into her head.

"Alright, Mrs. Baxter," she said, laughing, "can you run into the kitchen and check on Dean?"

Mrs. Baxter nodded and wondered off. She purposely muttered loud enough for us to hear that we were just trying to get rid of her.

I had told my mother I was simply going out with Phillip for the night. He had the same story to ensure she didn't find out the truth. Again, I felt like I was deceiving her, but at the same time, I felt like it was necessary. There was a knock at the door and my mother pulled it open. Phillip stood in the doorway looking very clean-cut in his suit. My mother gave Phillip a hug. We were almost out the door when Mrs. Baxter came running down the hall.

"Now Phillip don't you leave without giving me a kiss!" she said.

"Of course, Mrs. Baxter. I would never leave without kissing you."

Mrs. Baxter planted a large kiss on Phillip's cheek and pulled him into a hug that lasted longer than it needed to. My mother finally intervened and untangled Mrs. Baxter. Phillip led me outside and opened the car door for me.

"So, we are picking him up at Big Ben?" Phillip asked as he was getting in the car on the driver's side.

"Yes. I told him seven o' clock, so we better get going. It is already a quarter till."

"I hope this goes well."

Phillip had seemed very hesitant about the whole thing. I was too. I only hoped it did go well.

The three of us sat in silence for a while at the restaurant. We had decided to go to Kettner's in Soho. It was my favorite restaurant and also where Phillip had taken us for our first date. We all ordered our drinks and meals and waited in a silence that was thick enough it could be cut with a knife. Finally, Mathias broke the silence by speaking up.

"Do you two have a date set yet?" he asked, after taking a sip of his drink.

"No," Phillip responded, "we were thinking about summer, but I know Abigail wanted to wait a while before we got married."

"Yes. It is probably best she be focused on her studies right now."

I wondered which studies he was referring to.

"How long have you two known each other than?" he asked.

"Two years," Phillip responded. Why was he answering all the questions?

"Not very long at all," Mathias commented.

I couldn't help but give him a questioning look—I don't think he saw it though. How was two years not long? In some relationships, that was too long before waiting to get married.

I was going to say something, but Phillip piped up again before I could.

"How long were you and Abigail's mother together?" Phillip asked.

My body tensed up so fast I felt like someone had slapped me across the face. Why was he asking that? Just because Mathias didn't talk about my mother didn't mean Phillip had to fix it.

Mathias gave Phillip a look and then answered.

"About a year and then we were married."

"Not very long at all," Phillip commented.

Mathias' face went bright red—I knew it was anger—I had seen it before.

"Phillip," I intervened suddenly, "darling...could I have a private word with you?"

I didn't give him a chance to respond. I stood up and pulled him by the arm to the lobby of the restaurant, leaving Mathias brooding in his seat.

"What are you doing?" I asked.

"No offense Abigail, but your father is a prick!"

"Phillip, you are a prick."

"Okay, fine, but the guy suddenly wants to act all fatherly and say we haven't been together that long. Ever since you met him he has been the guy teaching you, not loving you. Now he wants to play father, just because I'm here. I'm not having it."

"Forget his intentions. This night is about trust. I want to trust this man. If this is what it takes, we will deal with it. Now let's go."

I pulled him back to the table and we sat down. The meals had arrived and Mathias was staring at his food, but not eating.

"I didn't want to be rude and eat without you," he said. I could sense a bit of sarcasm directed at Phillip.

"Thank you, Mathias," I said.

We all began to eat our meals and Phillip spoke up again once more.

"Abigail tells me I cannot enter your Headquarters until we are married. I quite understand. I'm just wondering why your wife was allowed to enter before your marriage. Abigail said you allowed that?"

I had stopped eating mid bite and stared at Phillip flabbergasted. Why were men so *stupid*? Seriously, I told him not to do something and he does it anyway.

Mathias gave Phillip a look. If looks could kill, Phillip would be buried already.

"My *wife*," Mathias said, "was allowed in because we were in our Headquarters in the Tower of London. It is a backup Headquarters we do not use anymore."

My attention was taken off Phillip for a moment.

"Did you say the Tower of London?" I asked.

Mathias was taken aback, and then I understood. He had not meant to say it. He had never told me where the location was before, why would he now? It was one of the many pieces of information about his past, and my mother's past, that he was keeping from me.

"I didn't say anything," Mathias said.

"Really? I'm not stupid Mathias. You didn't mean to tell me. Why don't you want to tell me anything about my mother's past?"

"Abigail, the circumstances surrounding your mother's death are already muddled. I left the place and haven't returned since. What concerns you are your Timekeeper preparations."

"No." I was livid. Once again, it was about teaching me, instructing me. "I came to you because I wanted to know who I was and where I came from. I wanted to know why my mother left me that night and find out what happened to her. I'm not saying Timekeeping isn't important to me—it is—but what's more important is having a father who cares about me enough to tell me about my mother."

Mathias was angry again. His face was bright red.

"Abigail your mother is dead. She left no information for me about you. She just disappeared and then she was dead. You say I don't tell you anything, but she was a very private woman and there isn't a lot to tell. I have accepted it and have not pursued the reasons why. You shouldn't either. I'm sorry, but I cannot even begin to understand why you have such an emotional connection to a woman you didn't know."

I stood up. This night was over.

"I invited you out tonight so that Phillip could meet you. So that we could talk about our lives and my mother. I came to you to find myself. Obviously, you have no emotion. I don't trust you at all. I'll see you at *class*!"

I left the restaurant with Phillip following in my wake. During the drive back to his flat, we exchanged no words. The silence was engulfed by my anger. I realized that I was being irrational and that I wasn't thinking. I knew that I shouldn't be continuing to see Mathias, but I needed to know, I *had* to know, about my biological mother. And if that meant spending my days with someone I didn't trust, I was going to do it.

I locked myself inside Phillip's bedroom and undid my hair. I let it fall down my back. Then I pulled off my shoes and unzipped my dress. I pulled open Phillip's dresser drawer and found a large shirt and put it on. I then put on his extra pair of pajama pants. I walked back out into the living room and he was in the kitchen putting dishes away.

"I like it," he said, grinning.

"Shut up."

I walked over to the window and pushed it open. It was hot in here.

"What the hell did you say that for?"

"Because you ruined the whole night!" I shouted at him.

"I ruined the night?" Phillip repeated. "How did I ruin the night?"

"You didn't have to provoke him!"

"The guy is a pretentious, self-righteous, and narrow-minded bastard, Abby! What did you want me to do? Sit there and let him talk about us and bring down our relationship just because he is obviously lonely."

There were no words I could say to respond to that. I stood there. My body was shaking with anger. I knew I was probably red in the face. My eyes were burning with tears that I wouldn't allow to fall.

"And please shut the bloody window," Phillip shouted. “It's freezing."

I turned around and pulled the window shut. Phillip walked up to me and pulled me into him. We stood there for a while, him holding me. Only did he let go of me when there was a knock at the door of his flat.

He walked over to the door and peeked out of the peephole and then opened the door. I looked around him, but there was no one there. A note was taped to the door however. He pulled it off and read it and then let it fall to the floor.

"Lock the door behind me," he said. He ran out into the hall, pulling the door shut behind him. I didn't have time to say anything. I didn't want to, but I ran ahead and locked the door. I looked down at the note and picked it up. I read it over and once again felt terror within me.

I enjoyed throwing her body off the Tower Bridge and letting it hang there like it was trash.

CHAPTER TEN

Phillip was gone for a while, but he returned. He had no luck in finding the person who had left the note. He was furious. He was even considering moving, but I said whoever it was would probably just follow us there.

"I was thinking," I said, changing the subject, "maybe we should go to the Tower of London. I want to try and find the old Headquarters."

"I thought he said it was dangerous," Phillip said.

"It could be, but clearly he relocated because he felt the need to. Maybe there are secrets there? He could be hiding something there and he doesn't want us to know."

"Well what if this person that is following us, follows us there?" Phillip asked. "That wouldn't be good, would it?"

"Phillip if they really wanted something that bad they would've busted through that door," I insisted. "Obviously they didn't. They are leaving these notes for a reason. And don't forget that not all of the notes have been threatening. There are two different people writing notes here and I think one of them is Mathias."

"What? How does that make any sense?"

"You saw the notes too. Who else could it be? I have no idea why he would do it—maybe he's terrible at being social because of being underground all these years and that is his way of communicating in a positive manner, or maybe—"

"Maybe he's the one leaving the threatening notes," Phillip finished. "Alright, fine." He reached up and scratched the back of his head. "Say we do go there. How are you going to find your way in? It isn't just going to be there. We can't just show up at the Tower of London and start looking around."

"I don't know. Maybe we'll get lucky."

Phillip rolled his eyes. "I'll think about it. I'm going to bed. Are you coming?"

I sighed and threw my hands up in frustration.

"I'll sleep on the couch," I said.

"Abigail! Wake up! They are coming!"

My eyes fluttered open. My mother was hovering above me. I could hear the sirens going off outside the house again. We had to get to the bomb shelter. I threw the covers off of me and got up, slipping into my shoes as I did. The house was warm and I was not ready to go out into the cold, freezing night. But we had to get to safety.

I followed my mother out onto the upstairs landing and we bolted down the stairs. My father was downstairs waiting for us—he was looking around in confusion. My mother grabbed his hand and we ran out the back door and down the path to the shelter.

"Wait."

I turned around and there she was. Her blonde hair was blowing around her face in the wind. Once again, she was barefoot and she wore the same white dress. It blew around her in the wind.

"Are you my mother?" I asked. Why did I ask that? My mother was behind me. "Are you my biological mother?"

"Don't go." The woman's eyes had a strong plead in them. She didn't want me to go. I turned around and looked at the shelter. I had to go. The bombs would drop and I would die if they did.

"I have to go."

The woman shook her head.

"Death," she spoke.

The bombs dropped.

My eyes opened. The room was quiet. I saw the ceiling above me and turned my head to look out into the living room. The room was dark. I was sweaty again. I stood up and walked across the room to the kitchen to pour myself a glass of water.

After downing most of it in one gulp, I set down the glass, walked into Phillip's room, and around to his side of the bed. He was turned on his side, facing me. I knelt down on the floor and admired him. He was beautiful when he was asleep. He was calm, peaceful, and vulnerable.

I heard a squeaking sound and turned my head to look out the bedroom door and into the living room. In the moonlight, I could see the silhouette of a shadow sneaking in under the apartment door. Someone was standing outside the apartment. I heard something touch the door frame and then the shadow disappeared. I walked up and looked through the peep hole. There was no one on the other side. I quickly unlocked the door and opened it. Once again, there was a note taped to the door. I took it off and shut the door—locking it.

The note was from the person that had left the first note. It wasn't from the person leaving the disturbing and threatening messages. However, my heart still dropped as I read it.

I fear that you are in danger. I know that another person leaving notes has threatened you. To find the old Headquarters, go to the Tower of London. Go to where the Tower overlooks the Thames. Here you will find the second entrance to the old Headquarters. The first entrance is no longer usable because your father closed it off. Jump into the Thames and swim downward until you see a hole in the wall under the water. Go through and you will know where to go. I will leave something there for you to gain passage.

I realized that this person had to be a Timekeeper, or something like a Timekeeper. It was the only explanation of why they knew so much. I despised the fact that I would have to jump into the Thames again, but I would do it anyway. I grabbed a torch, some clothes, and my coat, as well as Phillip's car keys, and left.

The drive to the Tower of London took longer than I thought it would. Maybe it was because I had not gone there in a while or because I was too busy worrying internally; and worrying internally made everything go slower. I saw the tower in the distance however and parked some ways off. I was fairly sure there would be someone somewhere here tonight and I did not want to draw attention to myself by pulling up in a car and then proceeding to jump into the Thames.

I made my way to where the tower was overlooking the river. The river was calm again tonight; however I knew the water would be freezing—and disgusting. I would have to swim fast to avoid catching hypothermia. I had dry clothes in the car so I would have to hurry up and swim back to change so I wasn't in cold clothes for too long.

Sitting down near the edge of the river, I looked over the side. I waited for a moment and considered the possibility that this was a trap, but then I also considered the possibility that every time I met with my father was a trip. Was this a risk I was willing to take? I thought of my mother and knew the answer. I took a breath and slipped into the river.

Unlike last time, where I felt outside of my body, this time I felt everything. The water was cold—freezing cold. I felt pain throughout my body as I swam further down. I turned the torch on so that I could see, hoping the water wouldn't damage it right away. I swam downward and found the hole in the wall and quickly swam through it. As soon as I was through the hole I swam upward and broke the surface. A ledge was nearby and I climbed up.

I shook myself off for a moment and then used the torch to find out where I was. There was a narrow hallway just ahead and I walked toward it. The hallway turned into stairs and I was walking down. The descent took longer than I thought and I wondered how far down this Headquarters was buried. Finally, I reached a solid wooden door. There was one large hole in the center of the door. I tried to peer through it, but there was only blackness on the other side. It was more like a place where you might set an object, like something needed to be put into it. I shone the flashlight on the door and there was a message carved into it.

That which is used to travel is used to pass.

The message clicked instantly with me. In order to travel with time a Timekeeper needed their pocket watch. But I didn't have one, at least not yet. I sighed in frustration but then remembered what the note had said. They would leave something there for me to gain passage. I pointed the torch in various locations, looking for anything out of the ordinary that may have been left behind. Hanging on the wall directly in front of me, was a pocket watch. I held out my hand and touched it, turning it around. The letter *E* was carved into the front of it. This was my mother's. It had to be. But did that mean that she was also a Timekeeper? Mathias had told me she hadn't been. Was this one of the secrets he had referred to?

I removed it from the wall where it hung and placed it in the hole in the door. A solid door slid down and the hole disappeared along with the pocket watch. Immediately the door began to ascend upward, revealing an archway. I stepped through and just as I did, the door lowered itself once more. My mother's pocket watch was lying on the floor in front of me. I picked it up and put it safely around my neck. I used the torch to look around the room I was now in.

I was in a study, similar to the one at Big Ben. Cobwebs were everywhere. The room had clearly not been entered in a long time, or if it had been, no one had bothered to clean it. The study was dark and there were several bookshelves, mostly empty as well as an old desk. A fireplace was in the middle of the room. Some old chairs and a couch were in here as well, but they looked torn and ratty. It looked like animals had gotten in here at one point, or mice.

At the other end of the room was a doorway that was completely boarded up. I assumed this was the usual entrance to the place that Mathias had closed off. I wondered why he left the other one open. Then again, it was hard enough to get to the place anyway so why bother?

I turned and there was an archway that led down into a hallway. The hallway stopped with a brick wall at the end. There were three different doors. Overall, this appeared to be it. The Headquarters was smaller than the one at Big Ben, which is obviously why it was used as a backup.

I tried the first door and it swung open. The room was completely empty. Only cobwebs and dust took up the space of the room. I shut the door and proceeded to the next. This room had a large canopy bed inside it as well as a dresser and some other pieces of furniture. I walked into the room and opened the first drawer of the dresser. I was not expecting it to be full, but it was. Women's clothes were inside the drawer. They were old and it looked like they belonged to the twenties decade. I realized then that these must've been my mother's clothes.

My eyes began to water. I decided I might as well get out of these wet clothes, I would probably be here a while.

I stood before an old mirror in a bathroom that I had found inside the bedroom. The mirror had a crack in it, but I could see my reflection all the same. I had found an old, cream-colored dress with a bow on it. My hair was pulled back into a pony tail. For a minute, I could see how similar I looked to the woman in my dreams—with the exception of hair.

I went back into the main bedroom and looked through the drawer of an old vanity. Inside, I found several different pieces of jewelry including a pearl necklace that I immediately tried on. I went back to the mirror and I enjoyed the way the necklace looked on me. But at the same time, it felt like something too extravagant for a time when things were supposed to be rationed and people weren’t able to have the things they wanted. It felt like something that I shouldn't be able to have.

There was a creaking sound and my head snapped to the right immediately. I had turned it too fast and cursed under my breath as a string of pain shot through it. I walked back out into the main hallway, but it was still empty. I remembered that I was underground as well as near water so I probably heard a sound from that.

One more door remained at the end of the hallway and I decided to check it out. I pushed the door open and again, it was something that wasn't meant to be.

The room was a nursery—my nursery I assumed. But I had never come home to use it. I slowly took in the sight of crib, changing table, and different baby toys. A rocking chair sat in one corner of the room. They had all of these preparations for something that would never be. Something that couldn't be.

My mother had touched these things once I thought, or at least, I hoped she had. I walked over to the dresser and opened a drawer. A few outfits remained—some little girl outfits that I never got the chance to wear.

Another creaking sound disturbed my attention. I turned around and looked at the doorway. I proceeded to check the hallway again, but it was once again empty. I decided I should get back to Phillip's. I didn't want him to wake up and find me gone. Whoever had left the note was obviously not going to make an appearance. I turned around and grabbed the handle of the door, but I stopped to admire my nursery for just another moment. I wondered—what would it have been like to grow up here? I immediately felt guilty for thinking it, thinking about my adoptive parents and how they had done everything for me, and went back to the first room to change into my clothes. I then turned back and left the way I came. I realized I still had the pearls on when I returned to my car. I placed them carefully into the inner pocket of my coat. I would take them back later, I thought, as I drove back to Phillip's.

I did not return to the old Headquarters for the rest of the week, nor did I mention it to anyone, including Phillip. I wanted to learn more about my past, and I wanted so desperately for Phillip to know, but I was also afraid. First off, the place was strange. I felt like someone was there. The creaking sounds made it sound as if someone was there, plus someone had given me the information to get there. Second, the place left me distracted. I knew if I went back I would probably spend hours there and I didn't have hours to devote during the day without people noticing I was gone. Finally, Christmas was in a few days and for the first time in weeks, I had the chance to do something normal.

"What do you want for Christmas?" I asked.

Phillip and I were at the library in his office. He looked up from what he was reading and I laughed. He was wearing his reading glasses. They always made him look different. He scowled at me.

"All I want is you," he responded with a flirtatious smile, "and I've already got you."

I got up off the couch and walked over to his desk. He swiveled around in his chair and pulled me into his lap.

"Well that's nice and dandy," I said, "but I think I could get you something."

He sighed. "I honestly cannot even think about what you could get me that I don't already have. I really am a lucky man."

"Of course, you are lucky," I responded, "if you weren't, I wouldn't be here. I'll find something for you though."

"Okay, what do *you* want though?" he asked.

"I've actually already got that planned out," I responded.

He gave me a questioning look. "So, what you are saying is, that you do not need anything else because you already have the greatest gentleman in the world."

"You are hilarious, but I was thinking we could have Christmas with your parents. That would be my present."

The look on his face went from jolly to a child who had just received socks instead of toys. I knew he would react this way. Phillip had only communicated with his parents through the telephone for the past few years. They lived in Scotland. They knew about me, but had never met me. Phillip only told me "what I needed to know" about them and that was that. He said to not expect them at the wedding. I couldn't even begin to understand why he was on such bad terms with them, but I wanted to try and fix that.

"Abby, we've been through this. They don't want to see me—I don't want to see them. Because you are my fiancée you are associated with me and anyone in association with me they also do not want to see."

"Fine," I responded. I had my own idea in place anyway. I knew he would say no, so I had a plan B, but I wanted to ask him in case he had one of those miraculous Christmas turnarounds. "I guess we will go with the second option. My mum wants you over for Christmas Eve dinner and she's going to set up the guest bedroom. We are going to stay up late and play games and then you'll stay over."

Phillip smiled. "That sound's lovely."

"So, what time did you want me for Christmas?"

Bridget and I were shopping out in London today. I figured it would be good for us to get out and do something for once since I had been so busy recently. She seemed to have let go of the conversation we had had outside Big Ben. I didn't know if she believed me or not, but she wasn't pestering me about it, and for now, that was enough. However, as soon as she had brought up Christmas, which she had every right to, a pang of guilt shot up and down my body. I had only just remembered a month ago when I had invited Bridget over for Christmas because she had no place else to go, but with everything that had been happening, I had forgotten.

"Abby?"

Bridget turned to look at me and I knew she knew before she even said anything. I had waited too long to respond to her and she could tell.

"I'm actually planning something secret for Phillip," I said.

"Oh."

Bridget turned and began to walk ahead of me. I had to walk faster to keep up. She was trying to get away from me. I grabbed her by the shoulder and turned her around. Her eyes were beginning to glass over with tears.

"I'll cancel it Bridget. It's okay. I owe you this Christmas. We'll spend it together."

She shook her head.

"No, Abby, it's okay, honestly. The two of you are getting married, and are about to spend the rest of your lives together. I'll be fine."

"Bridget, no. You come over to my house for Christmas. We'll have it together."

"No, it's fine."

"Please, Bridget, really, it's okay."

"Abigail, no!" She went red in the face immediately and then said, "I need to go." She turned on her heel and walked away. I didn't stop her.

Phillip had packed his bags and I told him that my mum and I would swing by and pick him up so that he wouldn't have to drive over. I was continuing to feel guilty over what had happened with Bridget, but I vowed that we would spend time together when I got back. I owed that to her as a friend, but I wasn't sure if we were even going to be that for much longer.

"You know he'll probably return whatever present he bought for you when he realizes what you've done."

"I know."

Phillip's grandmother, Marie, and I were on our way to pick up Phillip. Phillip loved her. She was the only relative I had had the pleasure of meeting. Together, she and I had set it up so that we would drive to Scotland for Christmas with Phillip's parents. His mother was apparently thrilled with the idea, which confused me.

"Does Phillip get along with your daughter then, Marie?" I asked her. Marie's daughter was Phillip's mother, Edna.

"Oh yes, sweetheart," Marie responded, "that boy is a mum's boy through and through. It's his daddy that he doesn't get along with. My poor Edna has to drive up here to London just to see him because he won't ever come home."

"Well, he's never introduced me to her."

"Yes, well, it took me a lot of hard work just to get him to introduce us. I suppose he didn't want you to meet his mum because he was afraid something like this would happen."

I smiled.

We arrived to Phillip's flat in no time and I went up to meet him at the door.

"I've missed you," Phillip said. He leaned down and kissed me and then turned around to lock up his flat door.

"I just saw you last night."

"It has been a long while for me."

Phillip and I walked down to the lobby and out the door, hand in hand. His hand dropped to his side however when he saw his grandmother and her car instead of my mother's.

"Abby," Phillip said angrily under his breath, "what in the hell are you doing?"

"I've planned an intervention darling," I responded, "just like you tried to fix my relationship with my father, I'm going to try and fix yours with your parents. We will have to put money on who is more successful."

Phillip didn't say a single word on the drive to Scotland. Phillip's parents lived in Glasgow, so the drive itself took around seven hours. I drove for a few and Marie drove for a few. Phillip refused to drive. He sat in the back of the car the whole time either with his arms crossed or asleep.

Phillip's parents lived in a wealthier area of Glasgow. His father was a doctor. Marie finally pulled into the driveway of Phillip's childhood home as the sun was beginning to set.

"Nana," Phillip said, "Could you give Abby and I a moment? We will meet you inside. I'll bring in the suitcases."

Marie gave me a look and nodded. She left us alone in the car.

"Why are you doing this?" Phillip asked.

"I haven't met your mother or your father. I'm sorry if you are not on good terms with either of them, but I would like to know the parents of the man I'm about to marry. I've known you for two years Phillip; this is absurd. I've only known my biological father for a month and I've already introduced you to him and you ruined the occasion. Just give me a chance here."

"Abigail this is different. And I hardly ruined the occasion with your father—he had a hand in that himself."

"How?" I asked. "How is it different?"

"My father has disapproved of everything I've done in my life," Phillip said. "He wanted me to go to public school, so I went to comprehensive school. He wanted me to go to university here, so I went in London. He wanted me to be a doctor, so I chose to be a librarian and studier of text."

"I still don't understand how that is different."

"Before I left for school, my father and I had a huge row. He hit me and I said I would not be around a man like that. He's abused my mother too. I saw him do it once, but they never knew I was watching."

My heart went out to Phillip. He had never told me any of this before. I suddenly felt sorry for bringing him here. His grandmother probably didn't know about it either. It wasn't a bad idea to try and fix this, but maybe Christmas wasn't the best time.

"Why didn't you ever tell me this?"

"I just didn't want you to know that not everything about my life is great."

Phillip's eyes began to water. I could tell, but he quickly tried to hide it by looking down.

"Phillip—" I started to say, but he intervened.

"No, it's okay. We've tried to fixed you up and now we can try and fix me."

He got out of the car and grabbed the suitcases out of the trunk. I watched as he walked up the garden path to the front door. I sat there considering how irrational I was and maybe how I needed to start thinking things through before reacting. I may have ruined the start of Christmas for Phillip, but we were here now and I couldn't change it. I vowed to make it better.

CHAPTER ELEVEN

A soft breeze swept against my skin as I made my way up the sidewalk to the front door. The first thing that caught my attention about the house were the wind chimes. They were everywhere—dangling from the hooks by the front door—to one merely hanging at the sidewalk gate. With the wind, they blew—chiming noises could be heard from all over. There was something about the sound that was peaceful.

"Abby."

My brief moment of peace slipped away and I realized Phillip was leaning outside of the front door.

"Are you coming?" he asked me.

I nodded and quickly made my way through the front door. The house was warm and inviting—the walls were adorned with many photographs of Phillip and his family as well as decorations. If I were an outsider, I would never have guessed that what Phillip had said about his father was true. The home seemed lovely and adoring, but I knew never to judge a book by its cover.

"Abigail," Phillip said, "this is my mother, Edna."

A tall, skinny woman stepped forward, extending her bony hand.

Her face was warm and inviting.

"Lovely to meet you, Abigail," she said.

"It's a pleasure to meet you, Mrs. Hughes."

The floor creaked and my eyes jumped to the archway that led into the kitchen. I was a little taken aback at first sight, because it was literally an older version of Phillip before my eyes. Phillip's resemblance to his father was strikingly similar, but where Phillip was warm-hearted, there was something cold about his father. I thought it might be in the way he carried himself. But perhaps it was simply because I had already known things about the man.

“Father,” Phillip said, "this is Abigail. I think now is the best time to tell you both that we are getting married, probably in the summer."

The look on Phillip's mother's face was like a young schoolgirl going giddy for a homemade treat.

"Why didn't you say that right away? I'm very excited for the both of you!"

I couldn't help but smile at her. She really seemed like a kind woman and I felt upset that Phillip didn't get to see her very often because of his father.

Phillip's father stepped forward and held out his hand. I took it.

"Michael Hughes," he said gruffly, "it is a pleasure to meet you."

"You as well, sir," I responded.

Phillip's mother led us all into the living room. Michael said he would talk to Phillip later, but said he had to make a run to the hospital. I found this to be odd since we had just gotten there, but I figured it was because of the problems between Phillip and his father.

"The wedding is in the summer, you said?" Edna asked.

"Well," Phillip said, glancing over at me, "we were thinking about summer, weren't we Abby."

"Maybe," I said smiling. "I would definitely love for it to be in the summer, but we would have to get started on planning very soon."

"I could help with that," Edna added in, "I love weddings."

She was clearly very excited about the prospect of Phillip getting married. She asked about my parents and I told her I was adopted. I left out the part of finding out about Mathias however. I explained that Phillip and I had met at university. Overall, the afternoon went very well. It was later on with Phillip's father that I was worried about.

That night I was lying awake in bed. My mind was racing. Phillip's mother had made a Christmas Eve dinner, but Phillip told me it was only the beginning. He said her Christmas feasts were like nothing else. He seemed happy to be around her and I felt saddened that he felt he had to stay away from her just so he wouldn't have to interact with his father. Phillip never started any conversation with his father at dinner. His father would ask what the librarian business was like. The sarcasm was clearly evident anytime Phillip's father spoke. A part of me was enraged that his father could think that way, but at the same time I was trying not to judge his father too harshly.

A dryness in my throat was killing me, until I couldn't take it any longer. I tore myself from the warm sheets of the bed and made my way down to the first floor of the house. I was about to cross into the living room in order to get to the kitchen, but I froze just at the archway. I could hear Phillip talking—to his father.

"I have to admit Phillip," Michael said, "that girl is probably the best thing you've done in your life. I like her."

I wanted to throw up. How did Phillip feel about this?

"Thanks," Phillip muttered.

"You need to come home more often though," Michael went on, "your mother has been very upset with you. Whines all the time about how Phillip isn't here."

I decided I should go back to my room. I turned to leave, but the floor creaked and I heard someone get up from the couch. I looked over my shoulder just as Michael walked into the hallway.

"Abigail!" he said, a grin on his face.

"I'm sorry Mr. Hughes," I said suddenly, "I was coming to get a drink of water. I didn't mean to listen in."

"Not to worry!" Mr. Hughes said smiling. "Please call me Michael. Come in, come in, I was just chatting with Phillip."

I hesitated, but followed him into the living room. The room had two divans—Phillip's father sat down on the longer one whereas Phillip was sitting in the love seat. I sat down next to Phillip and he pulled me in close to him. I realized that Michael had been drinking. One bottle of whiskey was on the table in front of me, along with Michael's empty glass that he now began to refill.

"So, how did you two meet?"

"I met Phillip in class at university," I said.

"Oh, you are in university," Michael said, clearly surprised. "Well, that I didn't expect."

"My father is very traditional," Phillip stated, "he doesn't believe in women receiving an education."

"Now, now, Phillip," Michael said, waving his hand. "I see no problem with Abigail receiving an education. She will need to be bringing in some money after all. I doubt this librarian business pays well. She'll probably end up making more than you."

"Phillip actually works in a very prestigious library," I told Michael, "he has an office and access to all the resources the library has available—including archived texts. We were recently sitting down to talk and it looks like I will be able to stay home and he'll be able to work."

"Well, isn't that fortunate," Michael said. “However, I cannot see why you would need to stay home. Not like this boy has the balls to produce children. He's always been on the feminine side."

I always felt the need to speak my mind, so I did. "He seems more masculine than you are now," I said. "He doesn't need alcohol to show off his toughness, especially in the presence of a lady."

Michael looked impressed.

"Well damn, Phillip," Michael said, "you've got yourself a tough little bitch."

Phillip immediately rose to his feet.

"Don't you fucking call her that!" he shouted at his father.

Michael stood up, swaying a bit, but pointed a finger at his son. Spit flew out of his mouth as he shouted.

"I'll call the little whore whatever I fucking please!"

Before I could say anything or react in any way, Phillip had socked his father straight in the nose. Michael tumbled to the floor, his hand covering his bleeding nose, mumbling incoherent words.

Lights came on from upstairs and Edna and Phillip's grandmother came running down.

"Phillip, what is going on?" Edna shouted. She looked at her son and her husband on the floor. Blood was pouring out of Michael's nose.

"I've had enough of his shit, mum!" Phillip shouted. "He's the reason I haven't been here. He just called Abigail a whore. Why should I let this man be in our lives? Why should he be in yours? There comes a time when enough is enough. I know he's hurt you in the past."

Phillip's grandmother's eyes widened and she looked at her daughter.

"Has he hit you?" she asked her daughter.

Edna looked unable to speak. She clearly did not know Phillip knew about the abuse. She looked at her mother and nodded. Her eyes began to water, and then tears were pouring from them. I could only stand in the background and watch in sadness as Phillip wrapped his arms around his mother. Michael continued to lie on the floor, moaning in pain, while Phillip and his mother embraced each other.

The events of the night before were still fresh in my mind the next morning. Phillip's grandmother had threatened to call the police if Michael didn't get some clothes and leave. The two of them had a shouting argument and at one point it seemed like Michael was about to hit Marie, but Phillip intervened and ultimately Michael left—surrendering his house keys.

Marie and Edna prepared a Christmas dinner throughout the next day. The four of us went to church in the morning. That night we feasted on turkey, potatoes, pies, and many other wonderful foods. Marie and Edna went to bed and Phillip and I stayed up to talk.

We both sat on the couch in the living room. Phillip was laying his head in my lap, staring up at the ceiling. I curled my fingers in his hair and played with it.

"Thanks for the present," he suddenly said.

I looked down at him. His tone had not been sarcastic, but serious.

"Are you serious?" I asked.

"Yes," Phillip said. "Besides you, my mother and grandmother are two of the most important people in my life. I've missed them so much. And my mum has finally realized my dad need some help."

"Do you think there is still hope for them?" I asked. I seriously wondered if there was.

"I do," he said, "I think that alcohol was a big factor in my father's behavior. I've seen pictures of when they were younger and dated. My grandmother said they were happy; or at least they looked happy. I think they can turn it all around. I believe they can. And if and when my father does, I'll forgive him."

I smiled. This was just one of the many reasons why I loved Phillip. Sure, he had a foul mouth at times and could be a little hot-headed. But he was also caring and compassionate, and he could still forgive someone even when they did horrible things.

"I want to show you something," Phillip said.

He got up from the couch and pulled me after him.

It was snowing again. I loved it when it snowed on Christmas. Phillip and I had thrown on our jackets and made our way through the snow. His backyard was literally a forest. He continued to pull me into the forest until finally we found our way into a small opening area.

A gazebo stood in the middle of the opening. It was fairly old, but still looked beautiful. It was white and the snow around it made it look even more special. Phillip pulled me into the gazebo, into the center, and began to kiss me.

We stood there, our bodies pressed against each other. It was a perfect moment.

Finally, he pulled away and spoke.

"I used to come here when I was a child," he said, "especially after days that my father and I fought. I would just sit here and let nature calm me—let it take away the problems of my life."

"It's beautiful," I whispered.

"Two more things," Phillip said. He reached into his pocket and pulled out a small box. It looked like a ring box, but I knew it wasn't a ring. I already had that. He opened the box and a delicate bracelet was inside it. The chain was golden and one charm was hung on it. Engraved on the charm were our initials, *PH + AJ*.

"Phillip and Abigail," Phillip told me as he put the bracelet on my wrist.

I looked up at him and knew there were tears in my eyes.

"Thank you," I whispered.

"Finally," Phillip said as he reached into his pocket and pulled out a sealed envelope, "This letter is one that I want you to save for our wedding day. I want you to write one for me as well and I'll save it too. If anything should happen to either of us, we can read them, but otherwise I think it will make our wedding day something special. Not that it isn't already special."

I smiled at him and took the letter, placing it carefully into my pocket. It was worth more than the bracelet. It was a piece of Phillip. A piece of him he was choosing to share with me.

"I promise I won't read it," I said, "But I think I'll keep it in my pocket as a constant reminder of you."

Phillip laughed at me and we kissed.

Edna and I sat alone in the kitchen the next morning. Phillip was out with his grandmother, so we decided to chat over a cup of tea.

"Do you approve of us?" I asked her. I knew it was probably a strange question to ask her, but after everything that had happened with Phillip's father, I wanted to know. I felt like I needed to know. She smiled at me.

"I do," Edna responded. "He seems happy with you. I'll be honest with you Abigail. I knew Phillip and his father did not get along and I tried everything I could to make it better. I feel that Phillip would have probably left sooner if it hadn't been for me. I should have told Michael enough was enough, but I didn't. I'm glad he found someone special in London though."

"You and Michael were happy at one point. Right?"

Edna nodded. "I admit we were happy together. I truly believe it was the drinking that caused so much strife in our marriage. Drinking can do terrible things to people."

I heard the front door opening and the voices of Phillip and his grandmother. They came into the kitchen, carrying their bags of groceries. They had gone shopping to replenish Edna's kitchen after the tremendous dinners she had cooked. Edna and her mother began to unload the groceries and Phillip pulled me out of the kitchen.

"Are you ready to go back to London tomorrow?" he asked me.

"Yes. I'll be sad to go though. Your mother is really nice."

He smiled. "So is yours."

We arrived back in London the day after next. I returned to my home for a late Christmas dinner with my family. Afterward, I was sitting at the table listening to my mum clean dishes. I had tried to help, but she insisted on doing it herself. As I sipped at my cup of tea, I thought of Mathias. Had he been alone at Christmas? Had Ian been with him? I had not seen him since our altercation at Kettlers and a part of me felt guilty. He didn't have anyone at Christmas and as much as I was suspicious of him and his behavior, I felt I should go see him.

The one dilemma with seeing Mathias late at night was that Ian was not waiting for me like he usually was. I clutched my coat tighter as the cold wind rustled against me. I was entirely unsure of how I'd be getting into Big Ben tonight. After a failed attempt at going in the usual way, as well as some strange looks from security guards, I wandered around the outside of the building. Hopefully the authorities would not be summoned because of a strange girl wandering around—hopefully.

"Hello, stranger."

I turned and saw Ian making his way toward me.

"Hello," I said, softly. I was freezing as the wind continued to blow against my cheeks.

"I saw you from the clock tower," he said, before I could ask.

"Do you go up there a lot?"

He grinned. "All the time. I kind of feel like a king in a fairy tale. A king admiring his city. So, what can the king help you with m'lady?"

"I would like to see Mathias," I said, adding in a curtsy. "I felt I should see him, since it's the Christmas season and all."

"Very well," Ian said, "Follow me."

"I haven't seen you for a while," Mathias said. He sat where he always sat when I entered his study—in his desk chair. Ian had left us alone.

"You shouldn't be too surprised."

"Perhaps," Mathias said, his concentration on a book before him, "but I would have thought since I paid the bill you would have showed me some consideration."

I took off my coat and laid it on the edge of the couch.

"I'm sorry Phillip reacted that way," I said, sitting down on the couch, "but I thought you would show him some consideration too. He is my fiancé. Why did you have to start playing the role of upset father?"

Mathias looked up at me and then sighed. He took off his reading glasses and stood up, perching himself on the edge of his desk and crossing his arms.

"I'm sorry Abigail. I just wasn't ready to be that involved with your life. I'm trying to work on it, but at the same time, I think it is important that you learn the essentials of being a Timekeeper."

"So, education before parenting?" I said. "That sounds lovely."

Mathias sighed again.

"I know you have another father, Abigail. I don't want to take his place."

"My father has dementia. He is deteriorating every day. Sometimes he can't even remember who I am. I need a father now more than ever."

The look on Mathias' face turned sad. I knew this information was probably a lot to throw at him, but I felt he deserved to know it.

"I feel like you don't trust me Abigail."

"I don't. Why can't you tell me more information about who my mother was?"

"I've already told you! I've said everything there is to say."

Mathias looked away from me and stared at the other end of the room. I didn't trust him. I didn't believe his response. I couldn't if I was going to believe the letter that my biological mother had left. He knew more than he was letting on. But I also couldn't tell him about the letter, not yet. Until I figured something out, I didn't think I could stay there any longer. Why should I stay there?

I stood up to leave and reached for my coat, but Mathias caught my arm.

"Wait," he said.

"Why? You aren't going to tell me anything or be anything to me."

My coat fell off the couch behind me and something fell out of the inside pocket and hit the floor. I turned my attention to it and my heart dropped. It was the pearl necklace. I went to pick it up, but Mathias pulled my arm so hard I landed down on the couch. He hovered over me, angry.

"Where did you get that?" he shouted at me. His voice was loud and booming. I suddenly felt very fearful. He was in a rage I had never seen him in.

"It's mine."

"You went there didn't you? Why did you go there? What have you done?"

"I haven't done anything!" I shouted back. "You wouldn't tell me anything, so I went to find out for myself."

"We aren't supposed to go back there!"

I stood up to leave again. I had had enough.

"No!"

Mathias grabbed my arm and pulled me back. I looked him square in the eye.

"Let go of me."

He did at that. I grabbed my coat and ran down the hall—leaving the necklace. Hot tears poured out of my eyes. I wanted to get away from this place. In the process, I longed to know the truth. The actual truth. I wanted to get the story straight. So, I decided to go back to the place where I knew her past was held.

The old Headquarters was dark once again. I entered it, shaking from the cold water I had just swum through. I walked to the room that had been my mother's and put on some of her warm clothes.

I was surprised to find an old photograph in one of the dresser drawers. I had not seen it the last time I was here. The picture showed, once again, a much younger Mathias. His arm was around a woman, but the woman's face had been cut out of the picture. I found this to be very odd. The frame of the woman did not look like that of my mother, but someone a little different. I turned the photograph over and found written on the back *Mathias and*, but the second part was scribbled out. I tried to read it closer up, but I could not tell whose name had been scribbled out. I placed the picture back into the drawer, while finding the person's head being cut out to be very eerie.

I went back to the main room and attempted to light a fire in the fireplace. I was taken aback however when I saw the dying smoke of another fire. Someone had been here.

I heard a creaking sound and I turned around. There was no one there.

"Hello! Who is there?"

I almost screamed because I wasn't expecting what happened next. A woman stepped out from the shadows of the hallway. She was older than me, in her middle forties. She had brown hair that was cut short and her face looked old and tired. She wore an old gray dress and plain shoes.

"Who are you?" I asked. My heart was racing.

"Please don't be afraid," the woman said. Her voice was soft and had a high pitch to it.

"I've been sending you those notes," the woman told me. "I saw you in the cemetery and left you the note on how to get here."

"Did you leave those threats?" I asked.

"No," the woman said, "those were left by someone you already know."

"Who?"

"Please, let me talk to you about everything first. There is so much to say."

"You can start by telling me who you are then."

The woman smiled a kind smile at me.

"My name is Bessie. I was your mother's best friend."

A part of me felt rather peaceful about this. Another part of me felt rather unsure. Was I ready for the answers I had desperately been wanting? I knew I was, but I was still fearful. The world of the Timekeepers seemed to be getting bigger.

CHAPTER TWELVE

January 1944

I did not stay long that first night with Bessie. I was still rather unsure of meeting an entirely new person and decided I was not ready to know everything just yet. I was afraid. I told her I would come back and talk about it some more. She explained that these things would bring up emotions I was probably trying to forget. She told me to take all the time I needed. So, I did. She continued to leave me notes however. Now that I knew who she was, it felt more like there was someone watching over me.

I spent the remainder of December away from Mathias. I didn't want to be around him after the way he had reacted. I knew the necklace probably brought back memories that he was not expecting, but I also think he overreacted. Phillip and I spent New Year's Eve together, and soon enough the cold month of January was upon us.

The word busy could describe how everyone felt. I was busy with a new semester at Birkbeck, whereas Phillip was busy at his job more than he had ever been. His parents decided to seek professional counseling for their marital problems, but more importantly, for Michael's alcoholism. I hoped they would be able to work through the problems that their marriage had been enduring for quite some time and that maybe Phillip would be able to forgive his father.

My father's health continued to deteriorate. He no longer had any recollection of who my mother was and it killed her heart. I could see the various emotions on her face, even though she constantly tried to hide them. As of late, my mother began working more hours at her job to help pay for the bills from December. Mrs. Baxter was around more than ever, she claimed she was just taking care of my father, but I knew she didn't want to be alone. Her husband had passed away several years ago, so when she left us each day, it was to go home to an empty house. My mother offered to let her move in with us, but Mrs. Baxter was too proud and said she wasn't old enough to be in a "home" yet.

One day when I was finally free of the reins of schoolwork, I decided to sit down and write my letter to Phillip. The letter he had given me was still in my pocket, where I kept it as a reminder of him. I realized how terrible I was at writing down my emotions. I talked about how much I loved him and that I couldn't wait to be with him on our wedding day. Overall, the letter was rather short, but I think the point got across. I figured he probably had a much better letter written. I sat there for a while, rewriting it until I felt it was the best it could be.

"Here you are," I said one afternoon in Phillip's office, handing him the letter.

"Thank you," he said. "Like you, I will keep this in my coat pocket at all times as a constant reminder of you."

He smiled at me and I sat down on the leather couch. He got up and plopped down next to me and pulled me into his arms. We kissed for a few moments before finally he lay down on his back, pulling me in to lie on top of him.

"Now that the holidays are over," he said, "we should be thinking about dates. I think summer is good, this summer definitely."

I laughed.

"Well?" he asked.

"This summer."

He sat up and looked at me.

"Are you being serious?" he asked me.

"Yes. I know it will be coming up rather quickly, and we will have a lot of work to do, but I want to be with you as soon as I can."

He smiled and we kissed each other again. We held each other close and he whispered into my ear.

"I love you. I feel like we are always honest with each other."

A feeling of despair shot through my body and I felt bad. I felt like I wasn't being honest with him. There were things I still had not told him. I had not mentioned the old Headquarters, what happened between Mathias and I recently, and finally about meeting Bessie. I hoped that could change.

The old Headquarters was dark and musty. I looked around everywhere, but Bessie was not there. I made my way to my mother's room and began to look through her dresser drawers. I was intent on answers.

My heart pounded when I found a false bottom in the bottom drawer of the dresser. I pulled up the false bottom and found an old chest underneath it. The chest was very small and wooden. I pulled it out and laid it on the ground in front of me. I opened it and was surprised to find it stuffed with several pieces of paper. My heart pounded again when I realized they were letters. There were two written in the same handwriting that I had been receiving, the ones that had been threats, not the ones from Bessie.

Elisabeth,

This is my first communication with you. I have been watching you and your husband for quite some time. I know that you are lying to him about something and I intend to find out what it is. There are things that you are keeping hidden from your family that need to be brought out into the light.

Please respond to me. Leave a letter in the same place you found this one. I will get it.

The next letter made me feel tense. I wanted to hurt the person that was talking to my mother this way. Why would they say such horrible things? But then I had to remember, this was the person who must've killed her.

Elisabeth,

You cannot hide from me, as much as you think you can. Either you set up a meeting to meet me, or I will find another way. And trust me, you don't want that.

I was sure there had to be more letters, but I had read everything that was inside the chest. I put the letters back in and placed them back inside the drawer. I would just have to keep looking until I found some more letters or clues somewhere in this place.

"We should go to Scotland."

My hair blew gently around my face. Phillip and I were walking to the London Library. He wasn't working today—we were just going to study together.

"Didn't we just return from Scotland?" I asked. I grasped his hand as we turned a corner. It was something I found myself doing a lot in the past few weeks. So many things had changed that I was afraid I was going to lose these moments with the people I cared about. I wanted to hold onto them. Even in something as simple as turning a corner.

"Yes, it's a lovely place. But I'm not proposing we go to Glasgow, but somewhere different."

I gave Phillip a stare and he smiled. We made our way up the walkway to the library and inside where it was much warmer. I didn't ask him anything else until we were inside his office with the door shut behind us.

"So, why are you bringing up Scotland?" I asked. "Like I said, we were *just* there."

"And like I said, a different part of Scotland," he responded. He put his hands around my waist. "A more private part, for just a weekend, and just for the two of us."

"My mum—"

He cut me off with his lips against mine.

"—won't care," he added. "She lets you make your own decisions. You are the one that pretends she cares."

"That doesn't mean she doesn't care."

I pulled off my coat and threw it on the couch.

"Abby, you are eighteen years old," Phillip pestered me, "your mother lets you make your own decisions."

"She should still be guiding me more and suggest what's right," I suggested. "It's what most mothers would do. She really hasn't questioned me at all lately about when I've stayed over at your flat."

"Well, she isn't most mothers is she?" Phillip laughed.

My body tensed and I turned abruptly. My hands were balled into fists.

"Maybe because she isn't actually *my* mother!"

My voice had risen. I caught myself immediately and brought my hand up to my mouth. It was as if I was checking to see if I had actually said what I had said. Phillip's face was contorted into disbelief. There was no anger, or hurt, just disbelief. I think the expression of disbelief was the most hurtful expression of all. It meant that a person was actually questioning, wondering, and trying to know if something was true. If I had said what I had said—and more importantly—if I had meant it.

I grabbed my coat off the couch and put it back on.

"I have to go," I said.

Phillip didn't stop me. I didn't look at him as I left. For all I knew, he still wore that same disbelieving expression.

"Are you hungry?"

I looked up. My mother stood in the doorway of my bedroom. I had come home and went straight there to read. It helped me get my mind off things.

"I'm fine," I said, looking back down at my book.

"You didn't come down for dinner."

My mother walked over to my bed and sat down on the edge, she pulled the book from my hands and set it down by my side.

"You usually come down for dinner," she added. "What's wrong?"

I didn't say anything for a moment. I tried to read her eyes. She was worried—I could tell. I wondered if she could read mine.

"Why don't you ever get upset when I spend so much time at Phillips?" I asked.

She raised her eyebrows. She was surprised.

"Well, he is your fiancé. Isn't it custom for two people who love each other to spend time together?"

"Yes, but don't you get upset when I stay over there, or when we went out of town together?"

"Abigail, you are eighteen years old. You are a grown woman now and can make your own decisions. Sure, you live in my home, but I'm going to treat you like an adult. Isn't that what you want?"

I nodded and looked away from her. I stared out my bedroom window and into the streets. It was already dark out.

I heard my mother get up and walk out. She knew I didn't want to talk right now and would leave me alone. She knew me, yet I felt distant from her.

I stood outside a house that was mine but wasn't mine. All the houses in the neighborhood were the same of course. But this wasn't my house. It was Mrs. Baxter's. Why was I here?

It was night. The wind was blowing hard—trees were blowing and snapping their branches against houses. My hair whipped around my face as I made my way up the steps toward Mrs. Baxter's door. The door came open before I reached it and I stepped into the house.

The door slammed shut behind me. It was dark inside the house. I reached around and tried to find a light switch so I could see my way around, but I didn't find one.

A creaking sound came from the end of the hallway in front of me.

"Hello?" I called out into the darkness.

No response came from the shadows. I felt chills go up my body. I felt cold. I felt like I should leave immediately.

I turned around and reached out for the door handle. I turned the knob, but the door did not come open. I tried to lock it and unlock it, but the door would not budge. My body tensed as I heard another creaking sound behind me.

I turned around, but there was still only darkness.

"Hello?" I called out again.

The sounds of hoarse breathing from another person filtered across the hallway. My body stiffened against the door. How far away was the breather? Were they dangerous? I slowly extended my hand—fearfully. I felt nothing at the end of my fingertips. They simply fell through the air in front of me.

My eyes burned as the lights in the whole house suddenly flashed on. I threw up my hands to shield my eyes from the sudden light. I blinked a few times, but finally my eyes adjusted to the light and I saw Mrs. Baxter standing in front of me.

"Well, it took you long enough to turn on the lights dear," Mrs. Baxter said.

"I—" I began, but I was startled. I looked over at the light switch. I had not turned them on.

"Mrs. Baxter," I said, "why am I here? I mean, it seems so late. I didn't mean to bother you."

"Well, you are here," Mrs. Baxter replied, "and you did bother me. So, you

might as well come into the kitchen for a spot of tea."

Mrs. Baxter turned and waddled away down the hallway and into the kitchen. I supposed I better follow suit. I followed her into the kitchen and took a seat at the table. She stood at the counter, pouring some tea into a cup and then placed it down in front of me.

"So why did you come?" Mrs. Baxter asked me.

I was bewildered. I had no idea why I had come.

"I told you I don't know," I said. "Don't you know? I mean you were out in the hallway and opened the door for me. Didn't you?"

"Only you can open doors for yourself," Mrs. Baxter answered.

I raised my eyebrows in wonderment. What did that mean?

"I'm sorry?"

"Abigail," Mrs. Baxter said, "I've known you since your mum and dad took you in from that orphanage. You've always been the kind of girl to find her way. Why are you so different now?"

"I didn't realize I was," I replied, "Mrs. Baxter, do you know something I don't?"

"You seem different these days," Mrs. Baxter responded, "Like you aren't sure of things. But I know you Abigail. You will find your way."

A grandfather clock began to toll now.

"I have to go now Abigail," Mrs. Baxter said, "I won't be able to come back anymore either."

"What do you mean?"

But Mrs. Baxter didn't answer. She stood up and walked into the hallway. The hallway was filled with more light, so much light that I could not see beyond that. Mrs. Baxter walked into the light and then there was darkness.

* * *

My eyes opened. I looked up at the ceiling above me. I brought my hand to my heart. It was beating fast and, once again, I was sweating profusely.

My dream had been so vivid. I could not remember the last time I had had a dream that vivid. What had happened to Mrs. Baxter? Why was she there anyway? Did it mean something?

I relaxed my body and closed my eyes. I let myself be consumed by thoughts and questions. What did anything mean?

CHAPTER THIRTEEN

Tap. Tap. Tap.

What was that sound?

Tap. Tap. Tap.

My eyes popped open and I veered them in the direction of the noise. A bird was simply tapping on the window, awakening me to the day. My thoughts turned to the dream I had had the night before. What had it meant? A knock sounded throughout my room suddenly, and my attention turned toward the bedroom door.

The door opened and my mother stepped into the room. She was dressed for work. I wondered vaguely what time it was.

"Abby," she said, "I need to be leaving for work. But Ian is here. He's downstairs. I told him I would have you get ready, but do it quickly. He really wants to speak with you."

Ian was here. I wondered if it had anything to do with Mathias, but nevertheless I tore myself from my bed and ran to the bathroom to get ready.

As I walked down the stairs of the house, I could see Ian standing in the living room. He was admiring some photographs of my family, his hands tucked into his trouser pockets. I noticed he often leaned forward on the balls of his feet when he was simply waiting around.

"Hello, Ian," I said, entering the living room.

He turned around and smiled at me. His smile was a work of art, painted on his face. It was a grin that would catch the attention of any young lady.

"Abby, I'm sorry to come without notice, but I really wanted to talk to you about Mathias."

I took a seat on the couch and he sat next to me.

"What about Mathias?" I asked rather coldly.

"First off," Ian began, "to make amends, he wants to give you your own key to the lift to the Headquarters." Ian pulled a copy of the same key I had always seen him use out of his pocket. He handed it to me.

"A key to the place," I responded. "And he thinks that will make everything okay."

Ian sighed.

"Mathias is a very disgruntled man. He isn't sociable, he lacks social skills for that matter. He's wasted away his life. The loss of his wife, the loss of you, well, it took a toll on him. He became a recluse. In fact, I think that night he went to dinner with you and Phillip was the first time he had really been out in a long time. I'm usually the one to go out and buy the supplies we might need. I just don't want you to think he's a terrible person, it's just, it's just hard for him."

For a moment, I sat there in silence. I considered what Ian had told me and related it back to Mathias. If I had my husband die and my child taken away, I knew I would be in pieces. I wouldn't have a clue where to go from there. Friends and family would still be there for me, but I would feel lost. I would want to be a recluse. But I knew I was stronger than that. It might be hard for a little while and it might seem okay to become a recluse, but I would save myself. I would get out of it. But it seemed like Mathias had not been able to do that. He had let it take him. But he had still been in a rage that night.

"He was just in such a rage," I finally said, "it just scared me. I can try and overlook that, but I just don't want another confrontation with him like that again. But I feel like it is unavoidable. I mean he never tells me more than I need to know and he doesn't act like a father at all. But the biggest issue of all is that I want to know, I need to know more about my biological mother. I don't know what it is, but I just have this strong desire to know who she was and why she gave me to that orphanage. I want to know what she was running from."

For a brief moment, I wondered if I should confide in Ian about the letter that had been left for my mother. The letter telling me to not go looking—the letter telling me that my biological father was dead.

"Let's go there then," Ian spoke up, "you should find out the name from your mother. And we will go there, me and you. If Mathias doesn't want to help you, then I will."

My eyes had watered up a bit. I looked at him. I could tell he was being honest, but I said it anyway.

"Do you mean that?" I asked.

"Of course," he answered, "I consider you a friend now and friends help each other out."

I smiled at him and then went to phone my mother at work.

The building was St. Agnus' Orphanage, located just a mile away from Trafalgar Square. It was the orphanage that my parents had come to in order to adopt a child. My mum had told me that late one night they got a phone call about a newborn baby who needed a home. That newborn baby was me and they had quickly traveled to the orphanage to complete the adoption.

The building was built in between two other buildings and felt hidden from society. Ian and I traveled side by side down the street. We hadn't talked much since we left Barton street. There was a feeling of excitement in my veins. I felt like I was going to find something out. Really, if I found out anything about my mother here, that would help.

Ian knocked on the door of the orphanage and a nun opened the door. She looked kind and gentle and quickly invited us in.

"You'll find it is rather quiet," the nun said, closing the door behind her. "Most of the children have been evacuated to the country, though a few remain. I'm Sister Margaret, how can I help you? Are you looking to adopt?"

I quickly shook my head, not thinking that the nuns might jump to that conclusion since I was with Ian.

"We were hoping that you could provide us with information about the night a young baby was left here," Ian said.

"Abigail?" Sister Margaret said.

Sister Margaret looked at me, a look of familiarity coming across her face.

"You look just like her," she said, "your mother."

"Elisabeth," I responded.

Sister Margaret beckoned us to follow her into an office nearby. We did and took seats in front of her desk.

"I'm afraid there isn't much to tell," Sister Margaret said, "the whole ordeal was rather short. But in the wee hours of December 8th, 1925, a young woman came to our door. She would not reveal her name, you said it was Elisabeth. She was very determined about not revealing herself. But she had you in her arms; you had literally just been born. The poor woman was distraught and she was weak. I tried to get her to stay, I was hoping to find out more information. But she needed to leave as quickly as she had come. She only told us to find you a home as quick as we could and to make sure that your parents were good people. She left you with us, told us your name, left a letter for your adoptive parents, and she was gone. We never heard from her again."

I had not realized until she was finished that I had been crying. My face was wet with hot tears. I quickly wiped them away and spoke.

"She didn't say if she was running from someone? We just, we have a feeling someone was hunting her. I don't think it was a suicide."

"She gave no inclination of such a thing," Sister Margaret said, "but whether that is the case or not, I am deeply sorry. She seemed like a very kind woman, and she was brave in bringing you to us. It must have taken a lot to separate herself from you."

I had no words. I found myself being consumed by my emotions. The only thing I recalled was Ian thanking Sister Agnus and then we were on our way.

Ian and I sat on a bench near the Thames. My thoughts were a tangled mess. I found my eyes veering over to stare at the Tower Bridge near us. The bridge loomed menacingly over the water. It seemed like a giant monster to me as I thought about the horrific events that occurred there that night.

"What are you thinking about?"

Ian's voice was soft, friendly. I looked at him, his expression was one of caring.

"She was trying to protect me. I know she was. I want to know who did this to her, and why. I want justice for her."

The idea that someone could tarnish a woman's life, force her to give up her family, and ultimately take her life away from her disgusted me. I wanted to see justice for the life my mother never had, for me, the daughter she would never know, and ultimately, even if the two of us could not see eye to eye, for Mathias.

CHAPTER FOURTEEN

The decision I made was to give Mathias another chance. After we talked by Thames for a while, Ian and I made our way to the familiar Parliament building and through the familiar passages to get to the underground Headquarters. This time around, I used my own key to gain entrance into the Headquarters and did all of the steps from there.

"You got in, all on your own," Ian said, as the lift began to descend far below the building into the Headquarters.

"I learn from the best," I responded.

I thought about Mathias and my reasoning to return. He was still my teacher if not anything else and there were things that I needed to know. I needed to know if my dreams were premonitions too, if something terrible was going to happen to Mrs. Baxter, and if I could prevent it.

Ian walked me into the study area and then disappeared through a door. Mathias sat at his desk—he looked more disheveled than usual. His attention seemed to be entirely on the papers before him. In fact, I didn't think he had even noticed us come in. I cleared my throat and he looked up. He looked at me for a moment and then looked back down again.

"So, why did you decide to return?" he asked, his attention still on the work before him.

"I'm still interested in learning," I said, "and you also gave me a key."

"Listen to me," he said. His eyes were at my level and they appeared menacing. "Did you meet anyone there?"

"Did I meet anyone where?" I asked.

"Where you found the necklace, damn it!" Mathias spat.

"No."

It was a lie. Even if I had felt some sympathy for him earlier, I still didn't trust him and I knew he didn't trust me so why should we share secrets? He owed me more answers than I owed him anyway.

"Are you being followed?"

I looked at him in bewilderment.

"Of course, I'm not being followed. Don't you think I'd know if I was?"

But then I thought about it. I remembered the menacing notes, that would be considered following, but then how would he know about it. Unless he was the writer of the menacing notes, but I shrugged this idea off. It couldn't be him.

"Listen," I said, "I'm fine. I won't go back there again." Another lie.

"Stay away from that place. No good can come of it. Otherwise, I wouldn't have left."

I walked over to the divan and took my usual seat.

"I didn't come back here today just to jump back into things. I want some answers." I hesitated. "I need them."

"Abigail, I am not in a position to speak about your mother right now if this is what you're referring to."

I shook my head in frustration. "Listen, it isn't that. I had a dream—it was disturbing."

"They are called nightmares," Mathias answered, a hint of sarcasm in his tone, "they are common in humans."

"That isn't what I'm talking about," I shot back. "I'd appreciate it if you would give me a moment to explain before you just give me your textbook answer."

Mathias didn't reply to me, so I continued.

"The dream was disturbing, but it wasn't a nightmare. It felt real. It was as if I could feel the intensity of the situation, as if I were there in the moment. When I woke up, it felt like it had actually happened, but it was too horrible to have happened, if that makes sense."

"Premonitions are something that Timekeepers have regularly," Mathias answered, "however it is not uncommon for Timekeepers to have very vivid dreams. While the dreams are usually not exact premonitions of the future, their events may contain messages relevant to things that may happen or have happened. Describe the dream to me."

I recounted the horrible details of the dream, including what had happened to Mrs. Baxter. I described how she had walked into some sort of light at the end.

"It sounds as if you are being prepared for something." Mathias gave me a questioning look as he said this, and I returned his look with one of curiosity. What was I being prepared for?

"What do you mean?" I asked.

Mathias looked at me for a moment longer and then turned away.

"We must continue. We have something important to discuss today."

For the first time, I decided not to press him. I was tired of pressing people for answers. What good did it do? Perhaps if I listened to what he wanted, he would tell me more later on.

"Abigail, this is what I wanted to discuss today."

He extended his arm and lifted a piece of paper off his desk. He held it out to me. I took it and began reading.

The Council of the Timekeepers is excited to announce the training of a new Timekeeper: Abigail Jordan, daughter of Mathias Benedict (Timekeeper of the United Kingdom). Miss Jordan's training is currently underway. All Timekeepers, as well as the Timekeepers elect, are invited to attend the traditional Timekeepers Ball to be held the twelfth of February, nineteen forty-four, at the Timekeeping Headquarters of the United Kingdom, located in London, in the ballroom. Formal dress is required in order to attend.

I looked up at Mathias in disbelief. "Isn't this something you could have told me about a month ago?" The fifth of February wasn't exactly a year away, it was in a few weeks.

"Time flies by doesn't it," Mathias said. An actual smile crossed his face. I simply frowned in frustration, but he turned away before he saw. "I do, of course, expect you to attend your own ball, Abigail. I will provide you with a gown, but I will need your measurements as soon as possible."

I made a mental note to get him my measurements tomorrow, but I needed to know more about the dream.

"What about that dream I had? The least you could do is tell me what to do. If something is going to happen to Mrs. Baxter, then maybe I could prevent it."

Mathias turned around so fast I was surprised and almost toppled over. I steadied myself, however, and looked into his face. His expression was dark.

"Abigail, there is nothing you can do. Death does not care. When it is time for a person to die, it will take them. And if you stand in its way, then it will take you instead. Even dreams can be considered premonitions and you cannot use them to help someone survive. Whatever happens, will happen. The dream was to prepare you, not to help save anyone."

I remained still—afraid of the future.

CHAPTER FIFTEEN

Bridget had not received much in the way of inheritance when her father had died. As a result, she lived in a neighborhood tarnished by the effects of poverty. The flat she had purchased after the death of her father was run down, but it was still a place to live, and that counted for something.

I traveled down the long narrow alley that made up Bridget's neighborhood. The area always sent chills within me because some of the individuals that lived in the area were involved in crime.

When I was standing in front of the building where Bridget lived, I reached into my handbag and pulled out the spare key she had given me. I quickly made my way into the building and up to Bridget's flat where I would be able to at least lock a door behind me and have a small sense of security.

I stood in front of Bridget's door and quickly unlocked it, making my way into the apartment. I could smell something baking. My mind suspected cookies. I shut the door behind me and locked the latches.

Bridget stood in the kitchen, hovering over an old stove that had not survived the effects of rust and age. She turned her head in my direction and smiled.

"Abby. I wasn't expecting you today. Did you have class earlier?"

I shook my head at her and took a seat on the torn and tattered sofa in the small living area. I began to contemplate what to say. I had come straight from the Headquarters, because I was afraid. When I was afraid, Bridget was the one that I used to talk to, before Phillip. But our relationship was continuing to grow worse, rather than better.

"How was your Christmas?" Bridget asked.

She took a seat across from me in her old rocking chair and crossed her legs. Her hair was tied up and she was wearing an old apron. She looked different, like she had aged in such a short span of time. Was I worrying her? Was she worrying about something else?

"It was..." I hesitated, how had my Christmas been? It had not exactly been the Christmas I had planned. I decided and said, "Pleasant."

"Why did you come?" Bridget was gazing at me, expecting some sort of answer.

"Because I was afraid," I responded.

It was not the answer I was planning to give her. In fact, I had no intentions of being *that* honest. What would I say next? How would she begin to question me?

Bridget focused her attention at something outside of the flat's windows. Her focus seemed to be on a bird that was sitting just outside her windowsill.

"Do you ever wonder what it would be like to be a creature?"

Her question caught me off guard. I looked away from the bird and at her, but she was still watching it.

"What do you mean?"

I turned my attention back to the bird. The bird was a robin—a very small and delicate robin with patches of white and orange. It pecked at something on Bridget's windowsill.

"The robin just lives each day," she said, "it has no worries, and no fears. It lives in the moment of everything that is happening. Don't be afraid," she said, looking at me with a smile that warmed my heart. "You are going through many things right now, some I hope you have confided in me, but don't be afraid."

A feeling of guilt ran through me. I had not been completely honest with Bridget about myself. If anyone deserved to know that there were things in this world beyond normalcy, it was Bridget. But I couldn't bring myself to mention it. I felt like Bridget was my only way to keep the life I had in intact; otherwise, I would be letting myself go into a life I had always been curious about but had never needed.

I returned a smile to Bridget, but kept my secrets hidden from her.

I shivered in my bed that night. The cold air managed to seep into the house and make the rooms horribly cold. It was hard for me to sleep as my mind was preoccupied with many different thoughts and feelings.

The night trudged by slowly, but finally sun seeped in through the windows. I felt exhausted because of my rough night's sleep. A knock came at my door and then it opened. My mother stepped in through the doorway.

She walked silently toward my bed and sat down on the edge,

placing her hand on my arm. I looked up at her through my groggy eyes and smiled.

"Abby," she whispered softly, "I have some sad news to tell you."

My heart pounded. I felt like I already knew what the news was going to be before my mother said anything.

"Mrs. Baxter passed away last night," my mum said softly. "She passed away in her sleep."

My heart dropped. I realized that this was the first time in my life that I had experienced someone close to me passing away. It left me feeling saddened in my heart, but also frustrated because I had dreamed about it. Should I have said something? But I couldn't have. According to Mathias, death would take me instead and would that be something Mrs. Baxter would want?

"I'm sorry to have to tell you this Abby," my mother continued, "it saddens us all. The funeral will be at the end of the week."

My mother left me feeling saddened, but also vulnerable.

At the end of the week, the funeral was over and Mrs. Baxter was gone. I was saddened, but at the same time I knew she was getting older and that death was an inevitable part of life that everyone had to live with. But the dream still haunted me. Was it some sort of sign? Was it to prepare me as Mathias had thought? Was this the torture of having the ability to look into the future to come as well as see what had already past? The questions consumed my thinking over the next several weeks. My mother was taking it a little harder than I was. She had been relatively quieter as of late whenever she was in the kitchen or outside in the garden. She would often just go sit outside in the garden for a while, even though it was winter and not had not come back to life yet.

Mathias and I continued our meetings and he continued to remind me of the upcoming Timekeepers' ball. A part of me was excited, but a part of me was slightly afraid. If I went to this ball, it would be a very large step into a world that I had no idea what held for me. I knew I would be introduced to several more people who had the same, strange abilities as me and while that should be comforting, it was also frightening. It meant that I had lived in a world for a long time that I believed had been normal, but actually had a fantastical power to it.

In everything that had been happening though, and all Mathias had taught me, I was still curious about the things he didn't want to share. I wanted to know the stories he would not tell me about my mother. He still refused to talk about her and this frightened me. Was he still in grief? Or was there an underlying meaning to his silence. Was he actually not my father? Was my father dead as my biological mother had suggested? Or worse, was Mathias my father and he was actually the danger I needed to stay away from? Because of these insecurities, I decided to return to the Tower of London. I told my mum I would be out late with Phillip, another lie, but I had still yet to confide in anyone about going there.

I called for a taxi and had him drive me to just outside the Tower of London. He gave me quite a strange look. I was sure I looked rather suspicious, a young woman being dropped off outside the Tower of London after midnight. But he took my money and drove off anyway. The night was cold and I knew it was about to get colder once I took that dive into the water, but I did so anyway.

The icy water made my bones go completely numb, but I pushed myself through the normal route toward the secret underground entrance. As soon as I broke the surface I took a rather large breath and pulled myself out of the icy river. I quickly found the entrance and used my mother's pocket watch to gain access.

I have no idea how I knew, but I had the strangest feeling that Bessie would be there and that she would be waiting for me. When I entered the familiar room, a fire was blazing in the fireplace, and I knew she was there. I made my way to what had been my mother's room and found a warm dress of hers to change into. I took my drenched clothes and placed them just beside the fireplace so that they would be dry before I left. After that, I hovered my hands just close enough to the fire to allow the warmth to consume my body.

"Abigail."

I fell backward in shock and focused my attention to the other side of the room. For a moment, I thought the voice had come from my own mind, but then the thin figure of Bessie stepped out of the shadows. She was as I had remembered her. Her brown hair was rather short and came just to her ears and her face was soft and kind. She wore no makeup. A part of me felt guilty for thinking it, but I thought a person would find her neither attractive nor unattractive, just simply plain. Maybe that was how she wanted it? We all judged each other for whatever unknown reason.

"I'm sorry," Bessie mumbled, "I didn't mean to frighten you."

Bessie walked forward and took a seat on the old withering couch. She placed her hands in her lap and smiled at me. She had a natural kindness about her.

"I'm glad you came back," Bessie said softly.

For the briefest moment, I hesitated. I let my thoughts come to me. What would I say? I had so many questions.

"Bessie," I said, "I just want answers." The tone of my voice sounded unsure.

"I understand," Bessie said. "There is so much that I would like to tell you Abigail. There was so much I wanted to tell you before, but I didn't feel it would be the right time. In fact, I'm not even sure if now is the right time."

"You said you were friends with my mother..."

"Your mother and I were very dear friends," Bessie said, "but I was actually friends with Mathias first. We were engaged to be married at one point."

I could feel my heart ramming against my chest. This woman was engaged to Mathias. Where did my mother fit in all of this?

"But my mother married Mathias." I spoke it as if it was truth. I spoke it as if I knew for sure the details of what had occurred, regardless of the fact that I didn't even know if Mathias was my father.

"She did." Bessie turned and walked casually to an old painting of a forest on a beautiful mountain top. She gazed at it for several moments. "Your father became too protective of me. He frightened me sometimes. I ended the relationship. Your father taught me about the Timekeepers though. He told me about the wonderful world in which they lived. The Timekeeping world was very interesting to me. I met your mother here in London. We worked together in a shop.

After your father and I split up, Elisabeth asked me to introduce her. I told her about him, but she was still interested. So, I introduced them and not long after that, they were married."

“He told you about the Timekeepers?” I asked, remembering that that was against the rules.

“Yes,” Bessie responded.

I wondered why Mathias had broken a rule when he seemed to be so concerned about making sure they were obeyed.

I decided to confide in Bessie what I had found out at the orphanage. I couldn't not tell herFor a brief moment, Bessie looked as if she had a sudden realization, but then it was quickly gone.

"That isn't surprising," she told me. "Abigail, your father is alive. Your father is Mathias. So, yes, your mother did lie in that letter, but I think she lied to protect you."

"Protect me from what? What happened to my mother?" I realized I had raised my voice unintentionally and quickly apologized.

Bessie appeared to be hesitant. She appeared as if she did not want to say anything regarding the death of my mother.

"Abigail," Bessie said, "I don't know if now is the right time for this. You seem very emotional and I'm afraid you won't understand everything."

"When is the right time?" I asked. "I've gone my whole life in the dark. I'm tired of it. I want to know the truth."

Bessie approached me. She placed her hand on my cheek and smiled. It was warm and friendly.

"Do you trust me Abigail?"

I hesitated. Why was she asking this question? I had only just met her a few weeks ago. I hesitated and so she broke the silence.

"It's okay if you don't," she responded, turning away. "I would be surprised if you did. But in time, I hope you will come to trust me. But that is why I think the information I know can wait."

"I had somewhat of a dream," I said, "or a premonition. It was about the death of a close family friend and she has since then passed away."

"I'm very sorry to hear about that." Bessie sounded genuinely sorry. She came forward and placed her arms around me, hugging me. I found it odd, considering this was only the second time we had met, but I returned the hug anyway.

Bessie pulled away and placed her hands in the pocket of her housedress.

"But why is Mathias so cold about these things?" I asked. "I thought about warning her, but he was furious because it is against the laws and could also get me killed."

"It is," Bessie responded, "but Mathias has always been very by the book. He doesn't like to test things unless he absolutely has too. But he could still have shared sympathy with you at least. And I think that is one of the reasons why your mother wanted you to stay out of all of this. Mathias isn't really a family man and she didn't want you mixed up in that. Like I said, she wanted to protect you."

"Exactly. He just doesn't share any type of emotion and it really bothers me sometimes."

The old grandfather clock across the room started to sound for the hour. Bessie turned her head to briefly look at the clock before looking back at me.

"It is probably best if you go, Abigail. You don't want to be out so late. But please return to me and, in time, I'm sure I can share more with you."

I left the old underground Headquarters slightly confused. She had information she wanted to tell me, but she didn't want to tell me. I understood her meanings. Did I trust her? The question was difficult to answer. Honestly, I think I was beginning to, but I did not trust her entirely yet. I did not trust Mathias entirely yet. I wondered who I should trust.

"He's an asshole."

I was sitting in Phillip's flat. I had gone straight there after leaving the Tower of London. I wanted to vent to him about Mathias, and he wasn't happy about the things I was saying. My body felt tired. I found it interesting how the body could be so drained from just mental stress. Phillip was furious that Mathias refused to answer my questions. I wondered why I even told things to Phillip sometimes. He usually got angrier than I was.

"Watch your tone, Phillip." How many times did you have to tell a person not to swear? But this was Phillip, and I just had to get used to it. I loved him regardless. Nobody was perfect after all.

Phillip walked over to the divan where I was lying and lifted me up. He sat down and then gently placed my head in his lap. I felt the warmth of his hand on my arm and his other hand stroking my hair.

"I don't like it when you do not get the answers you deserve, Abby," he said. "I care about you too much."

A smile crept onto my face.

"I know. I don't want to talk about Mathias though. I just want to pretend to be normal."

"You *are* normal."

"Phillip, I'm never going to be normal. I need you to accept that."

"We are all normal, Abby. Some of us just do different things."

I closed my eyes. I was going to have a hard time making him listen to me and I was too exhausted to try. I felt my body being pulled into sleep, and I drifted off.

CHAPTER SIXTEEN

At some point in the night, Phillip had woken me up and coaxed me into his bedroom. Light began to pour in through his window the next morning. I opened my eyes and looked over. He was still fast asleep. I smiled, his mouth was ajar just a bit and it made him look vulnerable. He still had his arms around me, so I gently moved them off me and got out of bed. I checked his watch on the nightstand. It was still early. I didn't have class that day, so I didn't have anywhere to be.

I walked to the bedroom window and looked out over London. While it was still early, the city was already beginning to wake up. I could see workers making their way toward the tube for their morning commute. Automobiles were abuzz, driving through the city to their desired destinations.

As I walked into the kitchen, I continued to think about what I knew about my biological mother, as well as Mathias. The more I thought about it the more I realized how cold and off Mathias was. He was also refusing to talk about Elisabeth, but why? He was furious when he found out I had gone to the old Headquarters. His only focus seemed to be trying to be a teacher instead of a father, and I already knew he was lying to me about something at least. I made the decision that I would not discuss anything with him. I would continue to go and learn, but I would need to find out a few things about whom it was I needed to trust.

A hand touched my shoulder and I felt Phillip's lips kissing my neck.

"Morning," he whispered into my ear.

"Good morning," I responded. "Don't you need to be getting ready for work?"

"Sure do. Want to conserve water and take a bath with me?"

"Very funny. Go take your bath. Coffee will be ready when you get out."

I heard him sigh and make his way to the bathroom. I could hear the running water of the tub as I returned to my thoughts.

Rain began to pour as I made my way to the tube. I ran down toward the train and got on. The train rolled away and soon enough I was ascending the stairs to the city once more. I started running through the rain again and turned down a street and turned again onto my street and made my way toward my house.

I unlocked the front door and quickly stepped inside, shutting it behind me. I could smell lunch cooking from the kitchen and made my way down the hall.

"Hello mum," I said, entering the kitchen.

She was wearing a long blue housedress with a white apron on over it. She smiled at me from the stove and then continued cooking. She had taken a few weeks of leave from work so that she could care for my father, now that Mrs. Baxter was gone. It was nice having her around the house more, but I knew she also worried about the income they were losing by her not working. I had offered to find a job somewhere, but she insisted I focus on my classes, so I did.

A knock came from the door down the hall and I looked up. My mother turned and was about to head out of the kitchen, but I stopped her.

"I'll get it mum."

She smiled at me and turned back to the stove.

I made my way down the hall and stopped at the front door. I peered out the window of the house and saw it was Bridget. I pulled open the door and she stood there, under an umbrella.

"Come in," I said.

Bridget stepped in and closed her umbrella. I shut the door behind her and took the umbrella from her and set it in the corner. We walked into the living room and sat down on the divan.

I looked around the room and took in the familiar sight of the fireplace as well as the many different family pictures that aligned the walls. My mum had collected my whole childhood through the use of photography. She had chronicled the days of when she first adopted me as a baby to now when I was a grown woman.

"How are you?" I asked Bridget, settling myself into the divan.

She smiled at me. "I'm okay, but I haven't seen you since the funeral and I just wanted to come over and see how you were doing."

"We're okay. It's tough, but death is a part of age so it is something that I've accepted. It is hard though, because she was the first person close to me I'd known who passed away."

Bridget was in silence for a few minutes. I realized she was probably thinking about her father that had passed away and I realized how potentially lucky I was to have both of my parents still in my life.

"I was wondering if you wanted to get together this weekend," Bridget said. "I thought maybe we could go out and eat and just have some friend time to talk about things. We haven't really done anything lately."

"Sure, that sounds like an excellent idea," I responded. "Does Saturday sound good? We can meet in the afternoon and stay out till dark or something like that."

She nodded. She seemed happier than when she had come in and I felt good that I was finally doing something non-Timekeeping with my closest friend for once.

The main hallway of the Headquarters was entirely too chilly. It might have been me however. I had goose bumps going in, not knowing what to expect from Mathias. He always seemed to be different on a daily basis. I walked slower than usual down the main hallway today. I admired some of the photographs and paintings of the past Timekeepers—my ancestors. The older paintings were beautifully done.

I continued my walk toward Mathias' desk and discovered that, for once, he was not in the room. But then he appeared from the area that led to the guest rooms. He looked like he had not slept and appeared rather agitated.

"Hello," I said politely upon his entrance into the room.

"Afternoon. Follow me."

I stood up and began to follow Mathias to the door that would lead down into the spare rooms as well as the ballroom.

Mathias led me into one of the guest rooms and opened up a closet. Inside the closet was a beautiful ball gown. It was black and made of very fine silk.

"I purchased your gown in London the other day," Mathias said. "It is a Charles James gown. He is very well known in Paris and the states as well as here in Britain."

"It's beautiful," I noted aloud.

Mathias turned and looked at me and I thought for once I might get a smile, but it was still the same hard expression as always.

"You will need to arrive early on Saturday so that you'll have time to get dressed before the Timekeeper's Ball," Mathias said.

"Saturday?"

I had completely lost track of time. Was the ball really this Saturday?

"Saturday the twelfth," Mathias answered, "is that an issue?"

"Well, I made plans with my closest friend."

"Cancel them."

I didn't say another word. I knew it would be pointless. This ball had been in the works for at least a month and other people would be attending it. I had to go. Guilt sprang up inside me as I thought about having to tell Bridget.

"That is all for today," Mathias said, "I have business to attend to. Be here around five o'clock Saturday to get ready. The ball will commence at seven o'clock."

"Won't it look a little suspicious if a large group of people arrive well-dressed at Big Ben?"

"Actually, they won't be arriving the way you think," Mathias said. "The Time Line uses an ancient magic, allowing us to travel. While we can travel through time, we can also travel through current time to another destination. This is something you have yet to learn."

I didn't press him for any more questions. He walked ahead of me, out of the room and I made my way out of the Headquarters.

Bridget's building was colder than usual. I made my way up to her flat and knocked on the door. She opened it and let me in.

"Abigail," Bridget said, "what are you doing here? I didn't think I'd see you again today."

I walked over to the divan and took a seat, crossing my legs casually. What I was about to say to Bridget was something that I didn't want to say. Once again, I had to completely cancel our plans for something else. I wasn't even sure where this would take our relationship.

"Well it's about Saturday," I said. The smile started to fade off of her face. "I forgot that my father had planned something and I cannot cancel it. It is important and I'm terribly sorry."

"Maybe if you talked to your father, it could be rescheduled."

"It can't be. It's pretty big."

"Well, maybe I could go with you."

"I'm sorry Bridget, but you cannot come. It is a private event."

The look on Bridget's face tore my heart apart. I was throwing away the things that were most important to me for the secrets of my past.

"Oh," Bridget said. "Well that's okay. We'll just figure something out for another time."

I stood up and walked over to her.

"Bridget, I really am sorry. I didn't mean to do this. It is completely my fault."

"Abby, it's okay. We'll figure it out later. But I have a class to get to."

"Alright."

I left Bridget's flat feeling even worse than when I had come.

February 1944

Music was in the air. I could hear it coming through the door of the bedroom I was in. I looked at myself in the mirror. The girl staring back was me—but she was not me.

The gown that my father had purchased was beautiful, but at the same time it felt like something I did not deserve to wear. With the war going on, clothes were being rationed and growing increasingly more expensive. My mother would not even consider buying this gown for any reason. There just wasn't a reason to go to a ball with a war going on. But here I was.

I looked at myself for a moment longer, admiring my hair, which fell in elegant curls down the small of my back. If my mother could see me, I knew she would say I was beautiful. My heart pounded however when I remembered these secrets that I continued to keep from her. I knew she did not need to know, may even want to know, but still I had a heavy heart.

There was a knock at the door and then it opened. Mathias stood in the doorway. He was wearing an elegant, black evening suit.

He appeared taken aback for a moment.

"You look so much like her. Except for your hair of course. My hair." He blushed and he turned away from me. "Sorry," he muttered quietly.

I walked forward. For the first time, I felt sorry for him and wanted to hug him.

"It's okay. Did she like to go to parties?"

He smiled a rare smile. "She hated the idea of having to go to a party, but when she was there she was the life of them. Anyway, it's time."

I followed Mathias out the door and closed it behind me.

"What exactly is going to happen?" I asked quietly. I was nervous. I was about to meet people I had never met; yet they supposedly knew all about me.

"You will be introduced to the party," Mathias said. "Then there will be food and dancing. It is expected of you to go around and mingle with the other Timekeepers. The council will be there and they will be watching. They like to see a Timekeeper be friendly and sociable. As you can imagine, I am not very high on their list of Timekeepers."

"Why do they let you stay then?" I asked him. I realized then that that was rather rude. Sure, I had been rude to him before, but I still did not believe he deserved such a harsh criticism. "I'm sorry, I was just curious."

He tried to smile, but I could see sadness in his eyes. I knew he knew. He saw what I saw. I saw him as a lonely man with no one in his life. I would not be surprised if none of the other Timekeepers called him a friend. Nor would I be surprised if this was the first time they had seen him in years.

"My family has been entrusted with the Timekeeping of this country as well as this Headquarters for years," Mathias answered. "They know that I am very knowledgeable in what I do and that I received the highest training. Because of those things, they tend to disregard my social inadequacies. However, that does not mean they show me mercy at parties. I'm sure I will be the punch line of many jokes tonight as well as the person being judged. Anyways, at the end of the ball, you will be recognized as a student of Timekeeping and recognized as a Timekeeper in training. Let's go."

Mathias led me through the usual doors that would take us to the grand ballroom. As we got closer to the ballroom's entrance, I could hear the music growing louder. It sounded like he had hired an orchestra for the ball. Judging by the expensive dress I was wearing, I would not be surprised.

Ian met us just outside the ballroom. He was also wearing a lovely suit and looked very handsome.

"You clean up well," I noted.

"As do you," Ian said.

Mathias smiled and reached out and opened the door to the ballroom. I nearly fainted.

Before, when I'd imagined the party and other Timekeepers, I thought there might be maybe twenty people or so. I did not think that for each country and each Timekeeper there would also be that

Timekeeper's family. The room was full of people. Granted it was a large ballroom, but still, I was expected to mingle with everyone here?

All eyes turned on me as my father led me further into the room. After a few moments, Ian seemed to disappear into the crowd. I wished he hadn't. I could feel the eyes staring me down, judging me. I could guess the thoughts going through their mind. Is she like her mother or her father? If she's like her father then she must be a cold, calculating, unsociable, Timekeeper. If she's like her mother well, well I was not sure because I did not get the chance to know my mother. I let my eyes wander up to the high ceiling. How far under Big Ben was this place? The ceiling was a vaulted ceiling and was fairly high. Did the Timekeepers build this place first? Perhaps Big Ben was built on top of the place.

"Mathias," I heard a gruff voice say. "Very, very long time and absolutely no see."

Was that supposed to be funny? The man standing in front of Mathias had a British accent. A long, jagged scar fell down the left side of his face. I caught myself staring at it for an unnecessary extended period of time. Much to my dismay, I realized this man was now looking at me looking at him and his scar.

"Stuart," Mathias replied. "What a pleasure it is. Abigail, this is Lead Councilor Stuart Winston."

"Pleasure to make your acquaintance Miss Benedict," Councilor Winston responded. He extended his hand and I extended mine.

"A pleasure indeed," I replied. "Also, sir, it is actually Miss Jordan." I saw Mathias give me a quick angered look out of the corner of my eye. But it disappeared as soon as it had come.

Councilor Winston smiled at me and I cringed at the horrible movement his scar made when he smiled.

"Ah yes, I forgot that you were orphaned. I must say it is a pleasure that you decided to search for your father."

I didn't really search for my father, but I guess I would let him call it that.

"Pardon my questions," I said, "but I thought my father and I were the only British Timekeepers? Or am I missing something in the system?"

Councilor Winston gave a hearty laugh before responding to my question.

"Ah, well you will find that many of the Timekeepers are actually British as well as Americans of the Caucasian race. We did have mixed Timekeepers at one point, but they were eliminated in the 1800's when we had, shall we say, a *bloody* disagreement. Pardon my pun. However, unfortunately, it appears that many of our Timekeeper men are choosing biracial women, so I'm sure we will begin to see more diversity here in the future."

I couldn't tell if he was deliberately trying to be, as Phillip would put it, a pompous arse, or if he was born that way. Regardless, the words he used really heated my blood. My parents had raised me to respect everyone, no matter who they were and what they did. I was not the judge of anyone and everyone was created equally. I truly wanted to stomp on this man's foot and turn on my heel. However, I knew that strong words had a strong ability and so I chose my next statement carefully.

"I must say. I think it is great that there was much diversity within the Timekeepers and I'm glad that that is returning."

"I'm sure you would be, considering you're a woman and all."

"I'd rather be a woman than an old bigot like you."

I turned on my heel and walked to the other side of the room where I could smell the delightful scent of good food.

A hand gripped my arm and I turned to look at whoever was touching me. It was a man I didn't recognize with vibrant blue eyes and sandy blonde hair that came down to his chin. He looked to be in his late thirties or early forties. His age did not detract anything from his handsome features.

"Can I help you?" I asked.

"I do apologize," he said. "But I wondered if I could speak with you privately?"

I looked around the ballroom and from a distance I could see Ian giving me a suspicious look. I smiled at him, hopefully sending the signal that everything was okay.

"I don't think now is the best time," I responded.

"Please," he insisted. And then he lowered his voice and leaned in close to my ear. "It is about your mother—your biological mother—Elisabeth."

I froze and looked him in the eye.

"What do you know?"

He shook his head.

"Not here," he said. "Privately? Please?"

I cleared my throat and then nodded. I led him out of the ballroom and into a hallway off of it. I closed the door behind us and then turned to him.

"Who are you?" I immediately asked.

"My name is Elijah, and that's all that I can tell you about myself for now. But you need to listen. I know—well, knew—your mother. I knew her very well and she didn't want this life for you. She didn't want you to become involved with your father. I spoke with her shortly before her death and she told me she would leave you with a letter saying that your father was dead because she didn't want you to search for him and find out about this world."

I stood there, completely silent. It felt like so much had been answered in a span of seconds yet even more questions came to my mind.

"How do you know all of this? How did you know her?"

"I can't talk about myself. I just need you to know that tonight will seal your fate. You are a part of a prophecy—a prophecy that was made thousands of years ago when there was only one Timekeeper—a Timekeeper that passed on her powers to a young girl. That girl was part of the original family. The stories that our people claim are only legends are all true. And this prophecy isn't good. You have to make sure you do not fulfill it."

"This is too much," I said. "Why would my mother not want me to be a part of this world? What if I made a mistake and saved someone from death? Death would take me instead. That is what Mathias told me. Why wouldn't she want me to know these things?"

He gave me a suspicious look and then shook his head.

"Abigail, I don't know what your father told you, but that only applies after you have been initiated. Tonight, you will be binding yourself to a contract with time. Only then do the rules and laws of our world truly apply to you. If you saved someone from death, death would only find another way to take them. After tonight though, the law will apply to you. But I'm afraid to say that it's different for you. Your mother was a Timekeeper. She was one of the last remaining descendants of the original family—until you.

"The original family is subjected to a harsher punishment. Essentially, they are a part of time. It is in their blood. They are the sole protector of the Time Line. Everything works differently for them. If they were to interfere with a premonition of death, it would upset the balance of our world. Time would literally stop. The world would be subjected to nature's harshest punishments until there was nothing left but the original Timekeepers and a wasteland where humanity once lived. You *cannot* interfere with a premonition of death after tonight. You will survive, but the world will not."

I just stood there. I didn't know if it was true. If it was true, then Mathias had lied to me in the most terrible of ways. He had taken away my *choice*. He had taken away my *free will.*

"How do I know you are telling the truth?"

"I have no way to prove that to you, except to say that how could I know about the letter your mother left for you?"

"Maybe you killed her."

I saw a look of hurt in his eyes and he looked away from me. "I would have never harmed her. And I don't know who did. She would only tell me that she was in danger, but not from who. She wanted to keep me out of it as much as she tried to keep you out of it. You have to believe me. Don't make her death meaningless."

"I do. I'm going to leave here tonight. I'm never going to talk to him again."

"I never got to know Mathias," Elijah said. "So, I cannot attest to his character. But Abigail, you have been discovered. Whoever is trying to make this prophecy come true knows about you now. They know who you are and they know where you came from. They were in the dark because your mother gave you up under a name only she herself knew with a letter she hoped would keep you out of this world. They will find another way to make this all happen. Leaving tonight won't do anything. I'm telling you now so that you have the advantage—so that you have the chance to do something—to fight back."

Footsteps could be heard coming down the hall. I turned around and looked to see where they were coming from and saw Mathias heading toward me. I turned back around and was surprised to find no one there. Elijah was gone. It was as if he had never been there.

"What are you doing in here?" I heard Mathias ask from behind.

I didn't look at him. I continued to look in the opposite direction. Once again, I was going to remain silent and not confront him. But I didn't trust him now. How could I? This was my life he was gambling with.

"I just needed to get away," I said quietly.

He walked in front of me to look me in the eye. "Abigail, that was not acceptable." It took me a minute to remember what he was referring to. And then I remembered—Councilor Winston.

"And what he said *was*?" I spat back.

More footsteps could be heard and I turned to see Ian heading toward us.

"What are we discussing here?" he asked. We told him about Councilor Winston and how horrid he had been.

"I despise that man," Ian added.

"But was what he said, acceptable?" I asked.

Mathias put his face in his hands and sighed.

"No," he responded, "but Stuart is the Lead Councilor. Believe me, I, nor many of the people on the council, agree with some of the things the man says. But unfortunately, we still have to deal with him. Besides, he won't be in the role for too much longer. The council members take turns serving as lead, and soon he will be leaving the council and someone else will take the role."

I looked at my father. "I don't care about any of that. He is a disgusting person and I want nothing to do with him. If there are others like him, then I'm not sure about this Timekeeping thing." If I actually had a *choice*, I wasn't sure about this Timekeeping thing. But of course, I kept that to myself.

"Abigail," Mathias said, "this has nothing to do with Timekeeping. This has to do with your own personal ideals and beliefs. Believe me, I have my own, and I hold yours in the highest regard. But it does not matter where you go in this world. There will always be a place where discrimination is found."

I looked away from him. I knew what he was saying was true. Even the kindest people could be judgmental toward others. It was what made us human. But I still could not fathom how someone like Councilor Winston could be so horrible or how someone like Mathias, my father, could keep secrets from me.

"So, what happened to the Timekeepers who were of a different race?" I asked Mathias.

"There was a lot of indifference in the 1800's about having only white Timekeepers," Mathias answered. "This came about just about the same time as it did in the world. Apparently, a group of white Timekeepers formed and announced a meeting one day. The sole purpose was to eliminate anyone who did not fit in with what they believed constituted a Timekeeper. Meaning anyone that was not white was killed. The group was punished and replaced. However, there was so much fear amongst the Timekeepers that anyone who was not white stopped practicing and left the Timekeeper's society. They were replaced. If you look around, you will see some Timekeepers here with their family and they are indeed a different race. Diversity is returning thankfully, but it is a slow process."

"That's horrible. Why would anyone do that?"

"If people see something different than them," Ian said, "they jump at the chance to despise that difference."

"Man is not all good Abigail," Mathias responded. "When someone lets themselves be lost to an unhealthy ideal they become hungry for power. It has been a part of this world for thousands of years. It was present when this society was founded by the Timekeeping family."

I looked at him and said it, even though I knew the truth now. "I thought you said that was a myth, one family starting it all."

Mathias smiled at me. "Someone had to have created it. They say it's a myth, but I believe in it."

"How about we return to the party?" Ian asked.

I nodded and followed Ian and Mathias back to the ballroom. Before I went back in though, I turned around one last time to look. There was no sign that Elijah was back there, hiding, or that he had even been there. I closed my eyes and took a deep breath before rejoining the party.

My attention turned after that to admire the guests of the party. I did begin to see the different Timekeepers there and while it was limited, there was still some diversity. An African family came up to Mathias and shook hands with them. Mathias introduced them as the Timekeepers from Africa.

"So, this is the orphaned one that Stuart was talking about," I heard a thick German voice say from behind me. I stood up from my chair and turned around at the same time that Mathias did. He smiled as a man came forward, with who I assumed was his wife. I could tell that she was expecting and she was very far long.

"Abigail and Ian," Mathias said, "I would like for you both to meet Hans and Ingrid Bäcker. They currently oversee the Timekeeping society for Germany. The both of you are stationed with the French Timekeepers right now however, is, that right?"

"Yes," Ingrid responded. "We have been there since the start of the war."

"We were just speaking with Stuart a moment ago," Hans said. "He had a few things to say about young Abigail here."

"The racist pig also gave us his views on how he just assumed, since Hans and I are German, that we must be conspiring with Hitler," Ingrid said.

"That's horrendous," I responded. "He just assumes who people are without even trying to understand them."

"Like I said," Ian added, "people jump at the chance when they see someone different."

Hans laughed. "The man has always been like that. He's never going to change. Anyway, it's a pleasure to meet you, Abigail. Stuart wanted us to let you know that he was ready to do the initiation ceremony. I think he is ready to get this ball over with. Unfortunately, he has never held Mathias in the best regard. Not that I am up there either for that matter."

"Well Abigail," Mathias said, "are you ready?"

Was I ready? Wasn't that the question of the day? I still wasn't ready for this ball let alone this initiation. Or as Elijah had called it—this contract. Mathias had lied to me and maybe, just maybe, if I had known earlier, I could still get out of it all. But did I want that? I knew that my biological mother wanted to protect me—to keep me safe—from whatever it is that caused me danger, whether that be Mathias or someone else. But I needed to know about her. I needed to know why she died. Because, unlike what I had previously thought, she hadn't thrown me out like I was trash. She was trying to protect me and I needed to know why. And her death wouldn't be meaningless. I would try to undo whatever prophecy had been made. I just needed to know about her. So, I nodded. Even though he was lying, Mathias was actually being nice tonight and I didn't want to ruin that. A part of me felt like he was probably doing it for the audience rather than me. I followed him, however, as he led the way toward the front of the ballroom where there was a raised platform for the ceremony. Ian disappeared into the crowd once more.

"I see the American Timekeeper didn't bother to make an appearance," I heard a woman nearby say.

"Isn't he the young, handsome one?" another woman gossiped. "I heard he has a scandalous reputation with the ladies." I heard the two of them laugh.

It didn't even cross my mind to look for an American Timekeeper. I had never been to America, but I had always wanted to go. I wondered why the man did not make an appearance.

Mathias led me up some steps onto the stage and we both turned to face all of the Timekeepers and their families. In front of me was a raised pedestal with an intricate wooden box sitting alone on it. Stuart walked up onto the stage. He looked at me like I was nothing with his smug face. I simply stared him down. I could play games too.

"Ladies and gentlemen," Councilor Winston began, "I am very excited to announce the joining of a new Timekeeper in training. We have here, Abigail *Jordan*." He spoke my last name with venom. I wanted to push him off the stage, but I figured that that would not be very lady like. "Miss Jordan has currently been in training with her father, Mathias Benedict, however because of her late initiation she has not been able to achieve the full extent of her studies. She will now have the opportunity to receive the full training that Timekeeping has to offer as well as the possibility to study abroad in a different country from other Timekeepers. We will now begin the initiation."

Councilor Winston reached into the coat pocket of his lavish suit and pulled out a small, withering book. He opened the book to the first page and began to read.

"Called to study," he began. "All individuals who possess the knowledge of the past, present, and future. Like those before them, these individuals have the ability to see beyond that of the normal human eye. Like many to come, they must let go of their life and move forth in the realm of Timekeeping. A special task has been assigned to them. Great power has been bestowed upon them. Hardships may lie ahead for them, but they must be battled with. A Timekeeper is who they are called to be. Nothing should prevent them from protecting the balance of time, nor should nothing possess them to abuse its tender heart. At this point, you will now sign a contract to obey the laws of time and our laws will officially apply, specifically, if you should interfere with a premonition of death, death will take you instead." A part of me was still hoping that maybe Elijah had been wrong, but now it was official. I looked at Mathias, guarding my knowing face with one of surprise. I saw him look guilty and he turned his gaze away.

Councilor Winston placed a piece of parchment paper onto the podium in front of me as well as a quill and ink. I looked at the contract. The words were written in Gaelic.

"Please sign here," Winston said, indicating to a place at the bottom of the document.

I hesitated for a moment and then took the quill, dipped it in the ink, and signed my name. It was done.

Councilor Winston turned and reached for the small box on the pedestal. He took out a key and put it into the lock of the box. It clicked after one quick turn and he opened the lid. Inside I saw what looked like a pocket watch, similar to Mathias' as well as the one that had been my mother's, but this one was silver and looked more like a necklace. Councilor Winston picked it up and stepped forward, placing the necklace-watch over my head.

"Record time well," he said to me before turning back to face the audience. "Ladies and gentleman, our newest Timekeeper in training, Abigail Jordan. Until we meet again for her placement ceremony, thank you for coming."

Clapping erupted in the audience before all the lights in the room went out. The room was consumed in a powerful darkness that threatened to swallow all of us in it. Several women screamed and many man were cursing loudly. I assumed this was not part of the ceremony.

"Mathias," I cried, "what is going on?"

There was no reply. I reached out into the darkness for Mathias' hand, but I did not find it. He was no longer standing next to me. I heard footsteps leaving the stage and a door shut.

"What is going on?" I heard Councilor Winston say. "Mathias Benedict, is this your doing? Someone turn the bloody lights back on or light a candle!"

The temperature in the room suddenly became very cold and drafty. I shivered and wrapped my arms around myself. The darkness was menacing.

"Bloody hell!" Winston yelled. "What in the devil is going on in—"

Winston made the most horrifying sound I'd ever heard and then I heard a body drop to the floor. Then, I heard footsteps from behind me.

I didn't have time to respond before something ruffled against my back and I turned quickly. My breathing was growing faster, my heart beat was increasing. I reached out into the darkness, but I felt nothing. I heard breathing though and it wasn't Winston. Was it Mathias?

"Who is there?"

Silence.

"Who is there?" I screamed. "What are you doing?"

There was no response and my body was suddenly pushed forward. I fell onto the hard concrete of the stage and hit my head. Pain shot up through my skull and my body shivered but it wasn't from the cold of the floor. I was lying in something hot and sticky.

I heard footsteps again and someone running off the stage. I heard several people shriek and a door slam.

The lights came back on and I was staring up at the ceiling. I could hear several people shrieking and I quickly rolled onto my side. I wish I hadn't. I was staring directly into the dead, empty eyes of Councilor Winston. His throat had been cut and it was his blood that I was lying in. I began to scream and pushed myself up off the floor away from the body. I turned to the people in front of me. Many of them were pointing at something behind me. I turned around and almost lost my balance again because of what I saw. Winston's blood was all over the wall behind the stage, and a message was left with it.

He killed Elisabeth.

My heart had been racing moments before, but now it almost stopped entirely. Who was "he?" Was it the councilor? Had Councilor Winston killed my mother? But it was an accident, a suicide is what they said. She hung herself. Or did someone hang her?

"Mathias!"

I turned, looking desperately for Mathias. Where was he? I wanted to get out of here. I wanted to leave this room, and leave the Headquarters. I wanted to go home. I had a man's blood all over me and a message that was quite obviously left for me, if not for Mathias as well.

Turning, I made for the stairs but slipped on the blood and went skidding off the stage. I landed on the hard floor and heard people rushing to help me.

"Get me out of here," I said. "Please get me out of here!"

I could not take the pressure of the moment anymore. I could not take the eyes looking at me. I could not take it. Period. I blacked out.

The bombs dropped, but they missed me. They missed my biological mother as she extended her hand out to me.

"Come to me dear," my mother said. "Please."

I walked forward, but every step I took it seemed my mother was two steps back.

"Come to me."

"I'm trying," I said. "I'm coming."

My mother's elegant white dress blew in the wind and bustled around her. The bombs were dropping but as soon as they hit the ground they simply fell straight threw, like the ground was smoke to them. My mother's long blonde hair blew in the wind and around her face.

"Abigail, please hurry."

"I'm trying."

It was too late.

The picture seemed to melt away and change. My mother was being lifted up by a noose around her neck. She was choking violently beneath the Tower Bridge, and I was sinking in the depths of the Thames. The water bustled around me as I continued to sink.

Mathias stood at the bridge's rail.

"No!"

I shrieked and sat bolt upright. My entire body was shaking and sweating and I was screaming and I couldn't stop. I clawed at my face and ran my fingers through my hair. It was dark. I was in a bed. Where was I? What was going on? I began to shake even more and scream even more. A door opened and light crept into the room and I felt familiar arms wrap around me.

"It's okay," Phillip said. He held me as I continued to writhe violently in his arms. "It's okay."

It was not okay. Nothing was okay. Nothing would ever be okay again. I had seen a dead man. I had fallen in his blood. I had seen my mother hanging from a bridge with no way to defend herself and standing above her, watching her die, I had seen him. I had seen Mathias. It was him. He murdered her. He'd been lying to me. It was true. But wait, no it wasn't. Or was it? I began to cry. Tears poured from my eyes. I didn't know what was going on. How did I even get to Phillip's? I was losing it. I was finally losing it. I realized then and there that I'd much rather be a mad girl hearing voices then be in the situation I was in now. But that was crazy talk. I didn't want to be locked up. Or did I?

"Abby," Phillip whispered, "it's okay. I'm here now and I'm not going to let anything happen to you." I could feel his clean shaved cheek rubbing against the crane of my neck. I felt safe.

I began to pull away from Phillip and lay back down in the bed. The scent of Phillip consumed me, and I was asleep.

The sounds of the city echoed through the closed window of Phillip's flat. My eyes peeled open to bright sunlight. I put Phillip's pillow over my face and signed. London was awake and alive outside the window, and it was screaming at me to get up and rue the day.

I heard the bedroom door open and pulled the pillow off my face. Phillip stood in the doorway of the bedroom in his work suit, a brown jacket and pants.

"Morning," he said, "I slept out on the couch. How are you feeling?"

I sat up in the bed and placed my face in my hands.

"I feel like someone beat me to a pulp. What happened?"

Phillip made his way across the room and sat down on the edge of the bed. He reached out for my hand and I placed it in his.

"Mathias said that someone turned off the lights wherever this ball was being held, and that some councilor, I couldn't make much sense of it all, was murdered. He said you fainted right after the incident and the whole place went chaotic. He brought you here."

He brought me here. Something about that did not feel right to me. I remembered then the message that had been left. *He killed Elisabeth.* And then I remembered my dream—Mathias was standing at the rail of the bridge. Did Mathias kill Elisabeth? My throat tightened and my heart rate picked up.

"Abby." Phillip's voice called me back out of whatever thoughts were running through my mind. I turned my focus back to him. A concerned look had appeared on his face.

"How does Mathias know where you live?"

Phillip gave me a questioning look.

"I assumed you told him. Didn't you?"

I shook my head.

"Well, maybe he looked it up."

"Looked it up where?" I shot back. "At whatever time of night it was, with a dead body lying around, and an unconscious woman to transport. He had time to figure out all that?"

"What are you saying?" I could tell Phillip was coming to the same realization that I had, but he didn't want to say it out loud.

"The notes," I said. "Your broken window. Someone's been watching us. It was him. It's all him."

Phillip shook his head. "No. No, it wasn't him. It can't be."

I was flabbergasted.

"Why are you so quick to discredit the theory?" I asked. "You haven't exactly been on board this train. You didn't get along with him. I haven't really got along with him until last night, and I assume that is because it was his big night to show me off. It all makes sense. He always has his mood swings too." And then I remembered my conversation with Elijah and immediately told Phillip.

"Fine," Phillip said. "If all of that is true than you are not going back."

"You cannot make that decision for me," I yelled. "I need to know what he did to her!"

"Who, Abigail?" Phillip snapped back, "What he did to who?"

"My mother!" I responded. "He did something, I know it."

"Well, you'll have to figure that out here and not there. I need to go to work. Please stay here, and don't do anything stupid."

He turned on his heel and slammed the bedroom door behind him. I sat there in disbelief. I knew he was trying to protect me but I needed to figure this out. I needed to know what was going on. I needed to have the answers to everything. I was so close to having the answers. My whole life was questions after questions, and now, I was so close. So close. I got out of the bed. I realized I was wearing only a shirt and my underwear. I quickly threw on a pair of pants I kept at Phillip's. He must have taken off the bloody dress. It was Sunday. I needed to get home so I could go to church with my parents and then, then I was getting an answer. An answer to something—anything.

I pulled open the bedroom door.

Bridget was sitting on Phillip's couch and I almost fell backward at the shock of seeing her there. She was red in the face and it was the red of what looked like anger, not embarrassment. I realized that Phillip was still here, standing in the kitchen, watching us both.

The first words that came out of my mouth were, "Bridget, why are you here?"

She looked at me for what felt like a good minute before a tear finally fell from her eye.

Bridget did not say a single word, so I turned my attention back on Phillip.

"Why is she here?"

Phillip only looked at me as well. Why was everyone only looking at me?

"Say something!"

"Bridget is here because she was worried Abby," Phillip finally spoke. "She came because she is your friend, and was worried about you."

I looked back at Bridget. She was standing up now.

"I was her friend."

My heart rate had increased again. I was getting upset with how much my heart rate was increasing. Why couldn't it just slow down for a while?

"Bridget."

She shook her head. "Stop, Abigail, please just stop. What is going to come out of your mouth? More lies? I cannot take it anymore. I just wanted to stay and make sure you were okay, but Phillip is the one who finally had to tell me the truth, and from what he said, I gathered that you were probably never going to tell me, so goodbye, Abby."

How could this be happening? Was she being serious?

"Bridget, please don't," I said. "Please don't leave me, I need you."

"Abby, if you needed me," she shouted, "if you truly needed me than you would keep our commitments. You would not break them. I understand this ball thing, but Christmas with him," she pointed at Phillip, who looked confused, "and all the time you have to spend with this so called unsociable father. You could have talked to me, you could have confided in me. I'm sorry that I recommended professional help. I was just trying to be a friend to you, because honestly Abby, most people would recommend that. They wouldn't baby you like he does."

The look on Phillip's face was one of fury. He clearly didn't understand how much Bridget had kept from him in regards to her feelings about him.

"I think you are going a bit over the line, Bridget," Phillip finally said.

"Phillip, you baby her, you treat her like your princess," Bridget said. "I'm not saying you can't do that, but I do not think it helps in situations like this. I have known Abigail her entire life. I'm just trying to be the friend she needs, the friend you haven't been. You are her fiancé, but you also need to be her friend, and a friend would be courageous enough to have told her to seek professional help."

I could not take this. "I do not need help though," I shouted. "I don't. I have a gift Bridget. It is real. None of it is in my head."

"And you've roped Phillip in this delusion?" Bridget asked.

"Bridget, I have a supernatural ability," I finally said. "I have power, I have premonitions, I can see the future and travel to the past. I'm a Timekeeper. It isn't a delusion."

Bridget looked at me. Once again, she wasn't saying anything. She just looked at me, and then, "Goodbye, Abby."

I stood there, frozen, watching my closest friend walk away. And then I turned on Phillip.

"Why did you tell her?" I asked.

"She deserved to know," he responded. "Listen, I am sorry. I didn't know that she'd react that way. I just felt like she should know."

"And to complicate matters, I'm now not even a normal

Timekeeper."

Phillip approached me and stood there and I buried myself into him and he held me tightly. He smelled like clean sheets. He must have been doing some laundry.

"I don't know what to do Phillip," I said, "I've been trying so hard to find answers to all of my questions. You said I was normal, but now I'm not even a normal Timekeeper. What am I?"

"You are you," Phillip responded. "You are my girl. I don't give a shit what kind of Timekeeper you are. Abby, the day you said yes to my marriage proposal was the day I became the happiest man on the planet. As long as we have each other, I promise everything will be okay. We will try to find the answers you need, but don't let them consume you."

My eyes turned up to his and I stared at him for a few moments. Before I knew it, our lips were on each other's. His hands were stroking my hair and we were connected, inseparable.

CHAPTER SEVENTEEN

My mind was racing as I made my way home. Bridget was gone. She had left me. I cursed myself for not telling her. Would it have been the same if I had told her earlier on? I didn't know. I feared it would have been—that she wouldn't believe me and she'd think I was insane. My mind turned to the night before. The only thing that I could think about was the councilor's blood. My body remembered the hot, sticky feeling I felt when I had fallen in it—not knowing it was blood at that point. I remembered his sliced throat and the message on the wall.

I shook my head vigorously to rid myself of the thoughts. The focus needed to be on where to go from here. Did I trust Mathias? The answer was no. He had lied to me about the initiation process and if the message had anything to do with it, he was lying to me about my mother. Did I trust him with my life? Most people would say they did trust their biological father with their life, but I did not.

The cold, bitter wind blew against my skin and I shivered. I pulled the coat I was wearing tighter around me and turned another corner. I don't know why I was walking. I had walked before, but it was a shorter ride by cab. I needed to think everything through and walking helped me think. Within ten minutes, I was at my house. I pulled out my keys and unlocked the front door, stepped in, and locked it behind me. Once the door was securely shut, I felt relaxed and warmer.

Footsteps sounded from the other end of the hall. I looked up to see my mother in the archway to the kitchen.

"Abigail, is everything okay? Phillip just phoned. He said you were distraught when you left his flat."

I nodded. Everything was fine. I was fine. Everything would be okay. I was a little aggravated with Phillip, though. He didn't need to phone my mother and "distraught" was hardly the word I would use.

"Sweetheart."

I could tell she was concerned. I turned toward the stairs, but she caught up to me.

"Abigail."

I turned to look at my mother. I realized I probably looked a fright. Cold from head to toe. I had not bathed since before the ball.

"Sweetheart, I can tell that you are struggling with something. Please talk to me about it."

I shook my head. "I'm fine, mum. Really." I took a step onto the stairs.

"Do not lie to me."

I froze. Why did mothers have to be intuitive?

"I do not want to talk about it," I responded, "just let it go. I'm sorry I was out and didn't come home. It won't happen again."

"Dear, if something is wrong, please tell me. I can help you."

I lost it. I never lost it with her, but I did.

"No, you can't!" Tears welled up in my eyes. "You have no idea, mum. You don't. Please just leave me alone. It's not like you could help me, even if I wanted you to."

"I'm your mother sweetheart."

"No, you're not."

I said it without thinking. I didn't even process it. The only thought that had come to mind was my biological mother, a woman who I had never known, and her standing in the wind, the bombs dropping around her.

"What?"

A hot, salty tear rolled down my cheek. Did I ever run out of tears? I turned to face my mum again and saw that tears were also falling from her eyes. It broke my heart to see her cry, but the only thing I could do was make it worse, because I was too angry to stop myself.

"You're not my mother. You found me, and you raised me. That's it."

I had stunned her into silence. I left her there and went to my room to change.

The church was cramped the next day. I sat in between my mother and father. My father was holding my hand for whatever reason. My mother's presence next to me was horrible. I thought I could feel the sadness seeping out of her body.

After the mass was over, my parents and I went to have lunch at a café nearby.

"We'll need to be getting into the shelter early tonight," my mother said as she ate the salad that she had ordered. "There is some talk about a possible raid." Her composure was like ice. She spoke the words in a monotone voice. I had broken her heart—it was written all over her face.

"I'm sure the alarm will sound," I reasoned with her, "it always does."

She gave me a look of fury. She didn't appreciate it when I argued with her, especially when it was about something as dire as this. There had been a few raids in the past two months, but nothing extreme. I didn't see why it was necessary to take the precautions.

"Are you going over to Phillip's?"

My mother was helping my father look over the menu as she was talking to me. He was having a very difficult time reading now. He was beginning to forget what even basic foods were sometimes.

"I don't think so," I said, "I'll probably see him tomorrow."

"Well if you do go somewhere, just make sure you are home before dark. I may not be able to get you into the shelter for the night, but I'll at least have you in the house."

The long hallway of the Headquarters seemed gloomier than usual. The walk to Mathias' desk was excruciatingly long. I could see the fire burning at the end of the hallway as well as the familiar shape of Mathias' figure at his desk. I made my way down the hallway, casually glancing up at the many different portraits of my ancestors.

"Hello, Abigail," Mathias said. He didn't bother to look up from whatever he was reading. I took a seat in my normal spot at the couch and crossed my legs.

"You lied to me."

He looked up at me.

"What would your choice have been if I hadn't?"

I didn't answer.

"That's what I thought."

"You're so hypocritical," I said. "You sit there and tell me we can't interfere with another person's free will but then you do it with mine. You took away my choice."

I wasn't shouting. I was calmly stating my feelings, and I think that made it worse for him.

"What happened last night?" I asked.

He looked at me stoically. For a moment, I thought he might gloss over it, like he did with almost everything else he considered "not related to Timekeeping."

"Councilor Winston was murdered," Mathias finally answered. "We do not have a suspect at this time."

"You disappeared right after the lights went out."

"And?" He looked at me quizzically.

"I thought that it was odd that the lights went out, and you so happened to disappear, and then the councilor ended up dead."

"Are you trying to accuse me of something?" A look of anger was painted onto his features.

I swallowed and considered my next words carefully. Either I was sitting in front of a cold-blooded killer who could easily take me out, or I was about to be verbally assaulted for false accusations.

"I'm only asking where you went." That was good. It didn't point fingers, but at the same time it didn't clear him.

"Where do you think?" he shot back. "I went to turn on the bloody lights. Why did you write that message on the wall?"

It took an extra minute to process the question that erupted from his mouth. Why did I write the message? He literally just asked it. He didn't ask me *if* I wrote the message, but why. I could not believe it. I stood up.

"Excuse me?"

"You heard me. The council was very upset by the murder of Councilor Winston, and they did not appreciate your antics against your own father."

I felt like invisible rocks were stoning me with each of his accusatory words.

"I did not write that!" I said, my voice growing louder. "Why would you say that?"

"The blood was all over you!"

He grew red in the face and stood up from his desk. He planted his hands on them and looked me in the eye, clearly waiting for me to lie and say yes. I would not.

"Because I fell in it! Someone pushed me in the dark! I fell in it!"

"Abigail," Mathias said, "I do not believe you had anything to do with the death of the councilor. For all we know, it could have been some kind of staged suicide, which is what the council is saying because he was a bitter man.

"Regardless, we need to begin making plans for your studies elsewhere."

"My studies elsewhere?" This threw me for a loop. I had no idea what he was talking about.

"Every Timekeeper must complete a separate study in another Timekeeper's country," Mathias told me. "Usually they go alone, but I will be accompanying you since you are still new to the business."

“I can't just up and leave, though. I also have university."

"Which is why we are planning it. What do you think about traveling with me this summer? We could go to several different countries as well."

He seemed excited about this. I felt guilt for being so distant from him as a daughter, but he was the one being distant from me. Maybe he was trying to finally be a bit closer.

"I'm getting married in the summer," I told him.

He froze, looking at me.

"Married?" Mathias repeated, "to whom?"

I stared at him incredulously. Was he being serious?

"To Phillip!" I almost shouted.

"Ah, yes. I forgot about the boy. Well, that will have to wait."

I stood up. I was furious at him. Was he seriously telling me that I would have to put off my marriage?

"It isn't going to wait," I said. "It is going to happen. I'm sorry Mathias, but I can't just up and leave to take some Timekeeping field trip with you for two months."

I regretted saying it like that. He looked like I had just slapped him across the face.

"Timekeeping field trip," he repeated. "Abigail this is your heritage. This is who you are. I thought that was clear when I introduced you at the ball."

"Maybe this isn't what I want to be," I said.

"It's too late for you to go back now."

"Thanks to you. Regardless, I'm also because of my mother. I want to know about her and you haven't helped me learn anything at all. You've kept me in the dark and pushed me away from figuring out what happened to her."

"Who cares what happened to her!" Mathias shouted. "She is dead!"

"How can you say that? She was your wife. I think it's clear that she was murdered. How can you stand here and not want to know what happened to her? How can you stand here and continue to be this Timekeeper, yet not know the basic answer as to why she is dead?"

"Because I don't care!"

I couldn't think. I couldn't feel. Mathias, my mother's husband, didn't care. He didn't care about Elisabeth. How could he even say that? After he said he had waited for me. After he said he had tried everything he could to find out what happened to her. Or did he? Perhaps he was just a liar. Perhaps he was just a con man. Perhaps the message was true. It wouldn't have been the first time he had lied.

"I don't know what my mother saw in you," I responded. "For all I know you didn't love her."

He just stood there. Either he was too hurt to say anything, or this was the truth. I turned to leave.

"Abigail, wait."

"No. You've had your chances."

I felt his hand on my shoulder and turned around to push him away, but he went frozen. His eyes were glassy and began to roll back into his head and he fell to the floor.

"Mathias!"

I fell to my knees to try and pull him up. What was happening? But then I realized. He was having a premonition. This was probably what I looked like when I had a premonition. It was powerful. It made people see. It was why we had to stay locked away. It was why I didn't want this life.

His eyes rolled back and he took a gasp for air.

"What did you see?" I asked.

He looked up at me and I thought I saw his eyes water, but I assumed it was just the light because he turned away too fast.

"Mathias," I said. "What did you see?"

"Nothing important." His voice was low.

"It looked pretty important to me," I responded.

"It was nothing," he said again. "Now go, like you wanted."

"Just tell me what you s—"

"Please, just go."

"Mathias, just tell m—"

"Get the hell out!"

His face was red. His eyes were cold. He looked like the devil, and as I left, I decided he was.

"He said that to you?" Phillip asked again. I sat in his flat and sipped some coffee he had poured for me. I wasn't sad or crying. I wasn't angry or yelling. I was just empty. I didn't care anymore about Mathias.

I nodded and Phillip stood up.

"I'm going to beat the shit out of him. And you said you wouldn't go back."

"Phillip, you don't even know how to get in. Just forget it. I'm done with him. And that was you that said that."

I had decided to go to Phillip even though I had said I wouldn't see him today. I knew if I had gone straight home my mother would have been able to tell something was going on. If her daughter had a cold, heartless expression on her face I'm sure she would be able to tell. I couldn't hurt her again. I had already done it earlier.

"Why does he think he can talk to you like that?"

"Look at how your father talks to you," I responded.

"That's not the point," Phillip responded. "You barely know your father. He shouldn't talk like that to a daughter he's only just met."

"I'm sure it has something to do with my mother."

"So, now you're defending him?"

"I'm not defending him. I'm just saying he has a lot of emotional issues and I'm sure they stem from that."

"Sounds like you're defending them."

"Phillip! Listen, both of our parents have made mistakes and I don't want us to repeat those when we get married."

"So, you're saying you think I'm going to turn out like my father?" Phillip responded, his face turning red.

"I didn't say that. I just don't want us to make the same mistakes. You do have a temper."

"I do not have a bloody temper!" Phillip shouted, standing up.

I crossed my arms and gave him a look that said I was right.

"You always do this!" he snapped. "You come up with excuses for people instead of stating it how it is. Your mother abandoned you.

Yet here you are on this grand mission to try and find out about her."

"You don't even know anything about her! Don't talk about her like you know her."

"And you know her, Abigail?"

I turned to leave. He didn't try to stop me. I slammed the door behind me. The thin walls of the building shook and a neighbor opened her door to look out and find out what was going on. I didn't say anything as I walked past.

How could he say that? He knew nothing about my mother. She was trying to protect me. She wouldn't deliberately put me in harm's way. He was just upset. I wasn't comparing him to his father—was I? Then again, maybe I was trying to fix people and make excuses for them.

The truth was I had no idea where my life was going. I didn't know what I was looking for. I had a fiancé who was right, a father who was wrong, a mother lost to me, and someone, supposedly the person who killed her, after me. Where was I going? What was I supposed to do?

It was getting dark and the sky was beginning to get cloudy. I turned in the direction of home and started walking. I needed to clear my head. It probably wasn't a good idea with night approaching, but I didn't care. I would take the risk. I could see the lights begin to go out and the ARP warden was out for the night.

I was less than a mile away from Barton Street when the air raid alarm sounded. The noise whirled loudly and left a ringing in my ears. It was dark and I stretched my head to look up at the sky. I didn't see anything, but I started to run. It sounded as if the alarm was getting louder. I made it to the front door, but it was locked. I found my key and quickly unlocked the door.

"Mum!" I shouted.

I slammed the door behind me. The house was dark and I could hear the screech of the alarm through the walls. The door to the backyard at the other end of the hall opened and my mother stood in the doorway. Her face was panic-stricken and she ran toward me, throwing her arms around me, and pulling me with her.

"Where were you?" she shouted, half crying. "You said you weren't going to Phillip's. I thought you might be stuck out in the city! Come on!"

"I'm sorry!" I yelled, running with her. "I did go! I'm sorry I should have called."

"It doesn't matter. We need to get in the shelter. I think this night might be worse than the others."

The sirens seemed louder as we ran through the backyard. The sound reverberated in my ears and it was painful. We made it to the bomb shelter and my mother pulled the door closed behind her. She turned on the light. My father was sleeping on the cot. How could he sleep through all this noise?

"The baby!"

My mother and I turned around. My father had sat upright in the bed and his face was screwed into a look of utter horror.

"What is it Dean?"

"Where is the baby?"

"What baby?" my mother asked him.

"Where is my Abigail Lu?" he asked.

I stepped in front of my mother and knelt down next to my father.

"I'm right here, papa," I said, taking his hand.

He gave me a look of confusion and then suddenly pushed me to the ground and got up.

"Dean, what are you doing?" My mother bent down to help me off the floor.

"The baby! We left the baby in the house!"

He pushed open the door of the bomb shelter and ran out into the night. My mother screamed and leaped forward.

"Dean!" she shouted, "come back!"

She turned to me and gave me a stern look.

"Stay here, Abigail," she said. "Do not leave this shelter."

She took off into the night.

"Mum!" I shouted.

"Stay there!"

I watched as she disappeared back into the house. I looked up into the sky. The clouds had disappeared and the moon was out. I could see the stars. It was a beautiful night. War shouldn't have been happening, but it was. The alarm continued to sound in my ears and sent shivers down my body. I continued to stare at the back door of the house. I crossed my fingers hoping to see my mother appear out of the door with my father and running back toward the shelter, but no one came.

Life is full of difficult moments—even more, it is full of difficult decisions. As I watched the back door of my home, desperately waiting for my mother and father to emerge, I had a difficult choice to make. My mother and father would want me to stay here and wait for them, but I needed to go to them. I ran up the steps out of the shelter and emerged into the dark backyard. I looked up into the sky and could see little dots slowly making their way into the city. I ran toward the house.

"Mum!" I shouted as I emerged through the back door into the kitchen.

There was no answer. I ran through the kitchen archway and down the hallway. There was no one in the living room.

Boom.

The whole house rattled, but the bombs were still several streets away from what I could tell. I quickly turned and bolted up the staircase to the floor above. As I stepped onto the landing, I could see my mother crouched at the door of her bedroom on her knees. She was crying and desperately shouting for my father.

"Dean," she said, "it's me, I'm your wife. Please come out."

"I will not let you hurt the baby," my father shouted from within the room. "Go away, you Nazi!"

My mother shrieked and began to cry harder. I quickly ran down the hallway and knelt down next to her. She jumped as I appeared, clearly not expecting me to be there.

"Abby! No, I told you to stay in the shelter."

"Not without you two," I said fiercely. I jiggled the door handle, but it was locked. I would have to break the door down; we did not have much time. It was an old house—so I felt it wouldn't be that difficult. "Move aside, mum."

My mum stepped to the other side of the hallway and pushed herself against the wall. I began to throw myself forcefully at the door, but it didn't budge. I began to kick near the door handle with my foot. It slowly began to give way. Finally, I threw myself against the door once more and it caved in to the room beyond.

My father was sitting on the bed, shaking. I walked over to him and he flinched away from me.

"Papa," I said, "I need you to come with me. The baby is in the shelter."

My father looked up at me. His eyes almost killed me. He had been crying as well.

Boom.

The house shuttered again. Planes had to be near us and more would be coming.

"Papa, we need to get back to the baby," I said. "We have to keep the baby safe."

I held out my hand. My father hesitated for a moment, but finally he reached out and placed his hand in mine.

The three of us ran down the landing and toward the stairs.

BOOM.

I heard the living room window crack below. As I looked over the landing, I could see glass flying everywhere. We made our way down the stairs and onto the landing below.

BOOM.

I tripped and fell after the last one. My face planted onto the floor below and I felt warm blood beginning to pour out of my nose. My mother grabbed my hand and pulled me up. But I knew it was too late and so did she. I could hear the eerie, whistling sound of a bomb falling outside and it had to be heading straight for the top of our house. The whistling sound filled my ears as it came closer, and closer, and closer.

BOOM. BOOM. BOOM.

The events that followed happened so fast I could barely keep track of anything around me. I saw pictures falling off the wall. I heard glass breaking. I heard what sounded like the horrid sound of a ceiling about to cave in on top of us. I heard the screams and cries of my mother. Darkness and dust eclipsed my view of the room and something hard hit my head.

Sirens.

I heard the sirens. Darkness continued to consume my vision, but the sirens I could hear. The air raid alarm was still going off, but these were the sounds of emergency sirens. The air raid that had happened had been one of the worst we'd had since a few years ago. Finally, I fluttered my eyelids and I could see.

Smoke filled my nose and eyes as I opened them. It exploded into my lungs and I let out a fit of coughing. I could see the smoke along with floating debris around the ruins of my home. I saw broken glass, furniture caught on fire, and pictures of my childhood crushed and littering the floor. It was then that I noticed a horrible excruciating pain in my right leg as well as my head. I looked over to my leg and saw a large piece of wood stuck cleanly in the center of my thigh. It didn't feel like, or look like it was touching the bone, so that was good. I supposed if this was the only injury I had from tonight that would be considered a blessing.

The feeling was still painful, however. I reached over and pulled on the wood gently and let out a horrifying scream of pain.

"Abby?"

My head turned sharply at the sound of my mother's voice. I could see her body a few feet away from me. The hutch from the hallway where we kept our good china was lying on top of her.

"Mum!"

I tried to move, but the pain in my leg was horrifying. I reached over and began to pull the wood out, but it continued to hurt.

"Just pull it straight out, Abby," my mum said. "Don't do it slowly or that will make it worse."

I grabbed the wood firmly with my hand and counted down to three. And then I pulled.

My scream of pain filled what was left of the house. Water blurred my vision as my eyes teared up.

"Now, rip off part of your shirt and use it as a tourniquet," my mum said. She worked in a hospital most of her life, so she knew what to do in times like this.

I grabbed the bottom of my shirt and ripped it. There was already a hole in it from being torn in the cave in so it was not too difficult. I quickly took the torn piece and wrapped it around my wound. I tied it tightly and then, even though it hurt, pushed myself up.

Wobbling over to my mother, I looked down at her.

"Wait," she said, "your father first."

I turned and saw my father another few feet away. I walked over to him, and my heart began to race when I realized that the top of his skull looked bruised and swollen.

I knelt down next to him.

"Papa," I said. I touched his shoulder lightly. He didn't move. "Papa?"

I quickly checked his pulse and my heart began to race when I realized his heart was not beating. He was gone. My heart was beating entirely too fast and my breathing was growing ragged. My father was dead. My father was gone. He was never coming back. How could this be? How could any of this be right? Where was the justice in this? Why was this happening?

"Abby?" My mother's voice drew me out of the darkness I was being enveloped in. "Is he alright?"

I didn't respond right away and she said my name again.

"Abby?"

I hobbled back over to my mother and knelt down next to her.

"He's gone," I whispered.

She was quiet. I stood up and began to try and lift the hutch off of her, but then I felt her hand touch mine.

"Why'd you have me check on him first?" I said, half crying. "We need to get this thing off of you."

"Abby, darling, we can't."

I realized then that her breathing was beginning to slow and she was talking softly. I knelt back down next to her and saw her eyes look at the hutch, and then I realized. She had been impaled by a large piece of wood. My stomach turned.

"Abby, listen to me," she said. "I will always be with you."

"Stop. The ambulances are coming. They will help us."

"They're not coming. We weren't the only people affected by this. By the time they get here it would be too late."

"No." I was biting my lip now. I was crying. "You are not going to die."

"I love you."

I could not look at her. I tried to her pull her out again, but she held up her hand.

"Mum," I said, tears were falling and staining my face. "I'm sorry." I was choking. "I'm sorry about what I said earlier."

"I know you are." She grabbed my chin. Her hand was shaking vigorously. She turned my face toward hers. Her eyes were blinking quickly. "Listen sweetheart. I love you. You are beautiful and wonderful. You are not a bad person. You *will* do great things. I know you will."

Her hand fell, and she was gone.

"Mum!" I fell forward and lay next to her. I leaned into her and closed my eyes. I didn't want to forget her scent. I didn't want to forget the way she felt. I didn't want to forget her.

I felt my whole world and everything I knew, began to leave me.

When a person you knew every day, like Mrs. Baxter, passes away, it hurts you. Perhaps you cry about it, or perhaps you feel saddened by it. A little part of you feels different. But when a person or persons who were close to you and raised you, your parents, pass away, you are consumed by it. After my mother took her last breath, I was consumed by it. I laid next to her in the rubble of my home and didn't care. The emergency crew finally did reach us, but like my mum had said, it was too late.

The next time I awoke, I was in a hospital. I saw the white ceiling above me and I felt a hand in mine. I looked over to see Phillip at my side. He was sleeping in the chair next to my bed, but he had not let go of my hand. I looked down at to the injury I had dressed in my home and found that it was now wrapped in gauze and hurt considerably less.

"Good morning."

I looked over to see Phillip's eyes opening as he spoke. I didn't say anything.

“Abigail,” he said, “how are you feeling?”

“The pain has gone down,” I said softly.

"I was scared today, Abigail," Phillip said. "I heard where the bombs had hit and came rushing to your house. When I saw the rubble, I felt like I had lost everything. But the crew told me they had found you alive."

"I did lose everything though," I said.

Phillip didn't reply to my statement. I think he realized I was right. Sure, he still had me and I had him, but I no longer had my parents. I no longer had the people who had raised me, a baby they had adopted as their own daughter. I had lost the people that had cared for me and loved me like every parent should. I no longer had that in my life. I felt empty inside and I felt unsure of where to go from here.

"The doctors said you could leave tomorrow," Phillip said. "They just want to keep you today to make sure your wound is healing okay. You did a great job dressing it."

"My mum helped me," I said.

I turned on my side, so that my back was facing Phillip. I began to cry again and I felt his hand on my shoulder. I felt his comfort, but this time it was not enough. This time he could not fix this. I was alone in this pain and suffering. I felt like I was lost in a hole. I felt like I was unable to climb out. I felt like the darkness was around me. I could not control it. I could not do anything to fix it. The only thing that I could do would be to live with it. Living with it was unimaginable.

CHAPTER EIGHTEEN

The backyard was alive with the colors of spring. My mother's flowerbed was blooming with different kinds of flowers I couldn't even begin to name. I was looking at all of this through the window in our kitchen—I wanted so badly to go out.

"Mummy?"

My mum looked up from the bowl she was mixing. She was making chocolate chip cookies—my favorite.

"Yes, Abby?"

"Can I go play in the backyard?" I asked. "It is beautiful out today."

"I suppose. Just be careful."

I smiled and pulled open the back door. The warm spring air hit my face and made my smile even brighter. It had started to smell like spring as well. I pulled the door shut and ran out into the open back yard.

Our largest tree in the middle of the yard was my favorite thing about the backyard. I loved to climb it in the spring and summer. I had been climbing it as long as I could remember. I began to climb and felt the rush that I would get from the heights. I had not climbed it since the summer before and had missed it throughout the long winter.

As soon as I got to the top, I sat on one of the branches and looked over the yard below me. I felt like I was a bird—a bird looking down from the sky above. I felt the nice breeze of the day against my cheeks, and my hair blew in the soft wind.

There was a tweeting sound above me and I looked up to see a small bird that was just a little higher up than I was. I wondered if I could get it to stay.

I reached out with my hand and it didn't move. I carefully stood up and then reached out for the bird. Suddenly, the bird flew right at me and I slipped. The feeling of falling out of the tree was amazing, but hitting the ground was horrifying. I landed on my left arm and heard the horrific sound of it snapping. And then I screamed.

My mum came flying out of the kitchen back door—followed by my father. All of the windows were open on the first floor so they had heard me.

They both knelt down next to me and I was crying.

"We'll need to get her to the hospital," my mother said. "I'll get the car ready."

My father held me in his arms as I cried.

"Don't cry, my Abigail Lu," he said. "I've got you. I've got you."

My eyes opened. I was staring out the window of a moving car. I quickly came back to reality and sat up in my seat. I was in Phillip's car and we were driving on the road along the countryside.

"Phillip?" I looked over at him. He turned his head and smiled at me.

"Hey there," he said. "You've been out cold since yesterday. I guess the medicine they gave you made you pretty sleepy."

"It's been a day?" I asked him.

"Sure has," Phillip replied.

"Where are we going?" I asked.

"Scotland."

"What?" I snapped. "We can't go to Scotland! My parents just died! I need to be planning their funeral! What are you doing?"

"That is exactly why you need to go to Scotland," Phillip said. "Because your parents just died. Abby you've been through a horrible ordeal. I've made arrangements with a funeral parlor and the hospital. We can plan the funeral while we're away. It will just be two days and then we can come back for the funeral."

I sighed and crossed my arms. There was no winning this argument with him.

"Not to mention," Phillip continued, "they are saying it is best to stay out of the city for a few days after that air raid. It was one of the worst we've had in a few years."

"Where are we going?"

"Edinburgh," Phillip replied. "My grandfather had a house up there that the family still owns. We used to go up there for weekends. My parents give you their condolences too."

Phillip reached over and touched my hand, but I pulled it away.

The house that Phillip had referred to was one in a row of old Victorian houses. It was beautiful to say the least, but nothing at the current time could pull me out of my desperation.

I took the bags Phillip had brought for me and went upstairs to a random bedroom. I threw the bags on the floor and then shut the door behind me and locked it.

With my back against the door, I began to lose myself again. I slowly slid to the floor and covered my face in my hands. The hot tears poured from my eyes and the emotions were let loose. My parents were dead. I wanted them back, but I knew that was impossible. I did not know how I could possibly go forward from here. A knock came from the other side of the door.

"Abby, let me in," Phillip said.

"Leave me alone."

"That is the last thing I'm going to do."

"I'll be fine."

I heard a sound on the other side of the door and realized he was doing the same thing I was.

"I'll just sit here and wait for you," Phillip responded.

"Why do people have to die?" I asked.

There was a moment of silence before he answered.

"Why are people born?"

"Because they are supposed to be born," I said.

"People are supposed to die, Abby," Phillip answered. "It's hard and they leave behind their loved ones to suffer, but it is what it is. We cannot control death, Abby. You know that."

"I wasn't ready," I said through my tears. "I wasn't ready for them to die."

"Who *is* ready? No one is ever ready for something like that. Abby, open the door. *Please*."

I reached up and unlocked the door. I moved forward a little bit and the door opened. Phillip came into the room and closed the door behind him. He bent down and pulled me up into his arms. He carried me to the bed and laid me down in it, then pulled the covers over me. I heard him take of his shoes and then he climbed into the bed as well. He pulled me against him and wrapped his arms around me.

"You can cry now," he whispered, "you can let everything out and I'll be here to help you and protect you."

I turned myself over in the bed so that I could face him. I let myself go.

Sleep consumed me. The following morning, I awoke to the smells of breakfast cooking from down below in the kitchen. Phillip was no longer in the bed with me. I climbed out and made my way downstairs.

I walked into the kitchen to find Phillip in his pajamas. He stood at the stove and was frying bacon and eggs.

"Good morning," he said.

I walked over to the kitchen table and sat down. A pot of coffee was in the middle of the table and two empty cups were set as well. I poured myself a hot cup of coffee and began to sip at it slowly.

"Morning," I finally responded. "Did I sleep through the whole night?"

"You did," Phillip said.

"Did I cry a lot?"

He nodded.

He distributed the eggs and bacon onto plates for us. I sat at the table and nibbled at my food with my fork.

"Still not hungry?" he asked.

"Not really."

We sat there in silence for a moment before Phillip finally spoke again.

"I thought we could go down by the ocean today and watch the sunset," he said. "Do you think that would be something you would be interested in?"

I nodded. "I wouldn't mind that."

He smiled at me and then finished his bacon. I continued to play with my food for a bit. I really wasn't hungry. There was too much on my mind right now and food was the last thing I was thinking about.

"Are you alright?" Phillip asked me.

I looked up at him in frustration. What kind of question was that? Of course, I wasn't alright. I shook my head and then pulled my legs up into my chair and hugged them. The tears began to flow. Phillip stood up from his chair and walked over to mine—kneeling down next to me.

"It'll be okay," he whispered, "I promise."

"My parents are dead, Phillip."

"I know, but you'll get through this."

I stood up from the chair and walked over to the kitchen sink. I turned the faucet on and began to run water on my hands and then brought the cold liquid up to my face and splashed it. The coldness felt good against my skin. Considering I felt coldness within me, I found the water soothing.

I turned off the faucet and turned around, leaning against the counter.

"I didn't want this to happen," I said, "I don't want to be a Timekeeper. It isn't me, Phillip. I'm not meant to do these magical things or whatever you call them. If I had never met Mathias, this probably wouldn't have happened."

"How do you know that?" Phillip asked me. "Abigail, just because you met a man who showed you the truth about yourself doesn't mean it led to the death of your parents. A war killed them Abby, not the fact that you are a Timekeeper, and not the fact that you were different from them."

"Phillip, I can't take this!" I screamed, and then I fell to the floor. "I wasn't ready to lose them. I need them. They were supposed to be at my wedding—our wedding. They were supposed to be grandparents. They can't be any of that anymore. What if it was me? If I had stayed in the shelter like they said maybe something would have turned out differently."

Phillip knelt down in front of me and pulled me into his arms. I let him hold me. I felt helpless and lost.

"You did nothing wrong," Phillip told me. "Do not think you could have done anything differently. You'll destroy yourself inside if you think like that."

"I can't do this anymore. This is all too much. My parents are gone, I've lost my best friend, my father hates me, and I have some maniac chasing after me. Why is this all happening? Why now? Is that what I get for trying to discover who I really am? Is this the punishment I deserve?"

"Listen to me Abby, sometimes life is hard and there are times that are worse than others. You will get through this. I know you will. I think all of this happening is a way for you to find yourself. It's a journey. It may not be a good journey, but it is a journey either way."

Knowing someone else is right is the hardest thing to accept. I knew Phillip was right. I knew I was at a time in my life where I had to find out who I really was. I was growing up and I had to accept that.

"Out of everything that has happened so far," Phillip continued, "what is the one thing that has kept you going?"

"My mother," I whispered, "my biological mother."

"Why?"

"She saved me. If it hadn't been for her I may not have met you. I would never have met my parents. She gave me this life. I owe it to her to find out the answers to the secrets that died with her."

Phillip took my face into his hands and held it gently. I looked up into his eyes and he spoke softly.

"So, keep going."

CHAPTER NINETEEN

The rain pounded against the windows of Phillip's flat. I stood in the bathroom—my reflection in the mirror before me. I had put my hair up into a bun and wore a simple black dress. I did not use anything on my face today. I looked different from the person I had been only a few months ago, but that is what death can do to a person. It changes you, whether you like it or not, whether you accept it or not.

I heard a knock and turned to see Phillip in the doorway of the bathroom. He was dressed in a black suit with a tie and his expression was somber.

"Are you ready?" he asked quietly.

"I don't think I'll ever be ready," I responded.

I walked past him into the bedroom and grabbed my black walking coat that was lying on his bed. He took it from me and put it on around me. I focused my attention on the pouring rain outside the bedroom window. A part of me cursed the rain—it shouldn't be raining, today of all days. But then a part of me embraced the rain. A shower amongst the city held a certain beauty that could not be captured or contained—it was only there and then it was gone. A roll of thunder broke my concentration and I turned to look at Phillip.

"Let's go."

The city of London was a flooding mess. It had been raining since Phillip and I had returned early yesterday afternoon. The streets were beginning to flood over and even though I had thought the rain was beautiful, I now cursed it. Today was supposed to be a sad day already, but the rain only magnified that frustration and anger inside me. I hated the war, I hated everything about it. It had taken away the parents I had loved—it had taken away the house I had grown up in. I felt selfish though, because I wasn't the only one suffering from the war.

Phillip pulled the car over at St. Patrick's church in Soho Square. Phillip got out first and opened an umbrella and then ran around to my side. I stepped out under the protection of the umbrella and we made our way into the church. There were more people here than I thought there would be. I looked around for Bridget, but I did not see her. A feeling of anger shot through me. I figured the majority of these people had worked with my father when he had been well, and I saw some of my mother's friends. Several people came up to me and hugged me and told me how sorry they were. I returned the hug and tried to smile, but it was difficult.

I saw Phillip's mother and grandmother sitting up front already. His father was not there. Phillip and I sat down next to them. I felt Phillip take my hand in his. I sat there and let myself take everything in.

"Would you like to see your parents?"

I looked over and saw the priest standing in front of me. I nodded and Phillip and I walked to the back of the church where my parents' caskets were. My heart pounded as I made my way toward them. They both looked peaceful. My father looked healthier than he had been when I had last seen him alive; his head bruise had been completely covered up by makeup, making it look as if it had never been there. My mother looked like she had whenever she would dress herself up for a party in her best dress.

I turned my face away and Phillip led me back to our seat.

I looked up as someone entered the row of our seats and saw Ian. He was wearing black slacks and a black button-down shirt. He smiled at me and sat down next to me.

"I'm really sorry," he whispered.

"Thank you."

It comforted me that he had come, even if Mathias probably wouldn't.

The funeral began, as well as the tears.

The burial took place immediately following the funeral mass. We followed the hearse in Phillip's car to the Cemetery of London where my parents were going to be buried. They had chosen their plots several years ago next to those of my father's parents. My mother's parents were buried in Scotland, so London had seemed the best idea for them.

Several minutes later, Phillip and I, along with many others, stood around the coffins. The priest began to say the final words before the caskets would be lowered into their graves. The rain had stopped during the mass, but just as the caskets were being lowered, it began again. Phillip opened an umbrella he had brought with him. Everyone quickly walked ahead and threw some dirt into each of the graves. As I did this, it all began to feel final. I looked below at the coffins of my parents once more, and then turned away.

I had said goodbye to Ian, and Phillip and I were walking away from the gathering of people.

"It was a nice funeral," Phillip said. "Your parents would be grateful."

I didn't respond to his comment. I simply nodded my head. My thoughts were racing over the last few days. As they did I remembered my last meeting with Mathias and how horrid he had been. I remembered the vision he had had and—

Lighting clapped as I remembered. Mathias had had a vision, something so horrible he wouldn't tell me. He would have told me if it had been nothing, but it had been something.

"He knew," I said aloud.

"Who knew what?" Phillip asked me.

"Mathias had a vision of the future. Before I left, on the night my parents died. He wouldn't tell me what it was. It was this. It was all this, Phillip. He knew they were going to die."

I felt Phillip's hand on my shoulder.

"Abby," he whispered.

I shrugged his hand off and turned around to face him, stepping out into the rain as I did.

"No, Phillip. Mathias knew what was going to happen and he wouldn't tell me." I felt the rain pour onto my face. My hair began to get drenched and I could feel the bun unraveling.

"Does it really matter?" Phillip asked. "What could you have done?"

"Of course, it matters!"

Lightning clapped again, and this time I could have sworn the ground rumbled as well.

"Of course, it matters Phillip," I continued, "He isn't even here. He's my father, he should have come. I hate him."

"Don't say that. Hate isn't something that is good. Hate is what led to your parents' deaths."

"I don't care. I hate him."

"This war is hate, Abby. This war started because one man used hate as a tool. He used hate to fuel people. Hate is ugly. It is horrid. Please, do not hate anyone."

"I'm sorry." The tears were coming again. "I just—I just can't do this."

My body was drenched in the rain now. My hair had come completely undone and was wet and sticking against my neck. Phillip looked like he was going to say something further, but I noticed his attention was drawn to something behind me.

I turned around, startled. A figure in a black raincoat was making its way toward us. The hood on the raincoat was pulled up, concealing the person's face behind it. The person then lifted their head, and I saw her face.

Lightning clapped again as Bessie looked up at me.

"Hello, Abigail," she said in her soft, almost childish voice.

"Bessie."

"You two know each other?" Phillip asked.

"Phillip, this is Bessie," I said. “She is an old friend of my mother’s.” I hesitated and then added, "My biological mother. Bessie, this is my fiancée, Phillip."

"It is a pleasure to meet you Phillip," Bessie responded. She then directed her attention back to me. "Abigail, I read what happened in the paper and noticed your last name and realized your parents had been killed. I'm so sorry."

For the first time in days, a small smile crept onto my face. This woman had come to honor the memory of my parents, something Mathias, who knew my parent's death would occur, had not done.

"Thank you for coming, Bessie. It really means a lot to me that you did."

"Abigail," Phillip said, "you are soaking wet."

I realized this, but did not respond to him.

"Abigail," Bessie said, "I was hoping we could talk about some things. I had hoped you would come to see me since our last meeting, but obviously great troubles have found you. I hope that by talking with you, we can work through some things. Has Mathias been appearing very off-centered and different lately?"

I nodded at these words immediately. His refusal to tell me what he had seen, his unkind words to me, and his anger that was out of control. Bessie knew what Mathias was capable of.

"Abigail, I think it would be best if we talked," Bessie said again. "Specifically, about Mathias."

"I think so too.”

I felt Phillip's hand on my shoulder.

"We should go," he said. "There's a small reception in the church hall."

"I need to talk to Bessie," I said.

"Abby, your parents only just died. Don't you think you should give yourself some time off from all of this?"

"Phillip, please," I said again.

Bessie spoke up. "Abigail, Phillip is right. You still need some time. I just wanted to make sure you knew that I was here for you. You know where to find me."

After that, Bessie retreated with her head once again bowed and walked away into the pouring rain.

"Please, don't do this."

Phillip held the steering wheel tightly. He wouldn't look at me. He only looked straight ahead.

"He's dangerous," I said. "He has been cold to me, to you. I don't trust him. I am not going to continue this relationship."

"That's fine!" Phillip shouted.

"How is it fine? An hour ago, you were upset at me for being hateful."

"I don't like the word, Abby," Phillip said. "I never have, but I do not like it even more because of this war. I fear every day that something is going to happen to you. I'm sorry for your parents, I miss them. I really do. But if something happened to you, I couldn't take it. But hate, hate is what is fueling all of this, like I said. I fear that hate is going to lead me to serve in the war. I will serve if I'm called. You don't realize how lucky we are that I haven't been called. I will go. I will go and help my country. But if I go, then I'm going to send you somewhere safe, because I need to know you are safe. But if you are going to end this relationship with your father, please do it in a way that isn't hateful. Just end it. Explain your reasons and move on. I don't want to keep going over this again and again."

"Okay," I said. I wasn't sure what else to say. I felt like he didn't give me enough credit sometimes, but I also understood what he meant. I didn't want to hate, but it felt like I should. I didn't know what to feel. I opened the car door and stepped out into the rain. We were at Big Ben. I left Phillip in the car and quickly ran inside. I hadn't grabbed the umbrella and the rain drenched me.

I took the familiar way to the underground Headquarters. Thunder clapped as the lift took me down. The room below slowly came into view and I was once again facing the hallway that would lead me to *him*.

Mathias must have heard the lift coming because he was standing at the end of the hallway, waiting for me. I didn't see Ian, and assumed he had not made it back yet. I walked slowly, but then picked up my speed as I thought about how angry I was. I tried to remember what Phillip said, but hot, burning tears fell down my cheeks. He knew. He had seen it happen. He saw them die. The idea returned to my mind that maybe Mathias had been responsible for Elisabeth's death. It was all I thought about. It was the thought that returned so frequently.

"Abigail," Mathias finally spoke, "I am truly sorry."

"You saw it. You saw it happen. Why didn't you tell me?"

"I couldn't tell you," Mathias said quietly, "you would not have understood. It was not your test to undertake. Time will test you, but it will do it through you, not through me. Time tested me and I passed the test."

I felt sickened.

"You passed the *test*?" I wanted to slap him. "How can you call it that? They were my parents! They loved me! They raised me! They aren't the questions on some test paper, they are people! They are people who died trying to keep me safe! How dare you degrade them to such a term!"

"I'm sorry. I should not have said that. Please calm down and we can discuss this. Please."

"I didn't come to discuss anything Mathias. I came to say goodbye."

"What?"

"I'm ending this. I'm sorry, but I don't trust you. I can't."

Mathias shook his head.

"Please, don't do this. I need you. Please."

Where had I heard that before? *No. You don't trust him.* That was right, I didn't trust him.

"I'm done. I cannot stay here knowing what I know. It may have been a test for you, but for me it's life. I have already seen enough here with the murder at the ball and all these notes and your cold and unfriendly attitude toward me. I don't need it anymore. It isn't healthy."

"Abigail, I have lived by myself for nineteen years. I rarely go out into the world anymore. I'm not good at being sociable."

"I don't think you ever were."

"Please, I beg of you, give me another chance."

He had shown a different side recently. He was truly trying here, I could see it on his face. *No. You don't trust him.* Did I say that? *No. You don't trust him. He lied to you, remember?* That was right, I didn't trust him. He had lied to me.

"People can change, Abigail." Mathias looked at me with pleading eyes and I realized I was making a final decision. As Phillip had said, I needed to make this decision and stick to it. *You know the decision. Leave. If you need to, you can make him pay for it later.* Make him pay for it? *He killed her, remember?* I don't know that for sure. *Yes, you do.* What was going on inside me?

"You killed her."

Did I just say that? I did. I hadn't meant to say it, but I did. What was going on?

"What?" Mathias looked confused. "Your mother, again? Why do you keep saying that? I didn't do it."

"Maybe you've just forgotten it," I said.

Why did I just say that?

Mathias put his arms on my shoulders. I shook my head.

"Are you making me say these things?"

He looked confused. I was confused.

"I didn't want to say you killed her! I thought it before, but I haven't been sure! Why am I saying these things! It's you, isn't it? You have some power over me."

"Abigail." Mathias looked concerned now. "I feel something is terribly wrong. Please stay here."

"I won't! I can't. I'm sorry. I'm *sorry*."

I took off the pocket watch necklace I had been given at the ball. I held it out to him. He wouldn't take it, so I put it on the floor and turned.

"Abigail, please don't!"

I started to run. I ran and ran. I couldn't look back. I didn't know what I was doing anymore. I didn't know if this was final. I didn't know if I was listening to Phillip. I only knew I had to get out of there. My mind was not in the right place and I needed to separate myself from this world for now. I needed to get away and think it out. I needed to be with Phillip.

I threw open the lift doors and shut them. I didn't want to turn around, but I did. Mathias was in the same spot, watching me. The lift began to rise and he was gone. My heart was racing. I had no idea what I had done. I had no idea if it was the right decision. I was the most indecisive person in the world. I had no idea if I was keeping Phillip's word. I just needed to leave.

The doors opened again and I ran. I ran down the stairs and out of Big Ben into the rain. I threw open the door to Phillip's car.

"Abby?" he said. "Abby! Please talk to me. What happened? Please say something at least!"

"I don't know," I said. I turned to him as the tears fell again. Why did I keep crying? I knew why, but why all the same? Why couldn't I have a break from this? It was one thing after another in this life and I just couldn't take it anymore. I spoke through my sobs, choking on my words. I spoke word after word. I wasn't sure if I was speaking coherently, but I just spoke what I felt. I needed to tell him how I felt. "I'm sorry Phillip. I don't know if that decision to leave was final or temporary. He seemed so upset. He really did. Maybe he is a good person and I'm a bad person. Maybe I made the wrong decision. I don't know. I'm sorry I'm so indecisive."

He looked at me for what felt like a good minute or two. Did he agree? Did he disagree? Was he really not going to say anything? I felt like it was Bridget all over again, except I was Bridget and Mathias had been me, and Phillip was the person on the sideline still not saying anything. Sometimes a person just doesn't know what to say and I think that for Phillip that was now. He just didn't know what to say and I didn't know how I felt about that.

We continued to look at each other until finally, Phillip put the car into drive.

CHAPTER TWENTY

The only place I had to stay now was Phillip's. I did not feel upset by it, but I felt like I was trapped. Two days had passed since the funeral and I found myself waking up every morning, expecting to find myself back at home with my parents. After a few minutes, I would realize my parents and home were gone. I would be upset and maybe cry before forcing myself to get out of bed and to face the world. I knew it was time to speak with Bessie and to try and find out more information from Mathias. I realized he could be dangerous, but at the same time I did not know for sure.

Before I knew it, I was showering and putting on the clothes I had been using lately to see Bessie. They were getting very ragged and rough looking, but I would use them to go through the underwater ritual without ruining good clothes.

I called for a cab and had it take me to the Tower of London. The wind blew powerfully today as I made my way through the familiar routine. I had to be extra cautious today however, since it was daytime, to make sure no one saw me jump in. It would be rather odd seeing a grown woman take a plunge into the icy water. I was sure someone would probably have a panic attack and dive in after me.

The icy plunge was even icier today, but I pushed myself through it. I was getting rather good at swimming. If I was ever in a terrible situation that involved water, I was sure I would be better off than I had before.

I lifted myself out into the familiar room and found where I had left an old gray dress. I quickly slipped out of the wet dripping clothes and into the dryer ones, taking the dry towel I had left as well and wiping my hair. I then took out my mother's pocket watch and used it to gain entrance. While I had parted with my own pocket watch, I would never part with my mother's.

I could smell the fire before I saw it, so I knew Bessie was there. My heart warmed a little when I realized she was probably coming here daily to see if I came. I knew she stayed here, waiting for me, wanting to give me answers.

"Abby."

Bessie stood in the empty room by the fire. She had her hands folded in front of her. I smiled at her and she smiled back.

"Are you here every day?" I asked. "I hate to keep you here, even if I don't show up. Maybe it is time we had another form of communication?"

"Do not be stressed, love," she answered. "I have a connection with you. Your mother willed me to protect you and protect you I will."

"Is it a power?"

"I feel it is more of a motherly instinct," Bessie replied. "I understand I am not your mother, but I believe we are given these instincts." She walked forward, until she stood in front of me. I felt safe with her. She truly was a kind, honorable person. She reached up and tucked a lock of my hair behind my ear. "I believe every woman has them, as will you too one day. I believe my connection with your mother, further strengthens that."

"Will you tell me about her?"

A smile crept onto Bessie's face and she nodded.

"Do you trust me?" Bessie asked.

I looked away. Did I?

"No," I replied. The answer came from my heart. I did not trust her, but it was not out of suspicion or inclination. I just was not there yet. It took me a while to trust people. I did not trust Phillip for a while when we had met. However, I also knew that it was my part of the bargain to keep going, to keep spending time with people, and eventually, you would trust them. I explained that to Bessie to and that it was coming. I was almost there. I was close.

Bessie smiled again. "I completely understand," she said. "I think you trust certain aspects, like coming here, but you do not trust everything and that is fine. However, I hope you are closer than you think, because that would be wonderful. I do want you to know that I trust you, and I would like to leave this place today for a walk. I would be delighted to tell you about Elisabeth."

I nodded. Bessie put out the fire and we left the way we came.

Unfortunately for Bessie, she did not have that second pair of clothes. As such, we were forced to call a cab. The driver gave us the most questioning look. I realized how odd it must be to see two women, completely drenched from head to toe, sitting in the back of your car.

"I guess this is not a walk after all," Bessie laughed aloud.

I laughed with her.

"It's okay," I reasoned with her. "I wasn't too excited about walking through London drenched anyway."

"Where too, Miss?"

Bessie told the driver to take us to the West End. She said she was going to take me to her flat.

Bessie's flat was small, but it felt like a home to me. The walls were white, but immediately upon walking in you were greeted to pictures upon pictures of family and friends.

"I truly am a horrible person in photographs," Bessie said. "There I am with my father. You can tell I was not too excited about being in the photograph."

The photos were very family oriented. I realized she did not have many friends in her life then, and I truly felt sorry for her.

"Do you have any photographs of my mother?"

Bessie took a quick intake of breath and responded haphazardly.

"I burned them!"

I had been looking at a picture of what looked like Bessie and her father together again when she said that. I turned to her quickly. Why would she burn them? Bessie looked confused. She turned away from me and walked into another room.

I hugged myself. It was rather cold in here. Why would Bessie burn the photos? I guess that would be similar to my father not wanting to keep any possessions of my mother, but still. Bessie had been gone five minutes when I decided to go and follow her. I opened the door of what I assumed was her bedroom. The room was dark, but I saw a light on in the crack of another door—I assumed it was the bathroom.

My attention turned to the disorganization of the room. Papers were everywhere. Newspaper articles were taped to the walls. It was the picture of Mathias and Bessie, framed, which drew my attention. The frame was sitting on a nightstand by Bessie's bed. I walked over and picked it up. Bessie was plain as usual, and rather cold looking. She stood next to my father and had a half smile on her face. My father smiled however, a wide, open smile. He looked handsome and well kept in a suit, whereas Bessie wore a simple black dress. I realized this must have been from when they dated. The door to the bathroom opened.

Bessie stood in the doorway and looked at me with the frame in my hand. She reached forward and snatched it so fast I didn't have time to be surprised.

"Abigail," Bessie said, "I appreciate your concern, but please wait around in the living area."

"I'm sorry."

I walked out of the room. I wondered why it was unkempt. Did she really need all of the newspapers lying around?

It was another few moments before the door to Bessie's room opened and she stepped into the living area again, closing the door to the dark room behind her.

"I apologize," she said, taking a seat on the couch. "I didn't want to keep any of the photographs of your mother. It was too hard."

"Was that photograph of you and Mathias when you were engaged?"

Bessie looked up at me. Her look was quizzical. What was she thinking?

"It was actually taken at your mother's wedding," she finally said. "Your mother was supposed to be in it, but she had to take a photograph with the flower girl who was bound and determined to have a photograph taken. I suppose I kept it because it reminds me of her without having to see her. It also reminds me what Mathias did to her."

My heart dropped. What Mathias did to her?

"What do you mean?"

"He was not kind to her," Bessie answered. "I'm sure he is cold to you. He was cold to her as well. If you are ready, I can tell you..."

"No."

"Abigail," Bessie said, "I really think you need to know the truth."

"I do," I replied, "But not now. Not yet. I'm still overcoming the death of my parents, and I need to hold onto reality right now. It is hard to live in both worlds."

"It doesn't have to be both worlds," Bessie replied. "It can be just the one. But I want you to know you can trust me. I will be here, when you are ready, which I *know* will be very soon."

She said it like she did know. Like she could feel my trust already showing. But it wasn't there. It wasn't there yet.

"I think I'm going to go," I said. "I appreciate everything. I'll be in contact."

"Please do."

Bessie stood and opened the door of her flat. I smiled at her and then turned away. It was odd, but I somehow felt like she was annoyed with me. Was she upset I didn't trust her? I felt her hand on my shoulder and turned around.

"I'm here for you," she said. The smile had returned to her face. I smiled back and then walked away.

I had not been to my classes since before my parents died; my professors had understandably given me some time off. Instead of going to class, or learning from Mathias, I spent my days on Phillip's divan.

The tears fell from my eyes. I was lying on Phillip's divan, my face down on the cushions. The cushions were being drowned by my never-ending tears. I did this every day since the funeral. I cried. I continued to cry when Phillip left for work, and I composed myself by the time he got home. I took a shower, washed my hair, and washed out my eyes. I looked as good as new. I didn't look depressed or upset. I got it together, for him. I failed today. I heard the door of the flat open and close before I even had time to do anything.

"Abigail?"

I heard Phillip set something down on the table and walk to my side. He knelt down by the couch and I felt his rough hand touch my cheek.

"Abby," he spoke softly, "my Abby. What is wrong?"

I realized how terribly I was shaking. The tears poured from my eyes. He had literally come in during what I now called "the worst fit."

I kept my face planted down and continued to cry. I felt him carefully turn my face to his however.

"Did you have a bad day?" he asked me. "It's okay to cry, Abby. It is."

How could I lie to him? How could I not tell him everything? How could I lie to Bridget? How could I not tell her everything? I realized it was time to tell everything. No matter how hard it was, I had to tell the people I loved everything. They needed to know.

"I've been crying every day," I admitted. "I just got myself together in time with your schedule."

Before I knew it, Phillip had stood up and lifted me up in his arms. We were both lying on the couch now and he was holding me tightly. My head was lying just under his chin.

"Listen to me," he said softly, staring up the ceiling. I closed my eyes and listened to his heart. *Beat. Beat. Beat.* "You do not have to compose yourself for anything. If you need to cry, you cry. If you need to laugh, you laugh. If you need to shout, you shout. If you need to speak, you speak! Be yourself. I won't judge you. The only thing I'll ever do when you cry, when you laugh, when you shout, and when you speak, is love you. I will always love you."

His words lifted something up inside of me. His words reached down into a pit of darkness and pulled me out. His words gave me life. I felt them in my heart. I knew them to be true.

"Abigail," he said. "You have always listened to my jokes, to my opinions, and to my criticisms with respect. Yes, I may see the look on your face here and there and yes you might have your own opinion in that righteous head of yours, but you never condescend to me. You never judge me. How could I judge you? I love you."

No more secrets. I told him about today, I told him about going to see Bessie as well as the times before that in more detail. I told him everything about Mathias. Everything.

"When I'm with you," he confided in me, long after the sun had gone down and the apartment was dark, "I feel like I can leave this world. I feel like I can leave this war. When I hold you, I feel like the suffering leaves the world. I will always protect you first, even if you try to protect me first. If someone were to try and hurt you, they would have to go through me over and over again. But I feel like you protect me too. You keep me in the light. You protect me from the darkness of this world."

We lay there for what felt like hours, but in his arms, I felt safe. In his arms, I left reality too. There was no Hitler. There was no death. There was no Timekeeping. There was no war, out there or in me.

CHAPTER TWENTY-ONE

My eyes cracked open. Phillip's side of the bed was empty and made up. I sat up in his bed and looked around the room. Some clothes were scattered across the floor, but the bathroom door was open and the lights were off. I forced myself to get out of the comfort of the bed and walk into the living room. He must have carried me to bed late in the night and slept on the couch. Phillip was not in the living room though, and his coat was gone. I figured he had left for the library. I turned to walk back to the bedroom to get ready, but there was a knock at the door.

I looked over at the door. A fear went through me that it could be Mathias, but I walked over and looked out the peephole. It was Bridget. I unbolted the deadbolt and opened the door.

"Why are you here?"

I didn't care if it sounded rude. It was the only question that went through my mind and actually came out in words when I opened the door. Bridget looked like she might snap at me, but I saw her think about it by her facial expressions and control the urge.

"I'm here to talk to you and be your friend. Can I come in?"

"A friend wouldn't have stopped talking to me in the first place," I told her. "A friend would have come to the funeral of my parents who were practically her parents to begin with."

"A friend also doesn't lie to her friend," Bridget counteracted.

I rolled my eyes and threw my hands up in the air. I walked over to the couch, leaving the door open for Bridget to come in. She followed shortly and shut the door behind her. I stared out the window, but I felt her presence when she sat down next to me at the couch.

"I didn't trust you," I said. "I'm just going to be honest and tell you that. If you find out one day that you are someone with some kind of supernatural ability, would you tell everyone you knew? I didn't even tell my mum, and she's gone now. She loved me no matter who or what I was. I know that."

"Well, I wished you could have," Bridget replied, "because I think that is what broke our friendship."

"If a friendship was true and strong it could be fixed."

Bridget grabbed my shoulder and tuned me to look at her. Her face was red and blotchy, and I saw the tears streaming down them.

"Do you honestly believe that?" she whispered vehemently. "Do you truly think that a friendship can be repaired? Are your questioning whether we even had a friendship?"

"'Yes' would be the answer to all of those questions," I responded.

I stood up and walked over to the kitchen sink. I began to scrub the dishes from last night, violently.

"How could you say that?"

My head turned. Bridget was standing up. She was shaking and looked like she was losing control.

"After everything we have done for each other!" she shouted. "After everything we've been through, you are going to question the validity of our friendship? Are you being honest with me Abby?"

My hand flung out from the sink and I forgot the dish was in it. I let go of it and it flung across the room and hit the wall; shattering into pieces.

"I am being honest with you, Bridget!" I shouted at her. "I don't know what is happening to us. I don't know if we were truly friends. I'm just trying to find out myself here. All of my life I have been in the dark. I don't know who I am. I just want to know who I am."

"You are Abigail Jordan," Bridget retorted back at me, "daughter of Dean and Annette Jordan. You grew up with me on Barton street. You are a strong and practicing Catholic. You attended school with me all your life, including Birkbeck now. You are in love with Phillip Hughes and are going to marry him. That is who are you are, Abby. I don't understand why you've been looking for yourself when you were here the whole time."

"You don't understand," I responded, "everyone has a name, a family, and someone they love. But everyone also has something in life that makes it life for them. They have a journey of self-discovery. I'm on that journey, I'm trying to grow up."

"But you are losing everyone you care about in the process," Bridget replied. "How close were you to your parents these past few months? How close have you been to Phillip? More importantly, how close have you been to this little mission of yours? You are forgetting about everything that is already here so that you can find what isn't. I wouldn't be surprised if karma killed your parents."

She immediately looked guilty for saying it, but before I knew it I was across the room and I had slapped her across the face. She went straight for the door, but before she walked out, she turned and spoke one last time.

"I *will* be there for you," she said, "when whatever it is you are searching for is found, or even if it's not. I just want you to be honest with me. I feel like you are trying to find someone that hasn't been lost."

She left, closing the door as she did. I fell back onto the couch and cried.

Hours later, I was still on the couch and it was dark again when I opened my eyes. I could hear the door of the flat opening, but I did not bother to look up and see who it was. I wondered why people did terrible things; sometimes the most terrible to the people that they loved the most. It was a strange concept to me. Never in my lifetime would I have thought that I would have slapped my closest friend. But never in my life had I thought she would have said some of the things that she had said.

"Abigail, what in the hell is going on?"

I finally turned my head toward the door at the sound of Phillip's voice. It was open and he was standing in the doorway, looking around the room in confusion. I realized the broken dish was still on the floor in pieces. There was a nice dent in the wall where it had hit. My face was probably streaked with tears and my eyes were most likely redder then, when my cheeks flushed.

Phillip shut the door and walked over to the couch. He looked down at me for a moment, and then took a seat next to me. I laid my head back down into his lap and closed my eyes. I took in his familiar, clean scent. I let it fill my senses. I felt his hand on the back of my head, his fingers running through my hair. I wished this moment could last forever. It felt like one of those precious moments. It felt like a moment that was so simple, yet so elegant.

"What happened, Abby?" Phillip whispered. His voice was gentle.

"Bridget happened."

Those two words were all I said to him. He didn't ask me another question. We were close enough now that he could understand without a detailed account of what happened. He understood my pain and he understood Bridget's pain.

I looked up into Phillip's eyes. He continued to run his fingers through my hair.

"Is it possible that I'm just a horrible person?" I asked him.

Phillip lifted me out of his lap and then slipped off the couch. He knelt down next to my knees and took my hands in his. I was looking away, but I felt his eyes watching me and I turned mine to look into his.

"I love you, Abigail Jordan," Phillip whispered to me. "And in my love for you, I have come to realize how much of a delicate, kind, and passionate person you are. You're only human."

A single tear fell down the side of my cheek. I didn't try to wipe it away. I let it fall.

"Do you think I've lost my way?"

Phillip did not answer for a moment. He continued to gaze into my eyes. It was as if he was looking for the answer, but I knew he knew it.

"Perhaps," he responded, "but that doesn't mean you're on the wrong path. Maybe you've just changed direction. There is still so much to understand and discover."

"Will she forgive me?"

It was the most important question. If no, I felt like I would break.

"I know she will," Phillip finally answered.

I pulled him up off his knees by his shirt. He lay on top of me and we kissed. The warmth and passion of the moment consumed me. His hands held me tight and I curled my fingers through his hair. It was our moment.

Phillip finally stopped kissing me and we both took a breath. I brought my hand up to his cheek and touched it. His skin was soft and warm against the palm of my hand. It was the vibrancy of his life.

"I'm ready to end this," I whispered.

"What do you mean?" he asked.

"Bessie promised me she had the truth," I said, "I've only been putting it off because I've been afraid. I'm ready for it. Maybe it will put me in a different direction again. I want to go now. I want to go with you."

Phillip nodded and then pressed his lips to mine again.

I stared out the window of Phillip's car as we made our way to the West End and Bessie's flat. I had to admit I didn't like the building she lived in. It was more rundown than where Phillip lived. We took the lift up to the floor that Bessie lived on and stepped out into the dreary, dark hallway. It was darker than usual; more lights had gone out since my last visit. I found flat number thirty and knocked on the door. My hand clenched Phillip's tightly. He stood by my side and was ready to take this next step with me. The door opened and the fragile-looking Bessie stood on the other side.

Her face lit up when she saw me, and a warm smile spread across it.

"Abigail. I'm so glad you've come."

Bessie pulled the door open wider and stepped out of the doorway.

"Please, come in."

Phillip and I walked over the threshold and into the flat. We followed her over to the couch and chairs by the window. I sat next to Phillip on the couch and Bessie took her seat in her chair. She crossed her legs and placed her hands on them, waiting for me to speak.

"Bessie," I said, "I'm ready to know everything. I know I've been skeptical and I haven't been completely accepting, but I'm ready now. Everything you have told me about Mathias appears to be true and it sickens me. But I need to know what happened to my mother. Maybe the one thing that keeps Mathias from being the good person he can be, is because he lost her."

The look on Bessie's face went from a smile to one of pain. She looked down at her feet and moved them a little, uncrossing her legs. Finally, she looked back up at me.

"Abigail. I'm sorry you've come to that conclusion. Because what I have to tell you is far from it. It is the reason I have waited so long. You truly had to be ready to accept this knowledge."

A feeling of dread pooled in my stomach. But I had come too far to run away now.

"I'm ready."

Bessie took a deep breath and then spoke.

"As I've told you before, your mother was my closest friend when Mathias and I broke up. When I agreed to introduce your mother to Mathias, it was with a heavy heart that I did. I could not even begin to imagine the horrors that would unfold within their relationship." Bessie paused and looked out the window of the flat. Her eyes seemed transfixed on the sky, until finally she looked back at me.

"The two of them became very close," she continued. "However, your mother soon confided in me the same problems I had seen in him. However, she was different than me. She liked to help people and she tried to help Mathias, but I soon came to understand he suffered from a mental disorder; I believe they call it schizophrenia. It would explain many of his outbursts at you, but it appears they are rather minimal toward you. I figure he has been controlling it. However, the truth is that Mathias also had a personality disorder. He began to send your mother threatening messages she believed were from another person. He used a completely different handwriting and everything. Finally, on the day your mother gave birth, they both met on the bridge, and it was to her horror that she realized it was Mathias. I followed her to the Bridge that night. He had a violent outburst with your mother when she tried to help him and he...he hung her from the bridge. He killed her."

My heart was racing. I could barely control my breathing. I stood upright and began to pace around the room. This was not what I was expecting. I thought Mathias maybe had some anger issues, but he disguised everything so well. He seemed genuinely concerned about how my mother had died; yet he had been the one to kill her. His disguise had been misleading, but not misleading enough. If I had not come into contact with Bessie, I feared what could have happened.

"Your mother left you the letter that said your father was dead because she didn't want you to fall into his clutches," Bessie continued, "which is why I have been watching you as much as possible. I knew you would seek out the truth of what happened to your mother. I knew you would be in danger around Mathias. It is why I have watched over you these past few months. Abigail, I'm sorry."

Phillip stood up and pulled me to him. I tried to break away, but he held me as the tears poured from my eyes. My father had murdered my mother. Everything had been a lie from him, as I had suspected all along. He was what I had feared of myself only months ago. He had a mental disorder. I couldn't even begin to fathom this knowledge.

"Let's go home, Abby," Phillip whispered.

I stepped away from him and screamed. Bessie stood up and walked toward me, but didn't try to comfort me.

“Why didn’t you go to the police, Bessie?” I asked.

She looked at me for a moment and then simply said, “I was afraid.”

"I want to go there," I said, "I want to confront him. He needs to be held responsible. We can report him to the council."

Phillip shook his head at me. "Abby, you are not thinking properly. We need to stay away from him, not fuel his desires."

"What about Ian?" I asked. "We at least need to go for him. He should know."

Bessie held up her hand.

"Abigail is right," Bessie said. "Mathias needs to be held responsible for what he has done. He is not suitable to be a Timekeeper. He has disguised his problems and actions well, but it is time we bring them to light. I have always feared him since I found out who he truly was, but with your help now, Abigail, we can expose him together. Abigail, will you take me to the Headquarters. I can call on the councilors and we can take care of this. And the boy, Ian—he can learn the truth about his teacher."

Phillip looked at me and I looked at him. I had to do it. He knew I had to. We had to resolve this. I had to do this for my mother. Her murderer had to be brought to the light.

"Only if Phillip can come," I said. "Mathias said he couldn't be trusted there."

Bessie laughed.

"That is only the talk of Mathias," she responded. "He likes to think he's powerful with his rules. Let's go."

Bessie grabbed a coat from her closet and we followed her out of the flat. A fear of the unknown beat within my chest. But I knew that the truth had to be brought to the light.

It was almost dark out as we made our way to Big Ben.

"Big Ben," Bessie said. "I'd heard rumors it was here. But it is still well-hidden."

The three of us got out of Phillip's car and made our way into the basement. I took out my key and unlocked the entrance to the lift.

"Abby," Phillip said, "are you sure you want me there?"

I could tell Phillip was nervous. I was about to reveal a part of me that he had only heard about for the past few months. Up until now, he had only my word as proof for what I was. Now, he would see everything.

"It's time you know what I am," I said. A smile was on my face. "I know you believe me, but I'm ready to show you. I want you there."

The three of us stepped into the lift and it began to descend downward. Darkness was upon us and then the lift doors opened and we all stepped out. Bessie leaned over me and whispered into my ear.

"Maybe you two should go first?" she suggested. "If I come in, out of the blue, it might be too much of a shock. I don't want him to have a violent outburst."

I nodded and Bessie lagged behind by the lift. She would be able to hear us down the hall talking to Mathias. Phillip followed me and we made our way to the circular room. Mathias was at his desk as usual, but his head was back in his chair and his eyes were closed. I realized he was asleep. He wouldn't have heard us come in.

Ian walked out of a side door and his expression changed quickly. It went from a normal expression, to shock at seeing Phillip, and then outrage.

"Abigail," he said, "what are you doing? He can't be in here."

"I'm here to settle who killed my mother."

Before Ian could say anything else, I shouted.

"Mathias!"

He jumped in his chair and then looked upright at me. He looked normal at first, but then his face turned bright red when he saw Phillip. He stood up.

"What the hell do you think you are doing? Get him out of here now! How dare you Abigail! Ian, did you know about this?"

Mathias pointed a long finger at Phillip, but neither of us budged.

"I'm done playing your games and mind-tricks, Mathias," I said. "Phillip has come to help me. I am here so that you can be held responsible for your crimes."

"What the hell are you talking about?"

I couldn't help it anymore. There was so much anger that was building up inside me that I started to scream.

"Stop lying to me! You killed my mother! You killed your wife! You killed Elisabeth!"

"Why are you still on about that?" He didn't shout at me. His voice was low and quiet.

"Because I know it is the truth," I responded. "You stalked her and sent her those vicious letters. You have a mental disorder and you need help."

Mathias began to laugh. Ian stood stock still at my side. I think my accusations must have left him speechless.

"Abigail, are you listening to yourself?" he said. "Why would you insist on any of this? What letters are you talking about? Is this because I have decided to be your teacher rather than your father? Is this some way of getting back at me?"

"Don't you remember the pearls?" I asked him. "And your angry outburst? You were angry because I had gone to the old Headquarters and because I had found something of my mother's."

"Those weren't your mother's," Mathias said to me. "I took everything of hers when I left. Except for the furniture, I took all of her clothes and all of her jewelry."

"Stop lying! All of my mother's stuff was there. You left it all. You killed her! I've learned the truth from someone other than you."

"Whom have you learned the truth from?" Mathias retorted. He pointed a finger at Phillip again. "Was it him? Has he been filling your head with these ideas?"

"She learned the truth from me."

My body went rigid. Bessie's voice sounded in my ears and I turned around to look at her standing in the entrance of the room. I looked back at Mathias. A look of utter horror I had never seen was on his face.

"Bessie," was all he said.

Bessie walked further into the room and stopped just behind me.

"Hello, Mathias. Long time, no see."

Mathias appeared to regain his composure and looked back at me.

"Abigail, I don't know what ideas this woman has been telling you, but it's all lies."

"That's just what he wants you to think," Bessie whispered to me. "He's lying."

"Bessie, shut up!" Mathias shouted. "Abigail, I'm your father. She is telling you lies. You must not believe them. She isn't even British; she's American and yet here she is, disguising her accent."

"If *she* is lying, then why did my mother leave me a note saying to stay away from this world, saying that you were dead?"

A look of confusion dawned on his face and I pulled the letter my mother had given me that had been left at the orphanage and walked up to him, thrusting it out. He took it and read over it, and sadness appeared on his face.

"Abigail." His voice was sad, dead. "I don't know why your mother would say this. I only ever loved her." He looked up at me and for the first time since I had met him, he was beginning to cry.

"It's because she knew you were dangerous, and as for Bessie, she's been kinder to me than you ever have. She was there when my mother and father died. She was there for me. Where were you? She comforted me. Why would I believe you?"

The tears streamed down his face. He was shaking. "Abigail, please listen to me. I'm telling you the truth. I'm sorry for not being there for you, but I'm telling you the truth. Who do you trust?"

The word trust caught me. I thought about the people that cared about me and did things for me. I thought about the good people in my life as well as the bad. But who did I trust? I continued to think. It felt like this question was the biggest question of them all. It all came down to this.

"I trust Bessie," I answered.

"And that's all I needed," Bessie whispered.

I felt a large blow to the side of my head. I heard shouts from Phillip, Mathias, and Ian as I went down. My head struck the hard marble floor and my vision was blurred.

"What are you doing?"

It was a man's voice. Phillip's. After that, I faded off.

***

My eyes opened. I was sitting behind Mathias' desk. My hands were tied behind my back with what felt like a pillowcase, from the couch I assumed. My feet were tied at the bottom. I looked over at the couch and Mathias was there. He appeared to have just woken up from being unconscious. His hands and feet were also tied. Ian was tied up next to him. I could not see Phillip anywhere, but in the middle of the room stood Bessie.

Bessie looked different than before. It looked like her body was almost glowing and she actually appeared more beautiful than she had before.

"Wakey, wakey, little girl," Bessie said. Her eyes were concentrated on me. She was now speaking in an American accent, very sarcastic and flamboyant. "You know my father always said I had a knack for acting. What do you think?"

The feeling of dread I had experienced earlier was suddenly intensified. Acting? It had all been an act. I knew it had all been an act, but I thought the act had been performed by Mathias. But it had been performed by Bessie. I looked over at Mathias. His head was down.

"What's the matter, Mathias?" Bessie said. She walked over and lifted his chin up to look at her. Then she wrapped her legs around his waist on the couch and began to kiss him. He shook his body violently and tried to pull away, but she held her grip until she was finished. She got off the couch and stood up straight, her hands on her hips.

"Oh my," Bessie said, "I remember that feeling. I have to admit

Mathias; you haven't lost your touch. Have you been shacking up these past twenty years? Or do you still yearn for Elisabeth? Let me tell you, she yearned for you when I pushed her body off that bridge."

Bessie cackled and I felt anger go through my body.

"You lied to me!" I shouted.

Bessie turned and walked toward me. She bent down so she was eye level with me.

"It isn't my fault you are the most pathetic excuse for a woman," Bessie said. "Seriously darling, you need to develop a thicker skin. Then again, you were the outcome of reproduction between Mathias Benedict and Elisabeth Callaghan. You really cannot expect too much from that mating."

"Bessie, shut the hell up!" Mathias spat at her.

Bessie turned and faced Mathias.

"Why don't you shut the hell up?" She extended her arm and pointed at Mathias. He began to scream in agony and I screamed as well. His skin began to wither into that of an eighty-year-old mans. Finally, Bessie lowered her arm, and he was suddenly his own age again.

"You see, Mathias?" Bessie asked. "Do you see now what your precious daughter has done? Do you see the formula?"

"What are you muttering about now Bessie?" Mathias asked.

"Let's run through the details, shall we?" Bessie announced. She began to pace around the room like a professor that was lecturing. "First off, I killed a Timekeeper, your wife, her mother."

"Elisabeth was not a Timekeeper, Bessie," Mathias said. "Sorry to inform—"

It was me that cut him off.

"She was," I said. Mathias looked at me, his eyebrow going up in questioning. "She was an original Timekeeper. The stories are true." He continued to simply stare at me.

"Indeed, they are," Bessie said. "Do you see, Mathias? Your sweet little Elisabeth was a very secret person of her own. What you don't realize is that I was her midwife. I tricked her, just as I tricked your daughter. Finally, it was on the Tower Bridge that I realized I didn't need you anymore. I originally wanted you back, but I realized there were more powerful things I could have. So, I killed her. Later on, I gave up my soul to the forces of evil and finally, tonight, your daughter finished the equation."

"I trusted you," I said quietly. I hung my head in shame.

"Exactly," Bessie said, "and now I possess the forbidden powers!"

Bessie walked toward me and grabbed me by the shirt. She pulled me up and untied my hands and feet and then she threw me hard to the floor. My head struck the marble again and this time I felt blood pouring from my nose.

"This should take care of you until I return," Bessie said.

She placed her palm on my forehead and my vision went dark.

CHAPTER TWENTY-TWO

A little while later, I came to again. My mind was racing. What I had a done? I had brought a murderer into the Headquarters of the Timekeepers. I had revealed the secrets my mother tried to keep from this woman so we could be safe from her. I had allowed myself to fall into this ploy of trying to find out what happened to my mother instead of realizing that whatever happened to her had been done to protect me, as well as my father. Finally, I had given a Timekeeper the ability to actually gain the forbidden powers. I felt horrible. I felt like a waste. What was the point of learning everything I had learned? I had let my judgment be clouded by lies.

As I pushed myself up off the cold marble floor, I saw the blood. Was it my blood? Was it Mathias'? I reached up to my head and touched it. It felt wet and sticky.

Standing up, I looked around. The room was dark. The fire was out. Mathias was gone. Ian was gone. Where did she take them? Why didn't she take me?

"Phillip!"

I screamed out his name. I knew he was here. He had to be. She wouldn't take him too, would she? There was no response.

I walked down the long, narrow hallway. Without the roar of the fire going, or the lights on, the hallway was very creepy and cold. Someone could be hiding in the shadows, watching me. The feeling was eerie.

Thump.

I turned my head. What was that sound?

Thump.

The thumping noise was coming from the closet door at the end of the hallway. I ran toward it and pulled open the door to find Phillip tied up and gagged. He had been banging the door with his feet.

I bent down and undid the gag and untied him.

"What happened to you?" I asked.

"She got me with those powers," he said. "Abigail, when the shock of her power hit me, I could feel the hate. I could feel it. I don't know how. I never went to feel it again though."

I pulled him up and he drew me into his arms. We sat there like that for a moment until I realized she had Mathias and Ian.

"We need to figure out where they went," I told him. "She has Mathias and Ian. I need to save them. I have to. You and he are the only people I've got left."

"I heard her say something about the Tower Bridge as she was leaving with them."

"How did she get them to go with her?"

"Abby, it was like she could manipulate them. Make them do what she wanted."

A feeling of terror leaped inside me. She was returning to the location where she had murdered my mother. She was going to take them to the place where she had left my mother's lifeless body hanging for the world to see. She disgusted me. She destroyed the family I could have had.

"Let's go," I said.

The night was cold, and the coldness was flowing inside my heart. I felt like was I turning into ice from the coldness. I didn't know how this night would end. Would I lose Mathias now, in the process of everything I had already lost?

Phillip drove as fast as he could. It was fairly late out, so traffic wasn't too bad, but we also didn't want to attract too much attention by racing in the streets. We finally made it near the Tower Bridge. Phillip parked the car away from the bridge so Bessie wouldn't know we had arrived. We quietly made our way up to the bridge. Mathias, Bessie, and Ian were not there. I looked up toward the walkway and pointed at it. Phillip understood. The walkway was closed to the public, but I had no doubt Bessie had taken Mathias and Ian up there to die.

"Abby..."

I turned and saw Ian slumped against a pole. He was easily concealed in the darkness, which was why we had missed him. I ran to him and bent down.

"Ian, did she hurt you?"

He shook his head.

"The forbidden powers," he said. "When she manipulated me, it weakened me. But it obviously didn't weaken you. It should have left you unconscious until she undid it. If your mother was an original Timekeeper, like you say, you are immune to the forbidden powers. You are dangerous in their eyes."

"Phillip and I are going to go up to the top," I said. "We'll be back for you."

He nodded and Phillip and I turned and made our way up the stairs.

Mathias and Bessie were in the middle of the walkway. Other than the two of them, the bridge was completely quiet and no one was in sight. Was it because of Bessie? Or was it because it was a calm late night?

Phillip and I moved up closer to the two of them, so that we could hear what was going on.

"Isn't this a sight?" Bessie asked. She immediately cackled loudly. Her voice was shrill in the night sky and sent another wave of iciness down the insides of my body.

"What is it Bessie?" Mathias responded. "Do you take pride in watching me stand on the place of my death?"

"You won't be dying right away Mathias dear," Bessie responded. "It will be rather slow and painful. To make up for the years of my life that were wasted away."

"Now Bessie, that's a little unfair, don't you think? You had every right to spend your life the way you wanted. If you decided to obsess over me, that was your choice."

Bessie suddenly screamed. The scream was anger and fury. It was hate. It was evil.

"You destroyed me, you pathetic bastard!" Bessie's voice was as shrill as the feeling of the cold night. "You will die in the same place your slut of a wife did."

Mathias responded, but this time his voice was cold.

"Don't you dare say another word about her."

I carefully looked around the pole that Phillip and I were trying to hide behind. Bessie strutted to Mathias and took his chin in her fingers.

"What's the matter, Mathias?" she said, a smile creeping on her face. "Did I strike a tender heart cord? I think it is time we share a little story. Oh, where to begin? It is quite an entertaining story."

She began to dance and parade around like a little girl. She clapped her hands together. I felt sick. She was more than evil, she was disturbed and twisted. She had problems, real problems.

"The story begins with a man named Mathias and a woman named Bessie," Bessie began. "These two came back to England from America together. Mathias was there, studying with the American Timekeeper. They met and became a couple. But then the man named Mathias discarded Bessie." Bessie slapped Mathias across the face. "Apparently, Bessie had too much emotional baggage for Mathias to control." Bessie took out a pocketknife from her dress pocket and made a quick slash across Mathias' cheek. I heard him grunt and try to control his reaction to the cut. "Well, then Mathias met Elisabeth and Bessie became rather upset over this. Mathias threw Bessie out of his life for good, but oh, she was watching. You see, Bessie was secretly planning to find out the truth about Elisabeth. She knew the blonde beauty wasn't all she claimed to be. So, Bessie began to sneak back in to Mathias and Elisabeth's old

Headquarters..." Bessie began to smile. "They really should have moved. Bessie began to spy on them."

"You little—" Mathias tried to say, but Bessie put her hand over his mouth.

"Now, now," she said, continuing to laugh maniacally, "don't interrupt the storyteller. Anyway, Bessie found out one of Elisabeth's secrets and began to send her threatening letters. She didn't know it was Bessie, of course. So, when Elisabeth became pregnant, Bessie became her midwife. You see, if only you had confided in Elisabeth who Bessie was and what she looked like, then maybe Elisabeth would have been smart enough to know that Bessie was up to no good." Bessie began to parade around again. She twirled in her dress and continued to laugh.

Mathias looked confused.

"After I'd poisoned her against you, she had her baby away from you," Bessie said, "but then she realized that Bessie wanted the child and the little bitch ran from us. She fled with the newborn in her arms and hid her from us."

The word "us" kept replaying over and over in my mind. Was there someone other than Bessie I should fear?

"Bessie tracked Elisabeth down to the Tower Bridge, Bessie continued. "Bessie knew Elisabeth must have hidden the child. In her rage, Bessie killed Elisabeth and told her the plan had failed. Now, wasn't that a wonderful story?"

"Why didn't you kill Abigail?" Mathias asked.

"Oh, I have further uses for her," Bessie responded. "You see that girl is going to be one powerful Timekeeper and I plan to use her to my advantage."

"What do you mean?"

"I think I've answered enough questions for you already," Bessie responded. "Story time is over, now it's time to play!"

Bessie raised her hand and the energy of time began to flow from it again. She raised it out over the bridge and I was blinded as everything was exposed to the light of this power. The power extended over the Thames, lighting up the water in the process. The water was glowing—it was being controlled by her energy. I would hate to fall into that water right now.

"I can use time's energy to make the elements react," Bessie told Mathias. "That water down there is now very dangerous. Imagine it like this—it is as if a thousand lightning bolts are striking the water at this moment. That is what the electrocution will feel like when I drop you."

"You are going to electrocute me, Bessie? Mathias reiterated.

"Oh, don't worry Mathias," Bessie said. "First, I'm going to make you suffer, just like I did to your wife."

She raised her hand and more energy extended from it, causing Mathias to wriggle in pain. He screamed in fury and agony. I could not take it any longer. I ran out.

"Abigail!" Phillip yelled, but it was too late.

"Stop it!" I screamed.

Bessie stopped and turned toward me. A look of surprise was on her face.

"How extraordinary," Bessie said. "The energy I used should have kept you unconscious until I returned. Obviously, you are immune to most of its effects."

She raised her hand and struck me with the energy. My whole body was on fire. I fell to my knees and began to scream.

"Not completely immune, though."

Mathias yelled and scrambled to his knees. He ran at Bessie from behind and clasped his hands over her eyes—clawing with his nails. Bessie screamed a loud shrieking scream.

Bessie grabbed Mathias' hands and energy radiated from hers. The energy shocked Mathias and he screamed and blasted backward off his feet. He flew across the long walkway to the other end. Bessie cackled.

"Don't touch me, Mathias Benedict!" she screamed. "I am more powerful than you now!"

Phillip ran forward and pulled me to my feet. Bessie turned around just then and raised her hand again. Phillip froze next to me, and then uttered a sound of pure pain.

"What's wrong, Phil?" Bessie shrieked. "Cat got your tongue? Or is it aging? You see, with the forbidden powers, I can increase or decrease the effects of aging. Phillip's body is reacting to the fast-moving effects of growing old. Quite the power."

I ran forward and pushed Bessie with all my might. The two of us tumbled to the floor of the walkway. Bessie rolled on top of me and grasped my throat with her hands. She began to choke me and my breathing began to slow. I saw Phillip's hands clasp Bessie's throat and she shrieked. He pulled her off of me and she grabbed his arm—twisting it. Phillip howled in pain. Mathias came out of nowhere and punched Bessie in the jaw. She lost her balance and stumbled backward. I took my chance, stood up, and pushed her out of the opening of the walkway, but she grabbed my arm and jerked me after her.

I felt my body being pulled by the force of gravity to the opening, but Phillip caught me by my right arm and I was holding on to Bessie's arm with my left. I was the only thing keeping her from falling to her death.

"Please Abigail!" she pleaded. "I'm sorry! I'm so sorry! It isn't me! I have a disease! I cannot control my emotions!"

I held onto her arm for a moment.

"Abby!"

I didn't, for one second, take my eyes off Bessie. But I could hear Ian. He was on the walkway now and was yelling my name.

"Don't trust her! Just let her go. It won't make you a horrible person."

Bessie's eyes widened and it looked like… was she starting to cry? I thought it looked like betrayal, but I rubbed it off.

This woman had killed my mother. I would never know her. I didn't know if it was the right thing to do, but I did it anyway.

"Goodbye, Bessie."

I let her arm go.

Bessie's shrieks of terror filled the air as she fell downward. She fell past the bridge itself and lower, toward the Thames. She fell into the glowing river. I watched as the water electrocuted her body. The skin peeled away from her bones. She sank into the water and then her power was no more. The river stopped glowing. She sank, and then it was over. It was all over.

***

I sat in Mathias' study. My body was numb. My mind was numb. Phillip was waiting in his car outside. Mathias had insisted we talk before I went home with Phillip. I didn't have anything to say to him. I just wanted to be alone. Ian was now resting in his bedroom. The power had truly weakened him.

My hands were clenched into fists. I broke them up and folded them into each other. I looked at Mathias. He was sitting at his desk, staring at me.

"What do you want me to say?" I asked. "If you want an apology, then I'm sorry."

"Abigail, you didn't trust me. Instead you believed the falsities of a mad woman. A woman who killed your own mother."

I stood up in a rage.

"Do you think I would have believed her if you hadn't been lying to me all this time? I've known her just as long as I've known you! I've been seeing her the same amount of time! I had to decide who to trust and I put my trust in her! I'm ashamed because of that. But she lied to me and did a pretty damn good job at it! Whereas you just sit there with no emotion in your face. You would think for a man who had just met his own daughter you would do a better job of being a father! You took away my free will by not telling me about the contract with time."

Mathias' expression was one of guilt. It was a human emotion. I sat back down and crossed my arms.

"I'm sorry, Abigail," he said.

"Well, so am I," I responded. "Who was Bessie anyway? Really?"

He looked like he was going to tell me, but then, like always he didn't. “I promise,” he said, “I will tell you one day.”

I stood up to leave.

"Listen—" he stopped. He was clearly unsure of what to say or do. "I loved your mother. She was everything to me. You are everything to me. I was just afraid. I didn't want to show emotion, because I was afraid it would make me vulnerable. I wanted to protect you."

I stood up. I didn't want to hear this now. Not after everything I'd been through today and the past few months. I grabbed my stuff and walked down the hallway.

"Where are you going?" he asked.

"I'll be with Phillip."

"Are you okay?"

I looked up at Phillip. I couldn't believe he just asked me that. Of course, I wasn't okay. I think he got the hint by my expression because he didn't ask me again.

"Abby, you didn't have a choice."

"What are you talking about?" I asked.

"I mean you had to let her go. Don't be upset because of her death."

I laughed and he looked taken aback.

"Of course, I'm not upset about it," I said. "She deserved to die."

A feeling of dread rose up inside me. Did she deserve to die? Maybe she did, but was I the one to decide. Could I have pulled her back up? If I had, she would've killed us all. I felt like I had let my mother down.

Shut up! I told myself.

Thinking these things wasn't going to help me now. It wouldn't make anything better.

"I'm going to take a bath," I told Phillip.

The warm water felt good against my skin. I felt dirty. I felt like the water was cleansing me of the dirtiness, the badness. I wasn't bad—I was just weak.

I let myself go beneath the water. But then, I closed my eyes and I saw Bessie. I saw her face as the skin was peeling off of it. I saw her being electrocuted all over again. I screamed underneath the water and broke the surface.

I opened my eyes. My breathing was heavy. I screamed again and flailed my arms around in rage. I banged on the walls of the tub and screamed until my lungs hurt. The bathroom door clicked open.

"Abby, are you okay?" Phillip asked. "I heard you screaming."

"I'm fine." I let out a cry at the end of "fine" and then the tears began to fall.

The curtain around the tub opened and Phillip stood over my naked body. He reached in and pulled the drain. He grabbed a towel and wrapped me in it. He lifted me up and carried me out of the bathroom and into his bedroom where he helped me into my nightgown.

Phillip and I lay in bed together. I leaned into the crevice of his arm around my shoulder. His other arm touched my cheek and caressed it softly.

"I keep seeing the image of her body," I told him, "being

electrocuted."

"It's okay. Think about something else. Think about your mother, Mathias, or your parents."

"Why am I like this, Phillip?"

"What do you mean?"

"I always have to try and uncover the hidden meanings," I told him. "I always want to find out why I am who I am. If I hadn't gone looking for answers, none of this would have happened."

"How do you know that? How do you know none of this would have happened? Maybe it would have come looking for you, Abby. Besides, it isn't worth going over again and again in your head. Everything has happened. You can't change it. The only thing you can do is to keep going on with your life."

Phillip and I continued to lay there in silence. It was peaceful. It was nice. For once, it felt like time was passing by slowly and I took advantage of every minute of it. I looked up at Phillip and kissed him. He returned the kiss. I admired his eyes, his face, and his beautiful unkempt hair. I thought about the memories we had shared together. I thought about everything we had helped each other get through. I thought about the time we met and everything in between. I thought about my mother and Mathias. I thought about my parents. I let myself be taken away from the horrors of what had happened today. I let myself be pulled into good memories.

I let myself forget as I fell asleep in the safeness of Phillip's arms.

CHAPTER TWENTY-THREE

My body felt numb to the events of the previous day. The image of Bessie falling from the Tower Bridge clung to my memory like magnets. The sun crept in through the windowpanes and touched my skin. I felt the warmth of the sunlight, and it made me feel better. I turned over on my side and looked at Phillip. His eyes were closed and he was in a deep sleep. He looked peaceful. I reached out and carefully touched his cheek, so as not to wake him. He took my hand in his and opened his eyes.

"I was watching you sleep," he said. "Obviously, I didn't hide it well, since you woke up."

I let him pull me into his arms. He held me tightly and his scent engulfed my senses.

"How are you?" he asked me.

"I'm okay," I replied. "It's hard not to think about it. I still see Bessie. I see her falling off the bridge—and I see me letting her go and not saving her."

Phillip caressed my cheek. "There was nothing you could've done."

I felt guilty—ashamed.

"I could have saved her. We could have helped her. Maybe we

could have reversed it."

Phillip shook his head. "She was gone, Abby. There was nothing we could do. She would have killed us with those powers."

"Mathias spoke of some prison," I responded, "where they keep criminal Timekeepers."

Phillip continued to shake his head. "Who is to say she could have been controlled? Honestly, you really don't need to think about it for a while. And I'm going to help you."

He leaned in then and pressed his lips to mine. They were firm and strong. Phillip rolled on top of me and covered my body like he was protecting me—protecting me from the darkness.

Phillip kissed my forehead, my cheek, and my neck. His hands began to move under my shirt as mine went under his. I knew we were going too far, but I didn't try to stop it. He was making me forget. Our love was removing the darkness, but we still needed to stop. I knew that.

His alarm is what stopped us. He rolled off me onto his other side, turned off the alarm, and then rolled onto his back; we were both gazing up at the ceiling.

"Time to get ready," Phillip said. "Abby, don't let it consume you. Remember, I'm always here for you."

"I don't want to get out of bed."

He laughed at me.

"Carpe diem. Or as your mother used to say, it isn't necessary to sleep in and waste another day on God's good Earth. You never know when it could be your last."

When he said 'used to say,' I felt a feeling of loss. But I knew he was right. It was time to seize the day and make the best of it.

We had lunch that day and then Phillip walked me to Big Ben. He said he would be at the library late tonight. I said I would probably stay at the Headquarters tonight and we kissed goodbye. I made my way to the basement and then down through the lift. Mathias and I studied Timekeeping throughout the day and eventually, I fell asleep on his sofa. When I awoke, I realized it was nearly midnight, and then I stopped breathing.

I was watching Phillip—he was sitting in his office—studying like always. One of his colleagues appeared in the doorway of his office.

"I'm out for the evening, Phillip," his colleague said, "don't forget to lock up."

"Will do, Professor," Phillip responded. His colleague left and Phillip returned to his book.

A picture of me sat on Phillip's desk. He started to look at it and put his book down, picking up the picture in return. He held it in his hands for a few moments before placing it back on the desk.

Time seemed to skip a little, because it was suddenly a while later. I looked at a clock and saw that it was nearly two in the morning. Looking back at Phillip, I could see he had fallen asleep. He suddenly stirred and looked at the clock—upon seeing what time it was, he cursed and then got up and left his office—locking the door behind him. I followed him into the hallway of the library and I could see the moonlight coming in through the windows. It was later than he normally stayed. And then the worst possible thing happened—the air raid sirens sounded.

I could see the look of panic on his face as he made his way to the back of the library, most likely for better protection. I ran to the front of the library and out the front door—it was as if I was made of smoke. As I stepped out of the library, I could see the familiar tiny dots, making their way into the city. I could see the familiar shape of the bombs, falling from the aircrafts above. I could hear the horrid whistle that each bomb made as they fell toward the city below and its citizens. One of them was heading straight for the back of the library.

I ran back inside and down the hall. Windows were cracking as I ran to where Phillip had taken protection.

"Phillip!"

I was shouting, but I knew he couldn't hear me. I knew this was simply something I was watching—not something I could control.

I found him—I found him just as the ceiling gave way and smoke and rubble eclipsed my vision and then time skipped again. It was days later and I was staring at his gravestone.

"Phillip Hughes," it read, "loving son, loving fiancé."

And then everything went dark.

"Abby."

Mathias had his hands on my shoulders, and when I opened my eyes, I saw his looking into my own. I immediately sat up and looked at the clock. It was after midnight. I had lost about thirty minutes.

"There is going to be an air raid tonight," I said. "I have to contact the library, Phillip is there. He is going to die. I have to get there."

"You can't."

I looked at Mathias. "Yes, I can, and I will."

"Abigail, you can't." His voice was rough. "Consider this a test. If you try and save Phillip, you will be changing the course of time and death. Death will take you instead."

"I don't care," I said. "Let it take me. There is nothing for me here. He has both of his parents, his grandmother even. He'll move on. He'll be fine. I won't let him die."

"What about that woman you told me about?" Mathias asked. "She died. You didn't save her. Her husband didn't get a premonition to allow him to save her. How is this fair if you get to save the one you love?"

I stood up. I was speechless. He was right, but that didn't change anything. I couldn't even begin to explain why. What was the point of me seeing this premonition if I couldn't change it? What was the point of any of it?

"People save their loved ones every day," I responded.

"Yes, but they do not know that they are saving them from their death. They did not have a preconceived premonition of what would happen. You do. If you did not have this premonition, then you would not technically be there to save him tonight."

Why was I standing here arguing? The man I loved needed me.

"I didn't ask for these premonitions," I yelled, "I didn't ask to be this Timekeeper. I didn't ask for any of this. I just wanted to know where I came from. I need you to help me, I need a phone so that I can call Phillip."

"Abby," Mathias began, but I interrupted him.

"Now!"

He sighed and led me over to a table at the far side of the room that had a black phone on it. I didn't say anything further. I simply picked up the phone and tried to dial the operator, but the phone wouldn't work.

"Why isn't it working?" I asked.

"It should be."

"Well, it isn't."

Mathias walked over, took the phone from me, and tried it, but couldn't get it to work. He hung it up and a look appeared on his face.

"Time," he said, "but also death."

"What?"

"Time and death are trying to stop you," he said. "I've never had this happen before, because I've never tried to change anything. They are both trying to prevent you from interfering with their course."

"Then I'm going to him," I said.

I turned and left and Mathias let me go.

I looked at my wristwatch. It was a quarter to one. I had to hurry. I didn't even think; I just started running. I turned onto Victoria Embankment and ran down the street. Some people were watching me. They didn't know what was going to happen. Surely people would be smart enough to get into their houses, but this wasn't like a few years ago when the raids happened almost every night. Everyone supposed they were just happening now and again, I'm sure. But it would happen tonight.

As I turned left onto Northumberland Avenue and made my way to Trafalgar square, a tree on the side of the road suddenly snapped and fell in front of me. I screamed and tripped, landing on the concrete. I took a deep breath and then stood up, examining the tree. There was no reason for it having snapped, but then I remembered what Mathias had said. *Time.* It would fight back.

After taking one more look at the tree, I continued on until I reached St. James' square. The library was there. The air raid had not come yet. I had time. As I made my way to the door of the library, I stopped. I stopped, because I remembered the night that I met Elijah.

It had only been a week or so ago, but I had buried it deep within me amidst everything that had happened since then. If I did this, if I intervened with death, it wouldn't take me. Instead, my interference would upset the Time Line. It would cause horrific and terrible things to happen—because I was not a normal Timekeeper—I was an original Timekeeper. In addition to that, time was already fighting back, first with the phone and then with the tree. It didn't want me to intervene.

My chest was heaving up and down, up and down, up and down. My heart was racing a mile a minute—because I knew, in that moment, that I was going to let the man I loved, the man I had poured my heart out to, die. I was going to let him die in the most terrible of ways. Because if I didn't—if I intervened—then everyone else would die too. Bridget would die. Mathias would die. Ian would die. People I didn't know would die. And I couldn't do that. I wouldn't allow myself to make *that* decision for other innocent people.

And so, I walked away. I didn't run. I just walked. I didn't care if the air raid started and it took me. Because in that moment, there was no possible way I could keep on going. Mrs. Baxter was dead. My parents were dead. And by the end of the night, Phillip would be dead too.

Phillip Hughes died on Ash Wednesday, February 23, 1944, shortly after two in the morning when a German airtime bomb was dropped in St. James' Square, where the London Library stood. The forensic pathologist's report said his death had been quick. He had been struck in the head by some kind of object as the library caved in. He was the only person there. He had died surrounded by what he loved. The library could be repaired—it would be repaired. While the damage had been severe, they said that if the bomb had been any closer to a certain point of the library, it could have been ten times worse. It was ten times worse for me, however, because Phillip was still dead.

At some point in my walk back to Big Ben that night, Ian found me. Mathias had sent him out in a panic to come look for me and he coaxed me into coming with him. It wasn't hard. I was practically lifeless. We made it back to Big Ben just in time, and even though Ian asked me not too, I went up to the clock tower to watch the bombs drop. It seems morbid now that I think about it, but in that moment, there had been nothing left in me.

CHAPTER TWENTY-FOUR

The next day, I sat in the study underneath Big Ben. I did not understand why everything had come to pass. I had wanted to find things out about myself. I had wanted to know where I came from. But in the end, I ended up losing everything I cared about. Where was the justice in it all? Is this always the outcome for someone who tries to find out who they are?

I looked at my leg. It was propped on a stool because I had cut open the fresh wound that I'd sustained in the air raid attack with my parents the week before. It had apparently come open as I had run to the library the night before, but I had not noticed amidst all the commotion. Mathias had stitched it back up and cleaned it. He was surprisingly good at doing that. I supposed it had come from living on his own for many years.

Mathias entered the room. I still couldn't call him father or papa—those names were reserved for the man I lost, the father I cared about, and for Phillip, who would now never be a father. I was meant to have children with Phillip. Or was I? Maybe everything was fate. Maybe this was how it was supposed to be.

Mathias sat down in his armchair by the fireplace. I didn't look at him. In some ways, I despised him. I know it wasn't his fault. He was just trying to protect me. There were laws. Even if I didn't want to be this person, I had to be. I hated time. I despised it. Time was the enemy. Time took my father, my mother, and Phillip. Time stole everything and in return gave nothing.

"Why did you not intervene?"

I looked at him, and then poured out everything I had been keeping from him. I told him about the threatening notes and the helpful notes and how I knew they both must have been from Bessie. I told him everything about the contact I'd had with Bessie. I told him about Elijah and how he had approached me at the ball and how I knew he was telling the truth because he knew about my mother's letter. I told him that if time hadn't been different for me, I would have sacrificed myself for Phillip. And I told him I chose to let Phillip die, because I couldn't make that decision for the rest of the world. I couldn't.

Mathias, the man I couldn't call father, looked at me. He didn't say anything. His eyes questioned me. They were my eyes. It was like looking at myself in the mirror.

Finally, he spoke.

"Your mother had her secrets, that is now obvious. Abigail, I believe you and maybe I will be able to speak with this Elijah at some point. But I don't want to worry about that now. I want you to know you made the right decision, and please don't think I'm saying that I knew Phillip, but from what I know about him and from what you say about him, I think this is the decision he would have wanted you to make."

I was shaking. I wanted to push him. I wanted him to make it right.

"Phillip is dead," I yelled. "My mother and father are dead. If I hadn't decided to go on this path, they would still be alive."

"How do you know that, Abby? Your choice doesn't affect what happens to them. Time didn't kill them. Bombs killed them. War killed them. The hate of one man killed them. Not you. Not your choices. Not time."

He sounded like Phillip as he said it, and my heart ached.

"I could have saved them!"

"No, you couldn't have!" He was yelling now too. "You have to let them choose their path. The gifts you've been given, the gifts that have been given to us, are given to us so we can keep things in check. We keep time in check. We keep the Time Line in check; we keep the clockwork in check. We aren't responsible for humanity. They are responsible for themselves. They have to be allowed to have free will and make their own decisions. Phillip decided to be at the library tonight, your mother decided to go back in that house. Hitler decided to bomb London. If we interfere with their free will, regardless of the reason, what does that make us? We are not God. We are Timekeepers. We don't have power over others. We have the ability to keep things in check. It isn't a power."

I knew he was right. I knew everything he was saying made sense. I knew from my upbringing that God gave man the will to act freely. I couldn't choose what my mother or father did. I couldn't decide for Phillip. No one could decide for me. We all decided for ourselves, but that still made it hard. To know that people would die, to have to watch them die, to not be able to have the ability to do anything about it.

"Why would people be given such an ability to live with?"

"Why are people given disease? Why are handicapped people handicapped? Why are people supposed to live with suffering? Everyone is given some burden to live with. But if you are a strong and live through it, I believe you will be rewarded in the end."

It was the same thing that my mother had told me. And until I had endured the suffering, I really hadn't known what it meant. I had thought hearing voices was my own personal suffering, but that was nothing compared to what I felt in my chest now. It was nothing compared to what I had endured over the past few weeks.

"I can make it through this," I finally said, "but I need *you* to be my father, not my teacher. Can you do that?"

"I can try. I promise you that Abby. I will try."

I began to cry. My father came forward and held me in his arms. He protected me.

A few hours later, we sat alone in the study. He was reading while I was curled up on the couch, beneath a warm blanket. The fireplace continued to roar with the crackling fire. I thought about how far I had come. How far I still had to go. I thought about how anything can change your life in a matter of seconds. In that moment, I truly believed life was meant to go a certain way, that things were meant to happen. That was how life worked. I knew that Phillip had lived his life. I knew I was never meant to marry him, but only be a short segment of his life. I knew I was meant to be raised by Mr. and Mrs. Jordan, my mother and father. But I knew that they were meant to die when I was only eighteen. They were meant to die in a war that had claimed the lives of other children's parents. I was thankful I had gotten to know them for eighteen years, because I knew that other children would lose a parent after having only known them for half of that. I was thankful I had found out about my father and the truth about my mother. I was thankful a man like Phillip had come into my life and changed it for the better. I knew that there was another man out there who would continue to change my life. I knew I had yet to meet him.

Finally, I knew my father loved me. I knew he wanted to get to know his only child, his daughter. I knew he would do anything to protect me, and he would be there for the tragic events that had rocked my life. I knew I loved him. I knew I forgave him for lying to me. I had to. Love was his reason for lying and while that may not be a good enough reason, people made mistakes. Love is something every person knows, or they should. It is something that is shared. It is something binding.

As I looked at my father, I admired the features that reminded me of myself. I knew I loved him. But in only that look, my life would once again change.

The click of heels against floor sounded. My father looked up from his book and I turned my head to see a tall, stern-looking woman walking down the hallway. She had hair as black as the night sky, and it was pulled back into a bun so tight it looked like her face was being stretched with it. She was in her forties, very thin, and wore a gray dress that covered her from neck to toe, as well as boring black heels.

"Councilor Headrick."

I looked over at my father and then back at the woman. She was a part of the council. This visit wouldn't be a good one.

"Hello, Mathias," the woman said. She didn't sound mean or angry. I thought I detected sadness or sorrow in her face. "I'm afraid I have some bad news."

My father stood up from his chair, leaving the book sitting on it.

"The council has voted me in after the death of Councilor Winston. I have been monitoring your activity with Abigail since the initiation. Due to recent events, I believe it is in her best interests if she was reassigned to a Timekeeper to whom she has no relation."

My father sighed.

"What if I don't want to be reassigned?"

I stood up. I was angry again. I wanted to know why this was necessary. Was my father not good enough to train me? Did he do something wrong? Did I do something wrong?

The councilor looked at me. "Abigail, it is important for a Timekeeper to stay outside of the Time Line. You must not be involved in any way. Every beginning Timekeeper starts out with difficulties. You almost allowed yourself to die in place of the person fated to die."

"Why does it matter if I want to sacrifice myself?" I left out the fact that I knew I was an original Timekeeper—I figured that was information to keep between Mathias and I.

"It matters," she responded. "We shouldn't interfere, regardless if the circumstances would affect others or not."

"But why do I need to leave Mathias? He didn't do anything."

"I didn't stop you." My father had spoken and I turned to look at him. He looked at me and smiled. "It is my duty to prevent you from changing anything, regardless of whether you want to or not. But I shouldn't have let you go."

"But you let me go because you love me," I responded.

"And that is why you are being reassigned," Councilor Headrick said. "A conflict of interest. The job that Timekeepers have is crucial. Free will is part of nature; you cannot try and take that away from someone. You almost did. If you had been with a Timekeeper with whom you had no relations, this would not have occurred. We cannot risk it happening again. You are being reassigned to America. You will leave tomorrow."

I opened my mouth to argue back, but Mathias stepped in front of me and began to speak.

"Councilor, if it isn't too much to ask, perhaps give Abigail a few more days. At least allow her to stay until after the funeral of her fiancé."

The councilor turned around and appeared as if she was thinking about Mathias' request. But I didn't allow her to speak. I had to speak for myself.

"What if I stop being a Timekeeper?" I asked. "Can I remain here with Mathias?" He was the only person I had left, I couldn't leave him.

Once again, Mathias interrupted before the councilor could speak and he turned to look at me.

"Abigail, please don't do this. I'm sorry I lied to you, but you've chosen who you are now." He pulled me into his arms and held me like a father should. "I know you will be safer there from everything."

I began to cry and didn't say anything more. I would go.

"She can remain until the funeral," Councilor Headrick said. "I will be there to pick her up immediately afterwards, so please have her luggage ready. Notify me of the date of the funeral, as well as the location. I will not discuss this further."

The councilor turned and left. I stood there, speechless. I couldn't even begin to understand what had just happened. I felt like my father and I had come so far and in the space of a few minutes, and now we were being ripped apart. Why, for once, couldn't I win?

Later that day, I was in one of the guest bedrooms. Mathias and I had just returned from Phillip's apartment, where I had collected the remaining things I had. There wasn't much, as many of my things were destroyed after the air raid on my home. After that, I contacted Phillip's parents, but someone from the library had already contacted them. They informed me of the funeral date and that it would be back in Glasgow. My father said he would go with me and that the councilor would be there. I packed what I had left and my father provided me with enough money to be on my own.

I sat in front of a vanity mirror in the room and I stared at myself. There was a slight cut on my head that was still healing from the injuries I had gained the week before. My leg was still in pain from being freshly stitched up. A knock interrupted my thoughts.

"Come in," I said.

The door opened with a squeak and Ian walked in, shutting it behind him.

"I'm sorry I didn't come see you sooner," he said. "I figured you needed to be alone with Mathias."

"That's okay." I looked back at my expression in the mirror. My eyes were red and my cheeks were pale.

Ian walked up behind me and put his hand on my shoulder.

"I'm here for you, as a friend. And I wanted to ask, well, if I could come with you."

I looked up at him.

"To America?"

He nodded.

"I have nothing here," he said. "My family has been gone for some time and I think it would be important for you to at least know someone there. And I also thought, well, I brought someone to see you—Mathias permitted it, just this once."

I gave him a questioning look, but before I could say anything, he opened the door to the bedroom and stuck his head in the hallway. And then he pulled the door wide open and Bridget entered the room. My heart raced when I saw her. She didn't look angry with me. She ran straight to me and knelt down at the chair.

"I believe you," she whispered.

"Seeing is believing," I responded.

She nodded and tears began to escape her eyes. I knew she knew about Phillip and I knew she wouldn't say anything. Instead, we just held on to each other. Because in that moment, I wasn't alone—in that moment, I had Bridget and I had Ian, and that was enough.

That night, after talking with Mathias, it was decided Bridget and Ian would come with me to America. After the funeral, Councilor Headrick would pick us up and we would depart on a ship with passage to New York City. And from New York, we would be going to San Francisco, California—the location of the American Headquarters. The thought of going to a new country was frightening, but it also seemed enlightening.

I was already preparing to pack, and as I did, I found the letter Phillip had written. My heart raced, as it had done many times over the past week. The letter was to be read on our wedding night or—of course—if something had happened. I took a deep breath and broke the seal of the envelope. Carefully, I unfolded the letter and began to read.

Dear Abigail,

I cannot believe we are finally together—married. I want you to know I know I can be an arse. I know you hate that I have a filthy tongue. I also know I can be a tad bit jealous—okay, maybe a lot. But I want you to know what I love about you is that you continue to love me even though I have those vices. That is why I fell in love with you. You always try to find the best in a person. Even when they are at their worst, you always try to figure out a way to make it better for them. I realize that is what you were doing when you surprised me with the visit to Glasgow, and I am honestly thankful. Because of you, my father is getting the help he needs. Because of you, my mother is out of a situation I worried she would be in for the rest of her life. I cannot wait to spend the rest of my life with you. Speaking of life, that brings me to my next point.

If you are reading this, not because we are married, but because something has happened to me, I want you to know that life goes on. Maybe not today, maybe not tomorrow, and maybe not even over the next year. But eventually, you WILL find someone who will love you and take care of you the way you deserved to be loved and taken care of. I'm sorry that person couldn't be me. If I could come back, I promise I would be that person. But I can't come back. Unfortunately, that is how life works. Please do not give up hope. There is so much out there for you and you have so much potential. I know you'd love to have me along for the ride, and I'd love to be there. But God works in mysterious ways.

So, to conclude, do what you want to do in life. Be what you want to be. Don't be something just because someone else tells you to be. Be it because you want to. Keep going.

Seriously...keep going.

Love,

Phillip

I placed the letter, now wet with my tears, down in front of me. I knew everything would be fine. In a couple of days, I would be starting a new journey. And, like Phillip had said, I would not be over his death or my parents' deaths tomorrow. Or the next day. Or maybe even in a year. But I had to keep fighting. I had to keep up the fight.

In that moment, I chose to keep going.

Acknowledgments

I honestly cannot believe this book is finished. Furthermore, I cannot believe it is self-published. If there were anyone in the world that doubts themselves and their ability to do things, it would be me. But regardless of that, there are so many people who helped make this happen and I am truly thankful to them.

First, I would like to thank my grandmother, Paula. She is no longer with our family on this earth, but I know she is watching over us. If there was ever a woman who could love a person unconditionally, it was her. She never judged. She always loved. And she taught lessons that were worth teaching. She, along with my other grandmother and my parents, was one of my first teachers in life. She is a prime example of why blood doesn't make you family, but those who stand by you.

Unfortunately, she died long before I was finished writing this story. The pain of losing her was unbearable, especially because it was so sudden. The last words she said to me were, "I heard you were writing a book." I told her yes, but like all of my other unfinished projects, I didn't think it would be finished. She said something along the lines of "you should finish this one." Her death had a profound impact on the way I viewed death, especially sudden death. And because of this, Abigail's relationship with her adopted mother grew even stronger. I went back and reworked parts of the story. I can honestly say Annette Jordan is very similar to my late grandmother. But I want to thank her, because I truly believe she inspired me to finish this book, to tell a story, and to teach a lesson about how life goes on, even without the people that you love.

I want to thank my numerous beta readers. I've lost contact with the first reader, but when I had them read it, they offered me tremendous advice. I won't name them, because they wished to remain anonymous. In fact, I don't even think they wanted to be mentioned anonymously. But I have to do that. I owe them tremendous gratitude. So, if you are reading this, you should know *who* you are. Thank you.

Thank you to Alexander von Ness for designing the cover for this book! It is amazing and felt true to me the first time I saw it!

Thank you to the following for reading this book in advance and giving me your thoughts: Beatrice Defenbaugh, Natalie and Mary Montgomery, Kimberly Wilson, Holli Dawson, Sara Kirkpatrick, Grandpa Jack and Grandma Leona, and my wonderful friend and teaching partner (who is also a published author…seriously, go check her out), Andrea Berthot.

Thank you to my advisers at Wichita State University, Dr. Katie Cramer and Ms. Nancy Sturm. These wonderful ladies took time out of their day to discuss my book with me and offer editing and publishing advice. Furthermore, it was from Dr. Cramer that I learned every writer has a distinct writing style, and all individuals write differently. Without that advice, I may have never had the courage to show this story to the world. For that, I am truly thankful.

Thank you Mom and Dad for not giving up on me and for pulling me along, kicking and screaming, through high school and then college. Not only do I love being a writer, but I love being a teacher.

And if you had let me drop out…well, that wouldn't be any fun at all. Thank you to my older brother, Anthony, who likes to write and record music. The creativity and inspiration you have is something other people feed off. I'm not sure I would have been able to pursue my own creative interests if I hadn't had your influence.

To my little brother, John, thank you for your wit and for sharing my uncanny sense of humor. You were my first partner in crime, and you always will be, no matter how far apart we are from each other. And thank you for pulling me out of a slump to finish editing this book. You asked me why I wasn't editing it when I could have been and I honestly couldn't bullshit my way out of it. So, thank you.

To my grandparents, Jack and Leona, thank you for both taking the time to read this book and to offer historical accuracies to the areas where there were none—I appreciate that!

To my closest friends, Sarah Olsen, Marcha Glenn, and Michala Taylor, thank you for being you. Thank you for laughing and crying with me. Thank you for being in my life and staying with me. Regardless of how far away we are from each other, we still need each other. And I know you will always be there, maybe not always in person, but somewhere in the back of my head…

To all of my other friends – there are too many to name – thank you for pushing me to do what I want to do and laughing with me along the way.

Finally, thank you to my students—past, present, and those to come. You teach me as much as I teach you. You teach me to have faith in the world and to have faith in the future. I love teaching you and I wouldn't change it for the world. You make my days brighter and for that, I owe you tremendous gratitude. I hope you always remember the motto I teach from day one: *write your own story*.

www.ingramcontent.com/pod-product-compliance
Lightning Source LLC
Chambersburg PA
CBHW020935310726
48980CB00007B/785/J

* 9 7 8 0 6 9 2 1 2 0 7 4 3 *